THE DARK SIDE OF YESTERDAY

Janet Tanner

This first world edition published in Great Britain 2007 by
SEVERN HOUSE PUBLISHERS LTD of
9–15 High Street, Sutton, Surrey SM1 1DF.
This first world edition published in the USA 2007 by
SEVERN HOUSE PUBLISHERS INC of
595 Madison Avenue, New York, N.Y. 10022.

British Library Cataloguing in Publication Data

Tanner, Janet
    The dark side of yesterday
    1.   Timesharing (Real estate) - Fiction
    2.   Missing persons - Investigation - Fiction
    3.   Suspense fiction
    I.   Title
    823.9'14 [F]

ISBN-13: 978-0-7278-6423-9

All Severn House titles are printed on acid-free paper.

Typeset by Palimpsest Book Production Ltd.,
Grangemouth, Stirlingshire, Scotland.
Printed and bound in Great Britain by
MPG Books Ltd., Bodmin, Cornwall.

THE DARK SIDE OF YESTERDAY

Recent Titles by Janet Tanner from Severn House

ALL THAT GLISTERS
FORGOTTEN DESTINY
HOSTAGE TO LOVE
MORWENNAN HOUSE
NO HIDING PLACE
THE PENROSE TREASURE
PORTHMINSTER HALL
SHADOWS OF THE PAST
TUCKER'S INN

Prologue

How well do we ever know another person? It's a question I often ask myself now, though once it was something that never entered my head. You could say, I suppose, that I was too trusting, naive even, but we have to trust, don't we? Conversely you might think that what happened has made me cynical and suspicious, but that wouldn't be true either. What it has done is open my eyes to an uncomfortable truth.

We can know every line on a person's face, every inch of their body, the way their hair grows – or doesn't. We can be familiar with their every expression, predict their reaction to any kind of situation, guess what they are going to say before they say it. We can know what makes them laugh and what makes them cry. What will cause them pleasure or disappointment, make them happy or angry, sympathetic or impatient. The music they like, the food they would choose. How they look when they are sleeping.

We may think we know what is in their hearts. But we can never know all that goes on in their minds. There are always secret places that are hidden from every other human being, however close – thoughts and hopes and imaginings we can never know. Sometimes they are tucked away out of sight because they are too precious to be shared; they make one too vulnerable. And sometimes because they are dark and shameful.

Inside every one of us is a secret stranger.

I know that now. It was a hard lesson to learn and one I shall never forget. It doesn't worry me too much any more – after all, I have my secret places too. But for all that I am aware – we can never know another person completely. And some we do not know at all.

*   *   *

1

There's another question I could pose – and perhaps I will. How does an ordinary life suddenly mutate into a nightmare? A web of blind alleys, unanswered puzzles and danger? How can your world turn upside down so that nothing is quite as it seemed and the people you trusted become people you do not know at all?

To answer that question I shall have to tell you the whole story, and I'm not really sure where to begin. Perhaps with the first time my instinct warned me that something was amiss. Even though, on the face of it, it really had nothing to do with me. And it did not seem to be anything I need worry about.

One

It began with the phone call.

I was in the garden, getting in the washing that I'd hung out before leaving for work that morning, when I became aware of the insistent double-purr tone. It came floating out through the kitchen window, which I'd opened to let the late spring sunshine and some fresh air into the house which had been shut up all day. At the same moment, the window directly above flew open and Molly's face appeared.

'Mummy – the phone's ringing.'

'Yes, I can hear it. Don't lean out of that window, Molly!'

Molly is my seven-year-old daughter and even as I automatically warned her, I knew I was being over-protective. She's quite a serious little girl and very sensible – far too sensible to fall out of her bedroom window. But I'm all too aware of how much a moment's carelessness can cost. Michael, my husband and Molly's father, had been a good driver. He had never taken unnecessary chances – or so I thought. But that hadn't saved him from being killed in a car crash two years ago.

The shock of having a policeman knocking on my door in the small hours has scarred me in ways I would never have imagined. I still go cold at the memory, feel the way my stomach seemed to dissolve and my knees go weak as I had when I'd seen him standing there, looking serious and almost apologetic.

'Mrs Lansdale? Mrs Michael Lansdale?' he had asked.

'Yes.' Breath constricted in my lungs, caught in my throat.

'Can we go inside?'

I knew then, before he said a single word. Knew with every fibre of my body, though my mind refused to accept

3

it. I didn't dare move. I didn't think my shaking legs would support me.

'Michael,' I said. 'It's Michael, isn't it?' My voice was shaking too, and rising a little towards the hysterical.

'Look – I really do think it would be better if we went inside, Mrs Lansdale.'

He urged me into the house, into the living room where Michael's suit jacket hung over the back of a chair and a motoring magazine he'd been leafing through lay, still open, on the coffee table. He made me sit down and then he told me.

Michael's car had gone off the road and hit a tree. Michael was dead.

What he didn't tell me then was that the car had burst into flames and that Michael had been so badly burned that formal identification had to be from the personal items that had not been destroyed – his wedding ring, his watch, the gold chain he always wore under his shirt. I suppose he thought I needed to learn the full horror of what had happened in stages, not all at once. And if he had told me then, I'm not sure I would have taken it in. I was too numbed by shock, fighting my way through a thick woolly cloud, struggling to breathe, able to say only one word, over and over, like an old-fashioned gramophone record stuck in a groove, but coming out like a sob. 'Oh – oh!'

But incoherent as I was I can still remember so clearly the way I felt, like nothing I have ever felt before or since. I can close my eyes and be back in that moment, silently mouthing that sob. 'Oh – oh!'

And I know, too, how terrifyingly easily your whole world can fall apart. That in a split second everything that you have taken for granted can be gone. Irretrievably destroyed.

That, I suppose, is why I am so protective of Molly. However much I try not to let it affect her, and the way I am with her, I can't quite overcome the fear that I may lose her too. Mostly I hide it, try not to think about it consciously. But it's there, all the same, a raw nerve deep inside just waiting to be touched. At moments like this, when I see potential danger too clearly, like her little fair head leaning too far out of her bedroom window . . .

'Phone, Mummy!' she shouted now, as if I hadn't heard her the first time.

'OK!' I dropped a handful of her socks into the washing basket and headed for the back door, the pegs still in my hand.

I was halfway across the kitchen when the phone stopped ringing. Either whoever had been calling had given up, or the answer phone service had cut in. I went back outside, collected the rest of the washing and dumped it all in the utility room off the back of the kitchen, ready for ironing. Then I picked up the phone and dialled 1571.

There was a message.

'Jo, it's Alison at the office. Can you give me a ring?'

Alison worked at Garratt Properties, the estate agency Michael had managed when he was alive; she now assisted Adam Garratt, Michael's friend and the name behind the business. She had come to the job as a junior, straight from school, but she had already been an institution there by the time Michael took the manager's job, and he had always had the highest regard for her capabilities. 'The office would grind to a halt without Alison,' he used to say. Nowadays Alison was even more indispensable, I imagined. Adam had never replaced Michael, preferring to run the business alone with the staff they'd trained themselves.

I was puzzled, I must admit, as to why Alison should be calling me. I had nothing to do with the business these days – never had, come to that. Michael had talked about it to a certain extent, of course – a particularly good sale, or one that had gone badly wrong – but mostly he liked to keep work and home life separate and if he had business conversations on his mobile, which I'm sure he did, he had them in the privacy of the small bedroom that he used as an office and never mentioned them to me unless he had to.

'I have enough of that all day,' he'd say, and I'd never pressed him. I'd been busy with my own work, in any case. I am a trained primary school teacher, and when Molly was old enough to start nursery I'd been lucky enough to get a job there. She'd moved on now, of course, to a 'proper school', but I was hoping a suitable vacancy might crop up there one day soon so that I could go back to real teaching.

5

But in the meantime I was more than happy to go on working with the tinies. My hours fitted in well with Molly's and if I had to stay later she could be there with me. She loved that – being particularly fond of the babies, and Greta, who was in charge of them, said she was a 'real little mother'.

To get back to Alison. I couldn't imagine why she should want to speak to me. Sometimes when I was in town I looked into the office to say hello, but that was about the extent of it. Perhaps she was ringing on Adam's behalf, I thought. That seemed altogether more likely.

Adam had, I have to say, been very good to us since Michael's death. At first I'd thought it was more from a sense of duty than anything else – after all, he and Michael had been friends since schooldays, and partners for several years. And Adam clearly had a strong sense of responsibility to old friends. He'd thrown the lifeline of the job to Michael when the packaging company where Michael worked in sales closed down and Michael was made redundant. He'd invited him for a game of golf and a drink at the prestigious local club where he was a member and mentioned, almost casually, that he could use a good office manager.

Michael had hesitated at first. He didn't want to feel Adam was offering him the job out of charity, because he had a thriving business and a lifestyle to be envied whilst Michael, with a wife and child to support, was agonizing over how he would pay the mortgage. But Adam had managed to convince him it was nothing of the kind.

'I want to be a bit freer to pursue other avenues,' he'd told Michael. 'I need someone I can trust to look after things when I'm not in the office. The job's yours if you want it. If not . . . well, I'll just have to advertise and take my chances with the best applicant.'

'What other avenues does he want to pursue?' I'd asked when Michael had talked it over with me later. For one thing I was curious, for another I wondered how what he was planning might affect the plum that seemed to be dropping into our laps like manna from heaven.

Michael told me he thought that Adam was interested in moving into foreign sales.

'You know he has a villa in Spain and an apartment in

Tenerife?' I nodded. *How the other half live!* 'I think he wants to be able to spend more time in the sun and I think he sees a profitable market with all the new developments that are going up there. He's quite the entrepreneur, you know. But I imagine that will all be quite separate from the estate agency, apart from maybe a poster in the window and a few fliers on the counter. Except –' he grinned, the first time I'd seen so much as a ghost of a smile since he'd been made redundant – 'we might get cheap holidays out of it, I suppose.'

'Sounds good to me!' I returned his smile. But it wasn't the prospect of freebies that pleased me. It was the thought that we could stop worrying about how we were going to keep our heads above water; that I wouldn't have Michael tossing and turning beside me each night, sleepless with anxiety.

And so Michael had taken the job and a year or so afterwards Adam had made him a partner.

I was never altogether sure, however, that Michael's heart was really in selling property, or the building society agency that they ran as a sideline. He and Adam were very different – Adam was a gregarious, outgoing type, who enjoyed nothing more than blarneying customers and cutting deals, while Michael, despite his background in sales, had been much quieter, less thrusting. He'd been a little withdrawn, I had thought, in the weeks and months before his death; short-tempered and brooding. I often wondered if he had been worried about something – the way the business was performing, perhaps, or even the direction his life had taken. But he'd brushed aside my tentative enquiries, saying everything was fine, and I had known he would never do anything to rock the boat whilst he had a family to support and a mortgage to pay. Perhaps the job wasn't exactly his bag, I'd thought. Perhaps one day when we were more secure financially he'll think about looking around for something he was more comfortable with, but for the moment he was going to stick it out. And whatever he did, he did well, I'd felt sure. Michael had been steady and thorough; the day-to-day running of the business had been safe in his hands and though he had never had Adam's skill as a negotiator, or his gift of the gab, he'd presented a figure that their clients could trust.

But that was all in the past now. Michael had never had the opportunity to change direction, if that was what he had wanted. He had died in a blazing car on his way home from a meeting with Adam and a couple of other business associates at Adam's golf club.

I could have gone with him that evening. I'd been invited. Not to the business discussion part, of course. Once we'd eaten, I would have been despatched to the members' bar with the other ladies while the men sat on the terrace with their drinks and cigars and talked about whatever it was they wished to talk about. And that was what I didn't fancy doing. 'I don't want to be lumbered having to make small talk with people I don't know,' I'd said, when Michael had told me Adam had suggested he bring me along. 'You know what Adam's women are like. Shopaholics who talk about nothing but their Jimmy Choos and the waiting list for the latest designer handbag.'

'Not to me they don't.'

'No, I can imagine. They're not my type, Michael. And in any case, we'd have to get a babysitter.'

'OK, OK!' Michael had held up his hands in submission. 'It was only a suggestion. No one's forcing you.'

'Good.' But I had been a little miffed all the same that Michael hadn't tried harder to persuade me.

Afterwards, of course, I'd thanked God that I hadn't been in the car that night. That Molly might have been orphaned was an unimaginable tragedy. But I also could not forgive myself for the guilty suspicion that if I had been there the accident might never have happened at all. If Michael had wanted a drink, I'd have offered to drive. Had Michael been drinking? Was that the reason he'd run off the road? Adam had said not, but we'd never known for sure, given the circumstances, and it had occurred to me at the time that Adam might not be telling the truth. Perhaps he had talked Michael into one for the road against his better judgement. That would be very much Adam's style. 'Come on pal – don't be a party pooper. It won't do you any harm. You're as sober as a judge. And you never see a police car on this road at this time of

8

night . . .' Yes, I could hear him all too clearly in my imagination. And if that was the way it had happened, then it was small wonder he felt responsible for Molly and me.

For without a doubt he did feel responsible. He called on us often in the early days, asking if we needed anything or if there was something he could do to help.

I was grateful, but at the same time I wanted to be left alone. Adam could be a bit overpowering and in my grief I didn't need that. Truth to tell, I didn't know what I wanted. No, I did know. I wanted things to be as they had been. I wanted Michael back – wanted it with such intensity that it tore me apart, left me hollow and aching, afraid and desolate. But I couldn't have that. Michael and our old life had gone forever and somehow, for Molly's sake, I had to go on. I needed to make her world as safe and normal as possible.

Adam was part of that. He was very good with Molly and she thought he was wonderful. He played silly games with her, making her giggle, and brought her presents she adored: a pair of Barbie sandals (high-heeled plastic things she shuffled around in), a diary with a lock and key, a teddy bear wearing sunglasses and a big sombrero that I assumed he'd brought back from one of his frequent trips to Spain or Tenerife.

'His name is Manuel, and he needs looking after,' Adam had told Molly. 'Will you take care of him for me?'

'Of course I will,' Molly had said earnestly – and so she did. Manuel lived in her bedroom, propped up against her pillows. He even had to wear a disposable nappy which she'd purloined from the nursery and which she pretended to change when she remembered.

Sometimes he took the two of us out for the day – to the zoo or the seaside; and once to a water park, where he'd changed into swimming gear and gone down the flumes with Molly.

Now, wondering why Alison was calling, it occurred to me that Adam might have asked her to ring me to fix something for the weekend. The weather had turned good recently and it was a couple of weeks since he'd been in touch. If he was busy it was entirely possible he'd leave his diary with Alison and get her to make the arrangements.

At least it wasn't likely to be an invitation to go out with him alone. He'd suggested it once or twice – a meal, a theatre trip. Once he'd said he had tickets for a concert. But I'd thanked him and refused with a firm 'no'. Adam was a personable man, good-looking and single. He'd been married once, to a girl Michael had described as a dolly bird, but that had been over long ago. And the way Adam looked at me sometimes made me uncomfortable. I didn't want to give him the wrong idea. I wasn't ready to let anyone get too close – wasn't sure I ever would be – and if I did, it wouldn't be Adam. He was too obvious for my taste, too flamboyant. Besides which, I was fairly sure he and Alison had something going. Very likely it was more on her side than on his, but all the same, the last thing I would want would be to upset Alison. I didn't think she was even very happy about the attention he paid to me and Molly as a family – which most likely accounted for the slightly strained tone in the message she'd left.

I should ring her back, I thought. I picked up the tele-phone and depressed the memory number for the office, still keyed in from the days when Michael was alive. The new junior answered – I wasn't sure of her name, though I thought it might be Claire – and I asked to be put through to Alison. A few moments later she was on the line.

'Alison. You called me.'

'Yes.' She hesitated slightly. 'It's about Adam.'

Ah – so I'd been right then.

'Yes?' I was thinking that Molly would be pleased to see Adam, not for one moment expecting what came next.

'I don't suppose . . . You don't by any chance know where he is?'

'Adam?' I said, puzzled. 'You mean is he here? Sorry, Alison, he's not.'

Another hesitation. 'Well, no, I didn't really mean now, this minute.' Alison sounded uncharacteristically flustered. 'I mean . . . have you seen him recently? He hasn't mentioned to you that he was going away somewhere?'

'I haven't seen him for several weeks,' I said, even more confused. 'Why – have you lost him?'

Alison laughed slightly, but more in what sounded like embarrassment than because she thought it was funny.

'Well – yes. Sort of. He hasn't been in to the office at all for over a week and I can't seem to reach him.'

'Perhaps he's in Spain,' I suggested. 'Or Tenerife.'

'I've tried the villa and the apartment. And his mobile. He's not answering that either.'

'I'm sorry then. I can't help you,' I said.

'Well, if you do hear from him, will you tell him I'm looking for him? And let me know? I really do need to speak to him.'

'Yes, of course.'

I replaced the receiver, stood for a moment with my hand resting on it.

How very strange. Alison must be pretty desperate to contact me. I wouldn't have thought I'd be one of her first ports of call. Unless Adam had given her the impression he had more contact with me than was the case. That wouldn't surprise me. He would probably like to pretend he was the indispensable friend, the one no one could manage without. He might even have insinuated that things between us were more personal and complicated than they really were. I hoped not. I didn't want Alison thinking I was stealing the man she had a fancy for, and I didn't want anyone thinking that I was looking to replace Michael in my heart or my life.

Oh, well, I'd made it clear enough I wasn't in contact with Adam now. And if he'd chosen to go walkabout and not let his assistant in on his movements, it had nothing whatever to do with me.

I opened the fridge, took out a cottage pie I'd made last night, and put it in the oven to warm for tea. Then I called up the stairs to Molly.

'Time to do some reading practice, sweetheart!'

'Oh, Mummy, no!'

'Oh, Mummy, yes! Just a couple of pages – come on. We'll do it in the garden if you like.'

Molly shuffled down the stairs wearing the Barbie sandals Adam had given her. I got her reader out of the clear plastic envelope in her schoolbag and waved it at her.

'I want to know what happened to the princess in the Magic Garden even if you don't,' I told her.

We went out into the garden, pulled two canvas chairs up

11

to the patio table, and sat down with the sun warm on our faces. And as Molly read aloud to me, slowly, laboriously but really very well, I forgot all about Alison's phone call and the fact that she had apparently lost Adam.

And I had not the slightest inkling that for me the nightmare had begun.

Two

'Mummy,' Molly said, 'can Daddy see us from where he is in heaven?'

She was in bed, her mauve duvet, appliquéd with silver fairies, pulled up to her chin, her long fair hair fanned out over the pillow. When I was her age my hair had been the same colour – I know because my father had a little snippet of it tucked in his wallet. Over the years, though, it had darkened to mid-brown. I hoped Molly's would remain that lovely sunshine colour, but somehow I doubted it.

A lump formed in my throat at her words. Funny how that sad sweet pang could still catch me unawares. Just when I thought I was beginning to get over losing Michael there it would be, as sharp as ever, choking me.

'I think so, Molly.'

'All the time?' She sounded a little anxious. I wondered what had precipitated this.

'Not all the time – or at least, I shouldn't think so. Why?' I asked.

There was a small silence. Then Molly said: 'I'd like it if he could see when Mrs Baines gives me a gold star for my pictures or my spelling.' Mrs Baines is her teacher. 'But I wouldn't want him to see me if I'm bad.'

The lump dissolved. I almost laughed aloud.

'Bad, Molly? You don't do anything bad, I hope.'

'Well . . . I do. Sometimes.'

I sat down on the edge of her bed. I knew confession time when I heard it.

'So what have you done today that you wouldn't want Daddy to see?'

Another silence. Then: 'I stole one of Jessica's tattoo transfers. Well, I didn't really *steal* it. She had a whole pile of them – roses and stars and things – and she gave them to me to look at. And I really liked the roses and she had such a lot of them and I thought I'd like one on my arm. And so I slipped one under my book when she wasn't looking. And I didn't give it back to her with the others . . .'

Her voice tailed away miserably. I could almost hear her holding her breath, waiting for my reaction.

'And you know you did wrong, don't you?' I said. 'It *was* stealing, wasn't it?'

'Yes, Mummy.'

'And you shouldn't steal from anyone. Especially not from friends.'

'I know, Mummy. I'm sorry. I won't do it again. But I really, really wanted it.'

'That is no excuse at all,' I said sternly. 'Where is the transfer now?'

'In my pencil case.'

'Well, I think you know what you have to do, Molly. Tomorrow, first thing, you give it back to Jessica.'

'But . . . I don't want her to know what I did . . .' Molly sounded on the verge of tears.

'Because you're ashamed. Well, I'm sorry, Molly, but you should have thought of that when you kept it. If you don't give it back it will just go on worrying you, and it won't do you any good. You can't use it because Jessica would know, and even if she didn't *you* would know, and you wouldn't enjoy it at all. Give it back, Molly, and you can forget all about it.'

'But . . .' She was crying now, I knew. She made no sound, but in the half-light I could see the tears running silently down her cheek.

'You could say it was under your book,' I said, offering her a lifeline. 'Just don't lie about it. You know telling lies is bad too, don't you?'

'Yes, Mummy.'

'I'm very pleased you told me. Now go to sleep and everything will be sorted out tomorrow.'

'Yes, Mummy.' She pushed back the duvet and her firm little arms went round my neck, holding on tight. Her skin smelled fresh and sweet from her bath, that lovely fair hair was silky soft against my cheek. 'I love you, Mummy.'

14

'And I love you, baby.'

'You won't go away, will you, to heaven, like Daddy did?'

The lump was back in my throat. 'I won't go away, Molly.'

'Promise?'

'I promise.' No one could promise such a thing, I know. But the most important thing was that Molly should feel safe.

I held her close, loving her, thinking that she had learned an important lesson today – that taking something that does not belong to us will bring no pleasure, however much we may want it. I didn't think Molly would do such a thing again.

Perhaps, I thought, I would buy her some tattoo transfers of her own when we went into town at the weekend. I wasn't keen on the idea of her plastering them on her tender skin, but I didn't suppose it would hurt if she wanted it so much. But I wouldn't tell her yet. She mustn't think she was being bribed to return the one she had taken from Jessica.

I dropped a kiss on her forehead. 'Night night, darling. Sweet dreams.'

'Night night, Mummy.' She pulled the duvet up to her chin again and turned on to her side, curling up into a ball.

I got up from the bed and crossed to the window to pull the curtains closed.

Outside it was still not quite dark. The sun had gone, but some light remained and the trees, planted at intervals along the opposite side of the street, stood like dark sentinels in the soft, pearly luminescence. There was a car parked beneath one of them, directly across the road from Molly's window – a medium-sized car, dark coloured; either graphite or black, in the fading light it was hard to tell.

I looked at it, a little curious. Ours was a quiet residential street and all the houses had their own driveways and garages, so it was only visitors or delivery men who parked at the kerbside. The Thomas family who lived opposite were away, I knew. Was someone coming to call on us? But I didn't recognize the car. Adam drove a rather flash silver Mercedes; Anna, my best friend, had a 4x4, old, but big enough to accommodate her three children in comfort; as for my parents, even if Dad had been persuaded to change the Saab he'd had for years, they lived two hours' drive away and never came to visit without phoning first. The car certainly didn't belong to anyone I knew.

There was someone in the driver's seat, a man. Not getting out, just sitting there. Suddenly I had the most disconcerting impression that he was watching me – or had been. Why I thought that, I don't know. He certainly wasn't looking in my direction now; he seemed to be staring straight ahead, his head angled slightly towards the Thomas's house. Had I subconsciously registered him staring towards our house and turning quickly away when I appeared at the window? I didn't know. But for some reason I couldn't explain, I felt a twinge of unease.

Impatient with myself, I pushed the feeling away. Perhaps he *had* been looking at our house, but it could only have been for want of something better to do. There was no reason on earth for a perfect stranger to be taking an interest in a three bedroom detached house that was identical in every way to its neighbours on each side apart from the cherry tree in the garden which dripped pink blossom over the wall and on to the pavement in spring, and the mock old-fashioned lamp standard Michael had bought to go at the end of the drive simply because it had taken his fancy. It wasn't even as if the For Sale board was there any more. A year ago I'd put the house on the market because it was so full of memories I'd felt I couldn't bear it; then, when prospective buyers had shown an interest, I'd taken it off again for exactly the same reason.

We'd had such happy times here, Michael and I, and so much of him was still here. The pond with a little waterfall that he'd built in the back garden, the new kitchen he'd put in himself, though he was no real DIY expert, all green wood, Shaker-style, and a cream sink that had looked wonderful when it was new but had a tendency to stain if I wasn't careful. Even the silly lamp standard reminded me of him.

'You'll be buying an old red telephone kiosk next,' I'd teased him.

'Don't mock, sweetheart. I just might!' he'd said. But of course, he never had.

'You're doing the right thing, Jo,' Adam had said when

16

I'd told him I'd changed my mind about selling and decided to stay after all. 'The last thing you need is to uproot yourself and leave all your friends behind.'

There had been something in the way he said it, something in the way he was looking at me, that had made me wonder for a moment if by 'friends' he meant himself. I'd dismissed it, of course. If I thought that Adam, who always made so much of his treasured freedom, might be interested in a grieving widow with a young daughter, then I was flattering myself. I didn't want to think it; I didn't want any awkwardness to creep into what was a reasonably comfortable relationship with a man who had helped me through the worst of times.

'Yes, I think it would be a mistake,' I'd said. 'At the moment, anyway. I'm just sorry to have put you to so much trouble.'

'Think nothing of it.' Adam had smiled; a smile that I knew could turn some women weak at the knees.

'Thanks, Adam. For everything.'

'My pleasure. I only wish . . .'

'I know. So do I.'

Why I was remembering the conversation now, I didn't know. Perhaps because for a split second the man in the car opposite our house had made me feel vulnerable and Adam, who I knew I could call on in an emergency, was missing.

No, not missing, I corrected myself. It was just that Alison didn't know where he was. Not the same thing at all.

The sound of a car engine starting up floated across the road and in through Molly's open window and a moment later the car pulled away. The driver had probably been early for an appointment, I thought, and was simply waiting time. Perhaps he was on his way to pick up a date for an evening out. My imagination, always fertile, pictured him ringing the bell at one of the flats further down the street. Some of the big old houses there had been converted into apartments for young professionals and bed-sits for students. I imagined a girl with long hair and a bare midriff coming out and getting into the car, laughing, happy, looking forward to a drink or a meal or a gig. The sort of girl I'd been in another life.

The bittersweet sadness was there again, just an echo, for

times that had gone and could never return again. I pulled the curtains against the gathering dusk and turned back into the room.

Molly was asleep already, her breathing deep and regular. My hand hovered over her golden head, my fingers itching to touch the silky hair, but I resisted. I didn't want to disturb her.

You are very lucky, I told myself. Whatever you have lost, you still have Molly. The loveliest, most precious little girl in the whole world. You have no money worries. You have a nice home, paid for by the insurance Michael took out on the mortgage, and a rewarding job that you enjoy. Looking back is a waste of time and energy. You have to look forward now. And make the most of each day. For you never know when it will all be snatched away from you.

For another minute or so I stood looking down at Molly as she slept. Then I tiptoed from the room, heading for the basket of ironing that was waiting for me downstairs. I forgot all about the mystery man in the mystery car. And all about Adam, who had taken himself off and not told anyone where he was going.

The phone rang as I was ironing the last of Molly's school shirts. I switched off the power, hung the shirt over the back of the nearest kitchen chair, and went to answer it.

'Hi, Jo! How y'doing?' It was Anna, my best friend.

We met, Anna and I, at ante-natal classes when I was having Molly and she was pregnant with Calum, her eldest, and we'd hit it off right away, perhaps because we were both new to town, and both of us with husbands who worked long hours – Anna's husband, Dave, was a policeman, a motorcyclist with the traffic department, on irregular shift patterns – or perhaps simply because we had personalities which instantly clicked. Whatever. We'd supported one another through the last weeks of pregnancy in the hot summer when our babies were born and we were both like beached whales, and Calum and Molly were born within a few days of one another. Afterwards we'd continued to meet regularly, even when the numbers of our group dwindled so that we called a halt to the regular get-togethers we'd all planned, and mostly gone our separate ways.

In those days Anna lived only a couple of streets away from me, and we'd push our prams to one another's houses, chat over a cup of coffee, and share our concerns and our triumphs – 'Molly only woke once last night! It's not going to be long before she sleeps through . . .'; 'I think Calum's teething. He's really fretful – and look at that red patch on his cheek . . .' We took them to the park together and later to Soft Play, the wonderful 'padded cell' as I called it, full of little slides and climbing nets and thousands of soft plastic balls for them to roll around in. These had been happy times and our friendship had grown and strengthened during them.

Since then, circumstances had changed. Anna had gone on to have two more children, both little boys she named George and Harry, and the maisonette they lived in was no longer big enough to accommodate their growing family. They'd moved to a village some seven miles outside Laverham – a lovely old cottage with a large garden for the children to play in – and at the time I'd been green with envy.

I'd suggested to Michael that we might move out into the country too – in his line of work he was in a position to know when all the best places were coming on to the market – but somehow it had never happened and now I was grateful for that. Bringing Molly up alone I was glad we were within easy reach of all the facilities the town had to offer and our modern house with its manageable garden made it reasonably easy for me to cope.

As for Anna, she'd been the most wonderful friend, and in many ways I felt closer to her than I did to my own sister, who lived a hundred miles or so away, in Surrey, and whom I rarely saw.

Tonight, as always, I was pleased to hear her cheerful voice, even though I still had a million things to do before I could put my feet up, have a cup of hot chocolate and think about bed.

'I'm fine,' I said in answer to her question. 'How about you?'

'OK. George tried to climb the apple tree after Calum and got stuck. I had to get a ladder and go up myself to get him

19

down. And Harry's having tantrums again. Just the usual, you know.'

I smiled. I envied Anna's big family too. It would have been nice for Molly to have a brother or sister. But it had never happened, and truth to tell I wasn't sure how I'd have managed to cope with three energetic, boisterous little lads as she did.

'Anyway – the reason I'm ringing,' Anna went on. 'You haven't forgotten it's my jewellery party tomorrow evening, have you?'

'Ah.' I had forgotten. A Freudian slip, perhaps. I'm not that keen on party-plan gatherings, I didn't think I needed any more jewellery – I never went anywhere these days to wear what I'd already got – and I didn't especially want to have to drive over to Anna's through the country lanes in the dark. It sounds pathetic, I know, but I'm not at all keen on night driving. My eyes never seem to adjust properly, the lights of oncoming vehicles blind me, and I keep imagining the shadows at the side of those narrow roads are concealing a pedestrian or two that I might hit. Road accidents are real to me. A ring at the doorbell in the middle of the night. A loved one who never comes home.

'Actually, Anna, I'm not sure I'm going to be able to make it,' I said, feeling guilty.

'Jo!' Anna said loudly and reproachfully. 'Why ever not?'

'I haven't got a babysitter.'

'You can find one, surely? I thought that girl you work with at the nursery was always on tap?'

'Maria. Yes, she's very good, but it's very short notice, and she may be going out herself on a Friday night.'

'You mean you haven't asked her.'

'No,' I admitted.

'Ask her then!' Anna could be quite forceful when she wanted to be. 'Ring her right this minute. She'll probably be only too pleased of the opportunity to earn a few extra pounds and watch your widescreen telly.'

'It's too late to ring her now,' I said weakly.

'It's only half past nine. She's a youngster, for heaven's sake! I don't suppose she goes to bed before midnight. And if she can't do it, ask your neighbour. She's always a good standby, isn't she?'

'I'm certainly not bothering Valerie tonight,' I told her firmly.

'Tomorrow, then. I'm not letting you off the hook on this one, Jo. You haven't had a night out in ages. It would do you the world of good. A glass of wine, a few nibbles, good company. There should be a dozen or so girls here, and you know most of them.'

'If you've got all those, you won't miss me . . .' It was a last-ditch attempt to get out of it; I knew even as I said it that it wouldn't work, and I was right.

'Be here, Jo Lansdale!' Anna ordered me. 'I'm not listening to any more excuses, OK?'

'OK. I'll try.' I had no option but to accept defeat. Anna meant well, I knew. I just wished she wasn't so bossy sometimes.

'You'd better.' Anna broke off. 'Oh, Lord, that sounds like Harry awake. I'll have to go. See you tomorrow evening. About eight, or as soon as you can make it. Bye for now.'

'Bye.' I put down the phone and sighed. But perhaps Anna was right. Perhaps it would do me good. It was all too easy to get stuck in a rut.

I picked up the pile of ironing, draped Molly's shirts over my arm, and headed upstairs to put it all away in the airing cupboard. Then I went into my room to put my clean tights and underwear straight into my drawer, and crossed to the window to pull the curtains closed.

My room, like Molly's, is at the front of the house, though it's much bigger, with an en suite. The bathroom and two more bedrooms, one which Michael had used as a study, are across the landing, at the rear, with views over the garden and the backs of the houses in the next road down. My room felt a little muggy. As usual I had kept the windows closed when we were out for reasons of security and I'd forgotten to open mine when we came home today, so the heat of the sun, surprisingly warm this early in the year, had become trapped. I opened the window wide to let in some air before I came up to bed, and leaned forward, my elbows on the sill, breathing in the scents of evening.

The street was quiet, as usual – just Frank Bowers from two doors down walking his goldie, Ben. Ben's getting on a bit; Frank was ambling along, Ben stopping to sniff at every lamp post. Idly I followed their progress, then froze, my eyes narrowing.

That car parked further along on the opposite side of the road – it looked very like the one that had been outside our house earlier. It was now about fifty yards away, but the light of the streetlamps clearly showed the dark silhouette of someone behind the wheel. For a couple of minutes I stared at the car. No one got out, no one came out of a house to get in. What on earth was the driver doing just sitting there?

Annoyed with myself for my curiosity, I straightened up and drew the curtains. Taking this much interest in some-thing and someone that had nothing to do with me was a clear sign of loneliness. It couldn't be the same car as before. Why on earth would it be? I was imagining things. Going a bit loopy.

Putting it out of my mind, I went downstairs to pack away my iron and ironing board and maybe catch the late news on the box before thinking about bed.

Next evening, somewhat reluctantly, I got myself ready to go to Anna's jewellery party. My excuse about having no babysitter had been shot out of the water as soon as I mentioned it to Maria – she'd been every bit as keen to do duty as Anna had suggested she would be.

Maria really was the ideal babysitter. She was a plump, rosy-cheeked girl who adored children and was adored by them in return. Molly had already left the nursery to start infant school by the time Maria joined the staff, but they'd found an instant rapport when Molly came in with me.

'If ever you need a babysitter, you know where to come,' Maria had said, and I'd had no hesitation about asking her when the need arose. I knew Molly would be well looked after and that Maria was glad of the chance to earn some extra money. She and Darren, her boyfriend, were saving to get married. Sometimes he came with her when she sat for me and I didn't mind that either. He was a good lad, big and solid, built like a rugby player, and though at first sight the bulging biceps under the tight T-shirts, the earring and the tattoo could be a little disconcerting, I now knew that underneath he had a heart of gold and was as gentle as a lamb.

Molly, at least, was pleased that Maria was coming to look after her this evening.

'I don't have to go to bed before she gets here, do I?' she asked when I went upstairs to change. 'I want her to sing with me.'

I smiled. Molly loved singing; so did Maria. Their favourite at the moment was *Amarillo* and they'd belt it out together, waving their arms and wiggling their bottoms, clapping their hands to the *sha-la-las*.

'No, but I think you should get into your pyjamas.' Friday night, so no need for a bath and hair-wash tonight.

In the event, however, Maria was late. She phoned me at about half past seven to say Darren had been delayed, she was really sorry, but it was going to be another hour or so before she got to us.

I wasn't altogether sorry. I wasn't looking forward to being pitched into the hard-sell of a jewellery party and the social chit-chat of a dozen or so girls I may or may not know very well. The only trouble was it would mean I'd have to drive both ways in the dark, and I didn't want to do that either.

I let Molly stay up until Maria and Darren arrived, full of apologies, and by the time I'd showed Maria the cold meats and cheeses I'd left for them in the fridge, kissed Molly goodnight and grabbed my jacket and car keys, the dusk was complete. As I went out to the garage the strains of *Is this the Way to Amarillo* followed me; both Maria and Molly singing at the tops of their voices.

Molly had a very nice voice, I thought, and she'd been able to hold a tune since she was two years old. She wasn't going to get ideas about being a pop singer, I hoped. These days everyone seemed to want that. When we were children, little boys wanted to drive trains or racing cars and little girls wanted to be nurses or air hostesses. Nowadays all they wanted was fame. The thought of Molly battling it out and inevitably being disappointed was not one I wanted to entertain.

I went into the garage through the side entrance from the utility room, pushed open the up-and-over door, and got into my little VW Golf. I manoeuvred on to the drive and got out to close the garage doors behind me.

I'd forgotten all about the car I'd seen parked opposite on the previous evening, and it was quite a shock when I saw it again – not opposite our house, but further down the road, more or less where I'd seen it from my own bedroom window.

That is odd, I thought. And then: Perhaps the Bowers or the Spurlings have someone staying with them and they're parking outside rather than blocking up the driveway.

I drove out into the street and turned on to the road that would take me out of town in the direction of Little Ryedale, the village where Anna lived. As I put my indicator on to turn left I saw lights in my rear-view mirror. For the moment I thought nothing of it, but when I hit the open road and they were still there I began to feel, not disturbed exactly, but distinctly curious.

A few miles out into the country and they were still there. I slowed down, expecting the following car to overtake me, but no, it seemed to me that it had slowed as well. I speeded up; the other car did the same, remaining equidistant behind me. It was almost as if he was following me. Alarmed, I immediately told myself not to be silly. But I couldn't escape the knot of nerves that had formed in my stomach, nor stop myself from continually checking the rear-view mirror, though I scarcely needed to, for the lights were still there, impinging on my retinas, even when I was looking at the road ahead.

They were quite distinctive, those lights, blue-white rather than yellow and I was almost sure that when the car I'd seen parked in our road last night had driven away his lights had been blue ones too. I couldn't see the shape or colour of the vehicle, of course, but I had the sinking feeling that if I could it would be the same.

Stop it! I scolded myself. *Of course it's not the same car, and if it is, why in the world should it be following you?* But I couldn't shake the unease that was slowly but surely gathering to something like panic.

I put my lights on to full beam, wishing they were more powerful, and put my foot down. The following car kept pace with me. And suddenly I was remembering the circumstances of Michael's accident on the night that he died and the statements made to the police by a couple of witnesses – a young couple who had been driving home along the same road.

They had been overtaken at speed by two cars, they told the police. First one and then the other, hot on its tail, had zoomed past them, going, as they had put it, like 'bats out of hell'. They'd thought at the time the cars were being driven by youngsters who were racing one another, called them 'crazy idiots' and predicted that they'd kill themselves and maybe some innocent motorist too. They'd turned off the road a couple of miles prior to the scene of the accident, but they'd come forward when they heard of it. At the time the police had speculated that it had been a case of road rage, that Michael had done something to annoy another driver, who had then chased him. But there was nothing to prove that either of the two cars had been Michael's, or identify the other one, and so they'd had to let it drop.

I'd never believed it in any case. I couldn't imagine Michael doing anything to warrant that sort of retaliation, though it has to be said I couldn't imagine him driving dangerously, full stop. But I'd had to accept that he had been. Now, however, it all came back to me. A car following Michael, panicking him into driving too fast. A car following me . . .

My heart was hammering in my throat, the palms of my hands were damp and sticky on the steering wheel. Again I told myself to take no notice – slow down – drive normally. Again I found my foot depressing the accelerator, rounding a bend faster than I liked too, easing off, pressing forward again. All I wanted was to get to Anna's house, the safety of the company of other people, the comfort of my friend.

Again and again my gaze was drawn to the rear-view mirror and those distinctive lights like tiger eyes in the darkness. They were mesmerizing me, though I knew I should ignore them and concentrate on the road. I reached the junction with the lane that wound for two or three miles between grassy banks and high hedges to Little Ryedale – and Anna's cottage – and swung into it. Too fast. For a horrible moment as I slewed across the lane I thought I was going to hit the bank on the opposite road. I overcorrected and the car went into a skid, throwing me back on to the nearside verge. For a moment that seemed like an eternity I was bumping along it, then my front wheels ran into something solid and I came to an abrupt, jolting halt.

My car seemed to be tilting at an alarming angle, and I was terrified it was going to roll over. But even worse, the lights were still there. Right behind me now, illuminating the hedge and the road. As the car passed me slowly I saw the man in the driver's seat. He was staring at me and pulling into the side of the road directly in front of me.

My heart hammered; my throat was constricted. Who *was* he? What the hell did he want, watching the house and following me? Was he a stalker? This couldn't be happening! But it was. And there was nothing I could do to get away from him now.

My car was firmly stuck and so was I.

Three

B lindly, I fumbled for the button that would lock my door. Why the hell hadn't I done it before? But my hands were shaking and awkward; in my panic I couldn't locate it.

The man was out of his car now, walking back towards me. A big man. Tall. Muscular in an athletic way. I knew I wouldn't stand a chance against him. Again I scrabbled for the lock, but before I could get the button down he had the car door open.

I felt in that moment the way you feel in one of those dreams when you try to run but your feet are bogged down, your legs as heavy as lead. I was trapped, totally, utterly trapped, and it was petrifying. He was there, his bulk completely filling the doorway, leaning in so that his head was only inches from mine. I could see the craggy line of his jaw and a nose that might have been broken at some time. A stranger. No one I knew at all. Suddenly I found my voice.

'Get away from me!' I screamed. 'Don't you dare touch me!'

He backed off a little, a sort of reflex action to my hysteria, but only a few inches.

'Are you all right?'

At first I didn't register that there was no threat, no aggression in his voice. That it was actually a rather nice voice, deep, with the faint burr of a rural accent and, if anything, concerned. I was still too shocked – and too scared.

'No – no I'm not!' I said sobbing. 'Get away! Leave me alone!'

'OK, OK!' This time he moved further away, holding up his hands placatingly. 'Calm down. I'm not going to hurt you.'

The moon had come out from behind a cloud; by its light, now that he was not so close to me, I could see his face more clearly. Though it was all planes and shadows, he didn't look like a rapist or a murderer.

'You were following me!' My voice, still shaking, rose hysterically.

'Sorry?' He sounded puzzled. How dare he sound puzzled!

'You've been following me for miles.' Suddenly I became aware again of the crazy angle my car was pitched at and I felt the beginnings of a new wave of panic. 'Oh, God, I'm going to tip over!'

'You're not going to tip over.'

'I am!'

'No, you're not. You're perfectly stable.'

'I am not stable! Oh – this is all your fault! Why were you following me? What do you want?'

He spread his arms helplessly. 'This is ridiculous. I saw you run off the road and I stopped to see if you were all right, or if you needed my help. But if you don't, I'll get on my way.'

There was something in the way he said it, a bit impatient and definitely offhand, that triggered a nugget of doubt in my mind. Had I overreacted – imagined the whole thing? Was he a perfectly innocent motorist who'd stopped to play the good Samaritan only to find a hysterical woman accusing him of God-knows-what?

'I . . . I . . .'

'Well, you're clearly not hurt. And I should imagine your car is perfectly driveable.' He walked round to the front, kicked something, came back. I noticed he walked with a bit of a limp. 'Looks like you ran into a boulder. You'll have a dent in your spoiler, I should think. Otherwise . . .' He started to move away, back towards his own car. 'Goodnight, then.'

'No! Wait! Don't go!' I was panicking again, not this time because the man was there – clearly he was no danger to me – but because he was going away and I was stuck at a crazy angle on a bank miles from anywhere.

He stopped but did not come back. He stood there, an athletic looking man casually dressed in sweatshirt, jeans and trainers. He did not look in the least threatening now. I began to feel a little foolish and ashamed, as well as frightened at the thought of being left out here all alone.

'Don't go!' I repeated. 'I'm sorry. Please don't go.'

'Well, make up your mind.' His tone was short – hardly surprising, really, given the accusations I'd levelled wildly at him.

'I'm sorry,' I said. 'Help me, please.'

He came back then, if a little reluctantly, I thought.

'You're OK. Just reverse along the bank and you can get back on the road.'

'I can't!' With the car at this angle, I was terrified of moving at all.

'Of course you can. Come on, I'll watch you.'

My hand shook as I turned the ignition key – the car had stalled, of course, when I hit the boulder. The engine started first time. Getting a grip on myself I eased the gear stick into reverse, inched back a fraction and stopped again, absolutely certain that at any moment I was going to roll.

'Come on.' His voice was even now, the sort of tone I might use to a nervous child at nursery. 'Straight back. You're fine.'

I took a deep breath and let out the clutch, moving only a few inches before stopping again.

'Do you want me to do it for you?'

'No.' I was almost as frightened of getting out of the car as I was of moving it. But I couldn't stay here all night, and I didn't want to look an even bigger fool than I already did. 'No, it's all right. I'll do it.'

'Come on then.'

Holding my breath, my heart hammering, my palms sticky with nervous perspiration, I crept slowly backwards. He was right – I didn't roll. A couple of feet and the verge flattened – the part where I'd mounted it, I suppose. With an enormous sense of relief I felt the car ease back on to a normal plane. I changed into first gear, turned the steering wheel to the right, and I was back on firm tarmac, moving back up the lane to where the man had stopped his car. My headlights shone directly on to the back of it and a nerve jolted again as I registered that it was dark grey or black. But I had no way of knowing if it was the same one that had been parked in our road, and even if it was, the brief conversation we'd had made it quite clear to me that I'd been wrong in thinking that he'd been following me. If it was the same car it was just coincidence that he'd been going the same way as me. He clearly had no sinister designs on me at all.

Something else was engaging my attention, too. There was something odd, heavy, about my steering. The car wasn't handling as it should. I pulled in and the man came alongside me.

'OK now?'

'No. I think I've got a puncture.'

He stepped back, looking at it by the light of the moon.

'Yep. I think you have.'

'Oh, shit!' Still shaky, my nerves in shreds, it was the last straw. I was close to tears. At least I'd kept up the recovery service Michael had always insisted on. 'I'll have to call the RAC. Oh, God – they could be hours.'

'Don't worry. You have got a spare? I'll change it for you.'

I was astounded by his kindness. Not five minutes ago I'd accused him of following me and causing me to run off the road. I'd been scared to death he was a murderer or a rapist. Now here he was offering to change my flat tyre!

'Oh, no – I can't put you to all that trouble,' I protested.

'Doesn't take much to change a tyre. As long as you can find the wheel brace and jack.' His tone was nonchalant.

'But you'll get yourself filthy.'

'The road's dry. If it was pouring with rain I might not be so ready to offer. Come on, let's get to it. As you so rightly say, it could be hours before your friendly RAC man gets here.'

'Well, if you're absolutely sure . . .' I didn't know what to say. I was feeling thoroughly ashamed of myself now and totally foolish. But I also wanted to be safe at home again, with Molly asleep upstairs, as soon as possible. No, not as soon as possible. I wanted to be there now, this minute. 'Thank you very much,' I said meekly.

I opened the boot and located the spare tyre, wheel brace and jack whilst the man fetched a halogen lantern from his own car.

'This is so kind,' I said as he came back with it. 'I really am grateful.'

He gave me an amused look, one eyebrow and one corner of his mouth lifting.

'Makes a change from yelling at me.'

'I know. I am so sorry about that. I thought . . .'

'I know.' The other corner of his mouth lifted – I could see it clearly in the now-bright moonlight, and the shadows made deep and rather attractive creases in his face. 'You made it pretty clear what you thought.'

'I'm paranoid. My husband . . .' But he wasn't listening to me. He was going down on his hands and knees, the brace in his hand, looking for the wheel nuts to loosen them.

'I don't even know your name,' I said foolishly.

'Tom Bradshaw.' He said it without looking up.

'I'm Jo Lansdale. Joanna, really, but everyone calls me Jo.' It came out sounding inane. My fright, receding now, was making me light-headed. But it seemed important somehow that we should introduce ourselves.

'Hi, Jo.' He loosened a nut. 'Can you pass me the jack?'

I went to fetch it. As I passed the open door of my car I heard the musical ring-tone of my mobile. 'Here it is.' I put the jack down beside him, went back to retrieve my bag from the passenger seat of my car and extracted my mobile.

'Hello?'

'Jo?' It was Anna. 'Are you all right? Where are you?'

'Anna!' My breath came out on a shuddering little sigh. 'Yes, I'm all right. But I've had a bit of trouble.'

'So where *are* you? Jo – I've been so worried . . .' She sounded it. In the background I could hear the twitter of female voices and someone laughing. 'When you didn't turn up I rang you at home and Maria said you'd left. Why aren't you here? What's happened?'

'I've got a puncture. I got too close to the side of the road and I must have hit a sharp stone.' Understatement of the year. But I didn't want to go into details now, and I didn't want to alarm Anna either.'

'You mean you're stranded! Where are you?'

'About three miles from you.'

'Have you called the AA?'

31

'Mine's RAC. No, I haven't called them. A passing motorist stopped. He's changing the tyre for me now.' I glanced at the man – Tom Bradshaw. He'd already loosened the nuts and was jacking up my car.

'A passing motorist? Who is it? Is it anyone you know?'

'No. But he's been very kind.'

'Are you sure he's all right, Jo? It's very lonely out there . . .'

'He's fine.' Strange I should feel that way now, when such a short time ago he'd been frightening the life out of me.

'Look – why don't I see if I can get hold of Dave? He'll be on his refreshment break soon – maybe I can get a message to him. If there's nothing much going on he might be able to come out to you, or get someone else who's in the area to stop by.'

I hesitated. Though I was no longer suspicious of Tom Bradshaw's motives I was still very shaky and the thought of a friendly face, especially one as solid and reassuring as Anna's Dave, who always reminded me of a big teddy bear, was a tempting one. But it would cause such a fuss – messages being passed over police radios, big throaty motor bikes roaring in the quiet night, with or without flashing strobe lights – and more than anything now I felt intensely foolish.

'I'm OK, honestly,' I said. 'I've got my mobile as you can hear, and if there's any problem I'll give you another call.'

'Well, if you're sure . . . Dave would come, I know, or get someone else to . . .'

'I'm sure. I'm not going to make the party now, though, I'm afraid. Once my tyre's fixed I shall go straight home.'

'Well, you are to call me when you get there.' Anna had gone into bossy mode. 'I mean it, Jo. I want to hear from you, whatever time it is. I shan't sleep a wink until I do. Promise me, now.'

'I promise.'

'It is such a shame! A night out was just what you needed. And there's the prettiest choker here – a sort of springy silver band with a stone like a topaz dangling on the front. I had it set aside for you. It's your birthstone, isn't it, topaz? I shall buy it for you anyway.'

'Anna . . .'

'Yes, I shall. To make up for you missing the party.'

She would, too, I knew.

'Well, you'll let me give you the money for it,' I said. With three children to bring up and a mortgage to pay on a policeman's salary, I knew money was tight. Much tighter than it was for me, thanks to Michael's generous insurance pay-out.

'We'll see about that.' Anna's tone told me there would be an argument and I would probably be the loser. She was generous as well as bossy, my friend. 'Now you take care, Jo, do you hear me? And ring me the minute you get home – or before, if you need to.'

'I will.' I clicked the button to end the call but I didn't put the phone back into my bag. Instead I slipped it into the pocket of my jacket and kept my fingers curled lightly around it. I might not think now that I was in any danger from the man, but he was still a stranger and knowing I could make contact with the outside world at the touch of a button was reassuring.

Tom Bradshaw had the wheel off now. He didn't even glance up as I went to stand beside him.

'That was my friend Anna,' I said. 'I should have been at a jewellery party at her home. That's where I was going when . . .' My voice tailed away. *When I panicked and ran off the road because I thought you were stalking me . . .* 'She'd rung my home and when she knew I was somewhere on the way she was worried.'

He glanced up at me briefly. 'What about your husband? If your friend rang your home and said you hadn't arrived, won't he be worried?'

'I don't have a husband.' My throat was tight suddenly. 'I'm a widow.'

'Oh, I'm sorry.' He slid the spare wheel into place.

'He was killed two years ago. In a road accident.' *And there was a suspicion he was being followed at the time and went too fast, just like I did. Only he hit a tree and all I did was run up the bank and get a puncture . . .*

It was all there in my mind, but of course I didn't say it. I didn't want to regale a complete stranger with my life history. 'That's probably why I'm a bit paranoid,' I said instead.

He didn't answer; he was too busy with the tyre. I watched in silence as he worked for a few more minutes. Then he lowered the car back on to all four wheels and straightened up. 'All done then.' He fished in the pocket of his jeans for a handkerchief to wipe his hands. I was mortified.

'Don't make your handkerchief dirty! I've got some wet wipes.' I opened the driver's door, feeling in the pocket. 'Here – use these. I always keep them handy for my daughter. If she has an ice-cream or chocolate she always manages to end up sticky!'

'You have a daughter?' He had pulled a wet-wipe out of the packet and was scrubbing his hands.

'Yes. Molly. She's seven.'

'You don't look old enough to have a daughter of seven.' It was the first personal exchange between us and it took me a bit by surprise.

'I'm thirty-five,' I said automatically. 'Old enough to have a daughter of seventeen, never mind seven!'

He grinned. In the moonlight I could see that craggy face clearly and I wondered briefly how old *he* was. About my age, at a rough guess. Maybe a bit older. It was hard to tell. Certainly not much over forty, if I was any judge.

He took the punctured tyre to the boot of my car. I followed with the jack and wheel brace.

'You'd better get to a garage first thing tomorrow,' he said, slotting the tyre into its compartment. 'You shouldn't drive on a spare more than you have to.'

'In case I get another puncture.'

'Well, that too. But the spare is smaller. It's just that – a spare. For emergencies. There's a speed restriction when you're using it.' He levelled a glance at me. 'You didn't know.'

I shook my head. 'What I know about cars could be written on a postage stamp. But I assure you, I shan't be speeding any more tonight.'

He grinned again. He really was rather nice-looking, I thought – and wondered why on earth I had been so scared of him.

'Better not. I shan't be on your tail if you do the same thing on the way home.'

'Don't worry, I won't!' He had replaced the brace and jack now, slotted the floor of the boot back into place. 'I'm really grateful. I don't know how I can ever thank you.'

'I'll think of something.' He closed the boot, looked directly at me. 'How about letting me take you out for a drink or a meal one night for a start?'

That really did throw me. It was a very long time since anyone had asked me out. When you are a widow with a little girl, working in an almost totally female environment and rarely going out socially, the opportunity rarely arises. And in the case of someone like Adam, who I'd suspected might have had something of the sort in mind, I'd been able to erect barriers, make it clear that such a suggestion would not be welcome, before the words were actually spoken.

Now I was caught completely off guard. Flustered beyond belief. Embarrassed by my own gaucheness.

'Oh – I don't think . . .'

'Why not? You said you aren't married any more, and neither am I, and we almost know one another. We did introduce ourselves, after all. When you stopped yelling at me.'

I could have told him there were a dozen reasons why not, but somehow I didn't.

'I can't believe you're asking me out after that,' I said instead.

'No, neither can I,' he said, and grinned again.

It was that grin that was my undoing. That half-rueful, half-mischievous little boy expression on a face that was unmistakeably all man. Quite suddenly I realized that I actually wanted to see him again. Given all my early misgivings it was crazy, but there it was. For the first time since Michael had died, I actually wanted to see another man.

'All right,' I said.

He looked surprised – as surprised as I was myself. I thought for a moment that he'd changed his mind, or never really meant it at all. That it had just been something to say, to tease me almost. I felt a little foolish again, awkward, that I'd taken him seriously. But before I could think of a way to extricate myself – let him know that I'd been joking too

– he said: 'When shall we say, then? Is Saturday a good time for you?'

'Tomorrow, you mean? Oh, I don't think I can. I can't ask my babysitter two nights running.'

'OK.' He leaned back casually against my car. 'You name a day then.'

My mind was racing. I could still get out of it. But I didn't want to.

'What about next Friday? A week today?' A Friday would be good, I thought. No work for me next day, no school for Molly. And time to come to my senses . . .

'Sounds good to me. Shall I pick you up? Where do you live?'

You know where I live. I almost said it, but I didn't want to start all that again. Didn't want to think about it.

'Lynton Road. Number Eighteen.'

'There's a recreation ground or something there, isn't there?'

'Opposite us. We're just along from the main entrance.'

'What time shall we say, then? Half past seven?'

'Better make it eight.'

'Oh, yes – you've got to put your daughter to bed first.'

'The babysitter can do that.' Molly would be pleased. Another chance to belt out *Amarillo* with Maria – provided Maria could make it. 'You'd better give me your phone number,' I said, 'just in case there's a problem. I wouldn't want you to have a wasted evening.'

He slapped the pockets of his jeans. 'I don't have any of my cards on me. Have you got something I could write on?'

I fished in my bag, pulled out my diary and opened it to one of the blank pages for January. My diary was mostly blank these days. Just dentist's appointments, hair cuts and concerts and sports days at Molly's school. I found a ball-point pen – one of the freebies they send you with requests for donations to charity.

'Here.'

He wrote, then handed the diary and pen back to me. 'There you are then, just in case. But I hope you won't need it. I'll book a restaurant and I shall be working up an appetite all day, so you'd better not stand me up.'

I smiled. 'I'll try not to. But let me give you my number too. I don't want to be stood up either.' I wrote my name and number on another of the blank pages, tore it out, and gave it to him. He glanced at it, folded it and tucked it in the front pocket of his jeans.

'You're all right now then? You'll remember to get to a garage first thing tomorrow?'

'As soon as I can, yes.'

'In that case I'll say goodnight.'

'Goodnight. And thanks again.'

'No problem.' He was heading back to his own car. As I got into mine I heard him gun the engine and then he was gone, his tail lights disappearing around a bend in the lane. I started my own engine and put the car into gear. I couldn't do a three-point turn here, the lane was too narrow and twisty, so I drove along until I found a farm entrance I could reverse into. My mind was racing, running over what had happened and full of unanswered questions, but I didn't stop to wonder about them now. All I wanted was to get home. But this time, as I'd told Tom I would, I drove very carefully indeed.

'Jo Lansdale!' Anna was talking in exclamation marks. 'I don't believe what I'm hearing! This man asked you out and you actually said yes!'

It was the next morning. I'd phoned Anna, as I'd promised, when I got in last night, but it had been a very brief conversation, just to let her know I was safely home, and now I was ringing to fill her in on the details.

'That's about the size of it,' I said.

'Well, I'm not sure that's a good idea.' Anna was going into bossy mode. 'You don't know him.'

'I know he's called Tom Bradshaw and he was kind enough to stop when he saw I was in trouble and to change my tyre for me. And I have his telephone number.'

'So what's the code? Where does he live?'

'I don't know,' I confessed. 'It looks like a mobile number.'

'Hmm.' Anna sounded suspicious, even though giving a mobile number these days is pretty commonplace.

'He must be some kind of professional,' I offered. 'He mentioned his business card, but he didn't have one on him.'

'Convenient.'

'Anna – please – don't spoil it. I haven't been taken out for a meal since Michael died.'

'Exactly. You're out of practice. Vulnerable. You're not thinking straight.'

She might be right, I conceded. But I was certainly *thinking*. I'd lain awake for a very long time last night going over it in my mind, wondering if I'd done the right thing or not, whether I should call the mobile number he'd given me and tell him I'd changed my mind. The very thought of going out with someone on a date – a date sounded like something teenagers did – filled my stomach with butterflies. And I still couldn't quite work out where he'd come from so conveniently if he hadn't been following me, whether his was the same car I'd seen parked in our road, and if it was, what he was playing at. I'd convinced myself it couldn't have been the same car – it made no sense at all – and besides, he was too nice. I'd really liked him, felt quite at ease with him once I'd got over my initial fright. I *wanted* to see him again – wasn't that enough? And yet a little nugget of suspicion remained. My own unanswered questions along with the ones Anna was posing now.

'Anna,' I said. 'Last night I was stuck with him in the middle of nowhere in the dark. If he'd been going to do me a mischief, he had every opportunity. I don't think I'm going to come to any harm in a public place like a restaurant full of people.'

'You're going to get in a car with him. That doesn't sound very sensible to me.'

'Mummy!' Molly had come into the kitchen. She was wearing her best flower-embroidered jeans and a sparkly pink T-shirt, and pulled her long fair hair up into two bunches, secured with pink bobbles, to frame her face. 'Are we going into town or not?'

I nodded at her – yes.

'Anna, I'm going to have to go. Molly's getting impatient. And I have to get to the garage anyway. We'll talk again.'

'OK. But don't do anything rash, do you hear me?'

'I won't. And it's another week anyway until . . .' I glanced at Molly, who was pushing one of the bobbles higher up her bunch and watching me critically. I didn't want to finish that particular sentence in her hearing until I'd had the chance to tell her . . .

What? How did I explain to my seven-year-old daughter that I was planning to go out with a man who was not her father? I quailed at the prospect. Oh, well – I would think about that later . . .

'Speak to you soon,' I said to Anna, then put down the phone and turned to Molly. 'Right, sweetheart, you're ready, I take it?'

'Yes. But if we're not going yet, I'm going to watch *Snow White*.' It was her favourite DVD, which she must already know by heart as she'd watched it so many times.

'We are going.' I was scouting round the kitchen, collecting my shopping list, purse and keys. And then the phone rang again. Molly raised her eyes heavenward and headed off into the living room and, presumably, the DVD player.

I reached for the phone, half expecting it to be Anna again with a new set of reasons why I should not go out with Tom Bradshaw.

Instead, to my surprise, it was Alison's voice on the other end of the line.

'Jo, I'm really sorry to bother you again, but I was just wondering . . . you still haven't heard anything from Adam, have you?'

'No – sorry. Haven't you managed to locate him, then?'

'No. Jo, I'd really like to talk to you. Are you coming into town today? If so, do you think you could pop into the office?'

'Well, I could, but I shall have Molly with me. Can't you . . . ?'

'Tell you now, on the phone? I'd really rather not.' Alison sounded reluctant. She also sounded very worried. 'I won't keep you long, I promise, and we'll find something for Molly to do while we talk.'

What could I say?

'I'll see you later then,' I said, wondering what Alison wanted to talk to me about so urgently that couldn't be said over the phone. It concerned Adam, obviously. But I couldn't see there was anything I could do or that it really had anything to do with me.

I put down the phone, picked up my bits and pieces again and called to Molly that we were going *now*, this minute. Never for one moment did I suspect that events had already begun to move that would suck me into a nightmare.

Four

We did a detour to the garage to leave my tyre for repair, then headed for the town centre and the spacious free car park that flanks the high street.

Laverham is a nice town – just the right size, really. According to the registers, it is home to about twenty thousand people, though it's growing all the time, with new estates swallowing up an alarming swathe of what used to be open country, and a business park or two springing up on the outskirts. The town centre itself, however, remains much as it always was – a long one-way street with a river running through it, a lot of interesting little shops, interspersed with a row of old almshouses at one end, and a square, more heavily developed, at the other. There's an Aldi these days, and a Sainsbury's, and even a small Boots. And a two-storey mall between the car park and the high street with a hairdresser's, a florist's, and a health food shop, amongst other things.

Adam's estate agency is situated on the frontage of the mall, looking out on to the high street – a prime position, really. Molly and I headed down the stairs from street level at the rear – there's a little escalator going up but not down, though more often than not it is out of order.

'I have to call in at the office,' I told her.

'Oh, no!' Molly's face fell. 'Do you have to?'

'Yes.' I wanted to do it first and get it over with. 'Tell you what. Why don't you go up to World of Wonder and have a look around – I'll come and find you there when I've talked to Alison.'

World of Wonder is a really superb toy shop, just a few blocks up on the high street. Molly loves poking about there, spotting new Barbie clothes and accessories, or furniture she wants for her doll's house, and jotting them down on her Christmas or birthday list.

She brightened visibly. 'OK.'

'And Molly – ' I got out my purse, took out some pound coins and a couple of fifty pence pieces – 'if you see some of those tattoo transfers you wanted, here's some money to buy them.'

Her eyes went round, her smile lit up her pretty face.

'Mummy! Thank you!'

The coins were still in my hand; I curled my fingers round them. 'You did give the other one back to Jessica?'

'Yes, of course I did.'

'OK then – get some of your own.'

She got out her little purse, pink with a butterfly appliquéd to it, and I dropped the coins into it.

'I'll see you in the toy shop, then. Don't go wandering off anywhere else, will you?'

'I won't.' She skipped off and I pushed open the plate glass door of the estate agency, which had Adam's name emblazoned on it in big green letters.

The junior who I thought was called Claire was behind the desk. She was handing out literature to a young man whilst his partner browsed one of the boards with pictures of property on it that stand in the outer office.

'Alison?' I mouthed to her.

With a tilt of her head she indicated the door leading to the inner sanctum. I went through. In the little room beyond, Alison was seated at one of two desks that were furnished with a computer screen, keyboard and telephone. A coffee mug stood on a coaster at her elbow.

'Jo! Oh – thanks for coming.' Alison is very attractive, not pretty exactly, but certainly striking. She's quite a big girl, and she dresses to flaunt it in the nicest possible way. She has a strong featured face, dark eyes and a sharp, sassy haircut that looks expensive. I think she must go into the city to get it done. I can't see any of the so-called stylists in Laverham having that sort of expertise or being so obviously up-to-the-moment. I'm always promising myself an appointment with someone trendier than A Cut Above, but somehow I never seem to have the time to get around to it.

'I can't stay too long,' I said. 'Molly's in the toy shop.'

'Can I get you a coffee?'

'No, I've not long had one at home.' I lowered myself into the mock-leather chair set at an angle at the corner of the desk. 'What did you want to talk to me about?'

'Adam.' Alison's face was serious; she pushed a hand through the wedge of hair at her temple. 'As I said on the phone, I'm really sorry to bother you, Jo. But I'm terribly worried and I didn't know where else to turn.'

'But I already said – I can't help you, Alison,' I said. 'It's a couple of weeks now since I saw Adam. I haven't heard anything from him, and I'm not party to his movements.'

'I know.' Alison chewed on a finger nail. 'I just wanted to talk it over really. Get another opinion as to what I ought to do. And you . . . well, you're practically family.'

'Hardly.' *It was Michael who was practically family, not me . . .* 'To be honest, Alison, I don't understand why you're getting so worked up about it. He just wants a bit of space, I expect. You know as well as I do that Adam is very much his own person. He hates being tied down or checked up on. It's just the way he is.'

'But his business is important to him,' Alison cut in sharply. 'He wouldn't just go off and not let me know how to contact him if something came up that I couldn't handle. Even if he doesn't spend as much time in the office as perhaps he should, he likes to keep his finger on the pulse. Surely Michael must have told you that? It caused a bit of friction, really. Michael thought Adam was too controlling. Forever looking over his shoulder and changing decisions he'd made.'

I bit my lip. It was true. Michael had mentioned once or twice that he wished Adam would let him have his head a little more and that there were aspects of the business that Adam still insisted on dealing with himself even though Michael was supposed to be managing the office. Presumably it was the same with Alison.

'So he's acting a bit out of character,' I said. 'But there could be any number of reasons. He's realized you're doing a fantastic job here and he's taken himself off for a holiday or to get some new project off the ground.'

Alison shook her head. 'It's more than that, Jo. I just know it is.'

'How can you be so sure?' I asked.

'Because . . .' She picked up a paperclip, twisting it between her fingers. 'The reason I asked you to come in this morning is because I found out something last night that really got me worried. I mean. I've been worried all week, hearing nothing and not being able to contact him. But last night . . .'

'Yes?' I prompted her.

'I got into his on-line bank statement. Oh, I know . . .' She raised a hand, waving it at me as she saw my look of disapproval. 'I shouldn't have done it, but I've just been so damned worried and I thought I might be able to see from any withdrawals he'd made where he'd been. The location of the cash point – you know.'

'How did you get into his bank account?' I asked, genuinely shocked.

'I knew that he had his passwords and memorable details jotted down in an old diary in his desk – I came across them once when I was looking for something. Of course, under normal circumstances I'd never have used them, but . . .'

'I'm surprised at him, leaving that sort of thing lying about,' I said.

'I suppose he thought it was safe enough. His desk – his office.' Alison had the grace to look a little guilty. 'And when you have to do random conversions of up to fifteen digits – I must admit, I've got mine written down too. Make a mistake a couple of times and they close down the access because they think you might be a hacker . . . anyway, rightly or wrongly, I opened up his bank statement. And that is when I really started to get worried.'

I looked at her questioningly, though I had already guessed what she was going to say. 'Why? What did you find?'

'There have been no withdrawals for the past two weeks,' she said. 'Apart from his direct debits, which go out every month, no movement at all.'

'Perhaps he hasn't needed to make any withdrawals.' I was unwilling to acknowledge what she was trying to tell me.

'Adam? He spends money like water, you know that. He always likes to have cash in his wallet – wads of it. I looked back to check. He usually withdraws several hundred pounds each week. But the last two weeks – nothing.'

'Maybe if he's in Spain or Tenerife he took traveller's cheques.'

'No, he wouldn't do that. He says they're the most inconvenient way of handling money that he's ever come across.'

'A credit card then,' I suggested.

'I checked his credit card statements too. Nothing. Zilch.' She leaned forward, her gaze meeting mine directly. 'Doesn't it seem just a little odd to you, Jo, that he hasn't drawn any cash or used his credit cards for two whole weeks?'

'Well, yes.' I was forced to agree. 'I suppose it does.'

'There's something else too,' Alison went on. 'The last couple of days before he went missing, Adam wasn't himself at all.'

'What do you mean?' I asked.

'He was . . . oh, I don't know . . . preoccupied. Bad-tempered too. You know what he's like usually – a bit full of himself, a bit brash, but really easy to get on with. But that week he was snappy and impatient – he nearly had Claire in tears over some silly little mistake she made with a client, and he bit my head off once or twice, too. I thought at the time maybe he wasn't feeling well – a hangover, or coming down with a cold or something – but since then . . . well, I've been thinking about it and it seems to me that something was worrying him.'

A small chill whispered over my skin. Hearing Alison say that was a little like déjà vu. I'd thought Michael was worried about something – n the days leading up to his accident. He'd been preoccupied and short-tempered too.

Alison had completely unravelled the paperclip in her agitation. She looked up at me, her eyes dark with anxiety, meeting mine directly.

'I think something has happened to him, Jo.'

Something terrible. She didn't need to actually say it. I knew what she meant.

'You mean . . . you think he may have done something silly?' I asked. As a euphemism for suicide it was the grossest understatement. But I knew Alison would understand the inference behind my words, just as I had understood the inference behind hers. And even as I said it, I was thinking: No! Adam would never do something like that. He just wasn't the suicidal type.

'Either that or . . .' Alison hesitated.

'What?' I asked puzzled.

'I don't know how to put this, Jo. But Adam is involved with some very dubious characters. Did Michael ever mention Kenny White to you? Or Mervyn Hiscox?'

I frowned, trying to remember. The names rang vague bells, but that was all.

'He may have mentioned them. I don't recall . . .'

'Kenny White lives in that big house on Proctor Hill – the one with electronically operated security gates, and Mervyn Hiscox has a stud farm, out in the country,' Alison started to explain.

'They've got plenty of money between them then,' I remarked dryly.

She nodded. 'Oh, yes, they've got plenty of that, all right. The leading question is – how did they come by it? Popular opinion is that it almost certainly was not legally.'

'You mean they're criminals?' I was shocked.

'I'd say so, yes. With fingers in all kinds of sticky – and very lucrative – pies. But they're clever enough to keep it pretty quiet. There have always been rumours surrounding them, nothing more. I believe Kenny did a spell in a young offenders' institution when he was a lad, but since then he's managed to steer clear of the law. Or cosied up to them. He has one or two good friends in the police force, or so I've heard – and I'm not talking your bobby on the beat, either.'

'Someone has turned a blind eye, you mean?'

'Exactly. Palms are greased – a brown paper envelope changes hands . . .'

'But that's corruption!'

'Happens, though. When someone has Kenny White's wherewithal, there's always going to be a weak link some-where in the line who will succumb to temptation.'

'But what is the connection to Adam?' I asked.

'He socialized with them,' Alison said. 'You know how

Adam likes a good time – well, he enjoys their company, I guess. They have money and they spent it freely. The best food and wine and cigars, the best hotels, access to a private plane, the most prestigious cars, and the most glamorous women. Adam likes that lifestyle too. I think he first got friendly when they met at his golf club . . .'

My heart missed a beat. Suddenly I had remembered where I'd heard Kenny White's name before.

'He was with Michael and Adam the night Michael died.' I said it almost to myself. 'It was him, wasn't it?'

Alison neither confirmed nor denied.

'He was certainly at the funeral,' she said quietly. 'A big man – six foot six tall and broad with it, black Armani suit, white shirt, black tie. You must have seen him.'

I shook my head. Michael's funeral had been a blur to me. I hadn't really been aware of anyone or anything beyond the coffin, covered with white roses and yellow sunflowers – Michael's favourites. I'd still been in a state of shock, struggling to hold myself together, hearing everything as if at a great distance, seeing everything through a blur of tears. There had been so many people there – the chapel had been full to overflowing – but I hadn't really seen any of them. I'd walked behind Michael's coffin looking straight ahead. And afterwards, when it had disappeared behind the purple drapes and the music from *Titanic* surrounded me, I'd walked out in the same daze.

I swallowed hard, trying to bring myself back to what Alison was trying to tell me.

'Anyway,' she was saying, 'I've always thought that Kenny White and Mervyn Hiscox were bad news. Adam should never have got involved with them. And now . . .'

'You're saying you think they're responsible for his disappearance?' I said.

'I'm very afraid it has something to do with them, yes.' Alison squeezed hard on the paperclip, bending it double. 'Kenny White came here looking for Adam in the week before he disappeared. He was far from pleased when I told him Adam wasn't here. And there were phone calls, too, that I wasn't party to. Adam packed me off out of the office while he was making them, and he never does that . . . No, Kenny

White and Mervyn Hiscox are behind this somehow. I wouldn't put anything past them, Jo.'

I shook my head, unable to take this in. 'You can't think, surely, that . . . ?'

'They're dangerous men.' Her face told me she was deadly serious. 'Nice enough when they want to be, but get on the wrong side of them and . . . they're dangerous, and ruthless too. And they have plenty of contacts with no scruples at all to do their dirty work for them.'

'But . . .' I was more bemused than ever at this talk of a murky world of which I knew nothing. 'If Adam only knew them socially, why would he end up on their wrong side?'

Alison's mouth set in a determined line. 'That, Jo, is what I intend to find out.'

'How?'

'I don't know yet. I had hoped you might be able to help, seeing you and Adam are so friendly . . .'

'We're not really,' I protested.

She continued as if I had not spoken. 'And seeing that Michael was Adam's friend and partner. But since you clearly can't, I shall have to find another way.'

A little frisson of alarm ran through me. 'But Alison, if they're the sort of men you say they are, couldn't that be dangerous?' I suggested. 'I can hardly believe it, but if you think they are capable of doing Adam some harm, well, they wouldn't take it very kindly if they were to discover that you were poking about in their affairs. Wouldn't it be better to go to the police and tell them what you suspect?'

'I tried to report Adam missing,' Alison said flatly. 'To the local police. They didn't seem to take me seriously. Adam is a free agent, with no ties, known to spend a good deal of time abroad. They implied that if he chose to take himself off somewhere without telling anyone it was no business of mine – or theirs. I was made to feel like a fussy, interfering child.'

'But presumably that was before you found out he hasn't been drawing on his account,' I persisted. 'Surely that's enough to make them take notice.'

'I don't feel like setting myself up to be humiliated again,' Alison said grimly. 'And besides, I already told you, I think

Kenny White has friends in the force. They'd cover for him, I'm sure, maybe even tip him off. I honestly wouldn't know who I could trust.'

Her words sent shock waves through me yet again. This wasn't the world as I knew it. Dangerous men living in mansions with security gates, disappearing businessmen, a corrupt police force . . . it was like something out of a thriller film.

'Well, I know a policeman I can trust,' I said. 'My best friend's husband. He's a motorcyclist with the traffic division and as straight as a die. Let me have a word with him, Alison – see what he thinks about it all.'

For the first time since I had come into the office, Alison's face cleared a little.

'Would you, Jo?'

'Of course. I must confess you've got *me* worried about Adam now. I'll speak to Dave as soon as I can and I'll let you know what he says.' I glanced at my watch. I'd been here much longer than I'd intended. Molly would be wondering what in the world had become of me. 'Look, I have to go now, but I'll be in touch, I promise. Just don't do anything rash in the meantime.'

'Don't worry – I won't. I shall be very, very careful,' Alison said grimly.

I left the office, my thoughts churning, and made my way along the precinct side of the river in the direction of the toy shop. It was busy now with the usual Saturday melee – some people walking purposefully, with store carrier bags bouncing at their side or shopping baskets over their arms, some idling or window shopping. A woman with two small children had stopped to feed a family of ducks who lived on the river. The sun was shining, bathing the whole scene in bright golden light and everything seemed right with the world. It was hard to give credence to Alison's suggestion that something terrible had happened to Adam, and a gang of ruthless and dangerous men were behind it. This was Laverham, for heaven's sake, a sleepy country town where nothing much happened in the way of crime beyond shoplifting, thefts from garden sheds and gangs of unruly youths getting drunk and smashing a few shop windows or spraying graffiti on the bus shelter. It was hardly the East End of London when the Krays ruled supreme!

But the fact remained, Adam was missing, and Alison – who had never struck me as the hysterical or over-imaginative type – was seriously concerned about him.

World of Wonder was a double-fronted shop in the older part of the high street. I walked past an automated parrot squawking and juggling brightly coloured balls inside his perspex pod, and pushed open the door. Two aisles ran the full depth of the shop between tall shelving units stacked high with everything from Lego to dressing-up kits, radio-controlled toys to hobby horses.

I couldn't immediately see Molly, but I knew where she would be – at the rear of the shop where the dolls and their accessories were arranged along the back wall. I headed down the first aisle, wondering how many outfits she'd picked out for her Barbie, or whether she'd set her sights on a fairy-tale castle or riding stables. If she had, she'd just have to wait for it until her birthday or Christmas. I don't believe in buying expensive toys for no reason other than that she's taken a fancy to them – she has more than enough already.

The Barbie clothes stand was immediately in front of me now, but no Molly. I looked to left and right – she was nowhere to be seen. Clearly I'd been so long she'd exhausted her interest in the dolls. I'd probably find her looking through the painting and puzzle books. I made for the second aisle, expecting to see her fair head bent over the rack, but once again, there was no sign of her.

I felt the first twinge of something close to panic. Where in the world was she? I must be just missing her round the high shelving units. It had happened before. Molly was a sensible little girl. I'd said I'd meet her here and she would never just go wandering off.

I went back to the door and started again, but my heart had begun to pound and the panic was rising. She wasn't in the shop. She wasn't *here*. Unless we were playing the most complicated game of hide and seek . . .

The counter with the till was to the right of the door. I went up to it. The middle-aged woman I recognized as one of the regular staff was serving a customer, but a youngster who looked like a Saturday girl was standing idly by, doing nothing more taxing than holding a big carrier bag open ready for the purchase.

'Excuse me – have you seen a little girl?' My voice was taut with anxiety.

The assistant looked at me as if I was mad – the shop was full of little girls.

'She's seven,' I said. 'She's wearing a pink T-shirt and embroidered jeans, and she's got long blonde hair tied up in two bunches.'

The Saturday girl shook her head, looking bored. 'No, sorry.'

I tried again. 'She was going to buy some tattoo transfers. She had her own money in a purse with a butterfly on it.'

Again the Saturday girl shook her head, but the older assistant must have heard me because she turned from keying in a cash card number to look at me.

'I served her just now. She went out to put the change in the Polly Parrot – I saw her standing there waiting for her sweets to come out. But she came back in, went down to the back where the dolls are. You'll find her there, I expect.'

'No – she's not . . .' But I hurried back down the aisle again to check anyway, then ran back to the till. 'She's not there. I can't find her anywhere. Are you sure you didn't see her go out again?'

'Sorry . . . we've been very busy.' The assistant was looking concerned now. 'It was only ten minutes or so ago. She can't have gone far . . .'

My heart was thudding; I was shaking all over. Suddenly I couldn't imagine seeing Molly ever again.

'Thanks . . .' Distracted, but striving to get a grip on myself, I turned to the door. Traffic was heavy, lined up along the one-way street, and the narrow pavement was heaving with people. I turned this way and that, desperately hunting for a glimpse of Molly. And suddenly there she was. Right in front of me.

'Mummy! *There* you are!'

'Molly!' I was so relieved it was all I could do not to grab hold of her, hug her tight and never let her go. 'Where have you been? I told you to wait for me in the shop!'

'Mummy.' I realized Molly, too, was close to tears. 'I did. But this lady came and said . . . Are you all right, Mummy?'

She took hold of my hand, her fingers wrapping tightly round mine.

'Of course I'm all right. Now I've found you. I was worried half to death, Molly.'

'But the lady said . . .'

'What lady? What are you talking about?

'When I was in the shop, looking at the Barbies. She said you were ill and you'd sent her to fetch me. I went with her, but I knew you were at Daddy's office and she wanted me to go the other way, up towards High Cross. Then she said to get in her car and she'd take me to the hospital. But I didn't want to. You say I must never get in a car with a stranger.'

'What?' I'd got myself into such a state I couldn't make sense of what she was saying. 'A lady tried to get you into her car. To take you to *me*?'

'That's what she said. To go to the hospital. I knew I shouldn't get into a car, but she said I had to, to go to you. I didn't know what to do, Mummy. So I pushed her off me and I ran all the way down to Daddy's office. And Alison said you weren't ill at all, that you'd just left to come up to the shop to find me, so I quickly ran back again . . .'

'Molly . . .' I was shaking, totally confused.

'I did the right thing, didn't I, Mummy?' Her anxious little face looked up at me and her fingers still curled tight as tendrils round mine.

'Of course you did, sweetheart. But . . .'

'Oh, thank goodness, she's found you!' Absorbed in Molly, I hadn't noticed Alison running toward us up the street. Now suddenly she was beside us, a little breathless, a little red in the face, but clearly relieved. 'You'd only been gone a few minutes when Molly came in saying you'd been taken to hospital. Well, I knew you hadn't. I told her you'd gone up to World of Wonder to collect her and she ran out again before I could stop her . . .'

'She said a lady tried to get her to go in a car.'

'She did! She did!'

I glanced at Alison over Molly's head. She looked as puzzled and worried as I felt. A woman pushing a double buggy tried to squeeze past us, giving us a dirty look.

'We're blocking the pavement,' Alison said. 'Why don't we all go back to the office. You can have a cup of tea. You look as though you need one.'

'I want to find this woman,' I said grimly. 'Where did you say her car was, Molly?'

'Further up – I told you. Outside the sports shop. But . . .'

'Come on!' Holding tight to her hand, I started determinedly up the street, Alison following. 'What kind of car was it? What colour?'

'It was red. I don't know what sort. It's gone now. It's not there any more.'

Sure enough there was not a single red car in the bay outside the sports shop. But then I didn't really expect there to be. If someone had been trying to abduct Molly and she'd run off to get help they wouldn't have been likely to hang around.

'She was there,' Molly said, pointing. 'Where that white van is now. Right there!'

I stared at the white van for a moment as if expecting it to metamorphose back into a red car like Cinderella's coach turning into a pumpkin, then looked around for anyone acting suspiciously. There was no one, just ordinary people going about their Saturday morning business.

'Come on, Jo. Let's go back to the office,' Alison urged.

'No way. I'm going straight to the police station. This has got to be reported.' I was furious now.

Alison looked doubtful. 'This isn't an adult male going missing,' I said forcefully. 'This is someone trying to abduct a child. Of course the police must be told about it.'

'A woman?'

'Have you never heard of Myra Hindley?' I was beside myself now that anyone should attempt such a thing in broad daylight.

Alison touched my arm. 'There probably won't be anyone at the local police station on a Saturday morning. Phone them from the office when you've had that cup of tea.'

I saw the sense in what she was saying. Nowadays it might take longer to go there in person.

Still holding tight to Molly's hand, I followed Alison back down the high street.

Five

Since the moment for dialling 999 had clearly passed, it took a lot of hanging on the line before we finally got through to the police. When we finally managed to speak to someone in the control room we were told to stay where we were and a patrolling policeman would come to us. It was almost another hour, however, before two uniformed officers – one man and one woman – walked through the door. We all sat in the relative privacy of Alison's office, mugs of coffee at our elbows, whilst I explained what had happened and Molly repeated her story.

'So what did this woman look like?' the policeman with the numbers 1289 on his shoulder asked. He wasn't a big chap, quite short really for a policeman, but his manner was quite aggressive. Maybe to make up for his lack of height, I thought.

Molly looked down at the picture she'd been drawing whilst we'd been waiting – Alison had found her a stack of copier paper and an assortment of felt tip pens. For a moment or two she didn't answer, just filled in the skirt of the lady she'd drawn with a vivid scarlet scrawl. She was having one of her shy spells, I knew, overawed by being the centre of attention and intimidated by the brusque figure wearing the uniform of authority.

'Molly?' I prompted her. 'Tell the policeman what you told me.'

'She was really pretty.' Molly was still scribbling with the felt tip pen as if her life depended on it. 'She had long fair hair like me.'

'How old do you think she was?'

Molly glanced up, rolling her eyes, then returned to her picture. 'I don't know!'

'Was she young . . . old?'

'Quite old really.'

'Older than your mother?'

'Maybe. Or about the same.'

Gee, thanks a bunch! I thought, but I was far too concerned to dwell on it.

'What was she wearing?' the policewoman asked. She had a gentler manner and Molly responded to her.

'She had on a really short skirt.'

'What colour? And what about her top? Did she have a coat – a blouse . . . ?'

Molly bent her head low. 'I don't know.'

'Think, Molly,' I urged her. 'It's really important.'

'I *am* thinking, but I don't know. I was worried about Mummy and worried about going in her car and . . .' She broke off. 'She had lots of jewellery,' she offered, looking up eagerly. 'I saw that. Gold bracelets. They were all jangling. And big sparkly rings. And chains round her neck.'

'Good girl, Molly,' the policewoman said approvingly, but the policeman – number 1289 – merely looked sceptical.

'Let's get on to her car, then. It was red, you say. What sort of car was it?'

'I don't know. I don't know cars. I'm not a boy!'

'Was it big – small?'

'Quite big. But not very big.' Molly frowned, then brightened. 'Oh, it had a hood, you know, the sort you put down when the sun's shining.'

'You mean a sports car?'

'Not really. Not like Jensen Button drives.' Jenson Button was Molly's hero. 'Bigger than that. And it had one of those smelly things hanging on the front window. I smelled it when the lady opened the door.' Molly hesitated for a moment, then rushed on. 'The lady smelled too. Well, I don't mean she *smelled*, not a pongy smell like the kitchen bin when it needs emptying. A nice smell really, sort of like Mummy smells when she's going out, but really strong.'

'Her perfume was the same as your Mummy's?'

'No!' Molly said scornfully. 'Not the same. Different. But that sort of smell.'

The policeman sighed. 'Is there anything else you

remember, Molly?' Molly shook her head. 'It's not much to go on, is it?' He fixed her with his intimidating glare. 'You're quite sure you're not making all this up?'

Molly pouted. 'No!'

'Are you sure you didn't just go off by yourself when you'd been told to stay in the shop, and then told your mother this story because you thought she'd be cross with you?'

'No! Mummy, tell him!' Molly looked close to tears again.

I was outraged. 'My daughter doesn't tell lies,' I said coldly.

'It's the sort of thing children do,' Number 1289 replied implacably. 'She starts off by remembering nothing at all, then suddenly we have soft top convertibles and perfumes and bangles. She has a pretty fertile imagination, doesn't she?' He indicated Molly's rather elaborate picture.

'If my daughter says a woman tried to get her into a car, then it happened,' I said furiously. 'I believe her even if you don't. And I want something done about it.'

'Trouble is, Mrs Lansdale, there's very little we *can* do.' The policeman began gathering his things together. 'The woman – if she ever existed – is long gone. And do you know how many red convertibles there must be in our force area? Unless your daughter can come up with something a good deal more concrete we haven't a cat in hell's chance of finding her.'

'You mean you're going to do nothing? Some nutcase is driving around trying to entice little girls into her car and you're just going to let her go on doing it?' I was shaking with fury now.

Number 1289 closed his notebook with a snap.

'Molly's complaint will be recorded and details circulated. And if she remembers anything else that might be useful, then let us know.'

'I don't think I shall bother!' I snapped.

The policewoman's personal radio was crackling; I realized she was speaking into it: 'OK, we're on our way . . .'

'That's right – go and harass some poor motorist!' I shouted after them as they left.

'You see?' Alison spread her hands as the door closed after them. 'I told you. They're just not interested. I remember a time when I looked up to the police, but now . . .'

I was still shaking with anger. 'Are they going to wait until some other innocent little child is snatched off the street? Oh, it doesn't bear thinking about . . .'

'I wasn't on the street, Mummy. I was in the shop. She came into the shop. And she knew my name.'

I froze. 'She knew your name?'

'Yes. She said "Molly?" And I turned round from looking at the Barbie clothes and she said: 'Your Mummy is Joanna Lansdale, isn't she?' And I said: 'Yes.' And she said: 'She's not very well and she sent me to fetch you. So you'd better come with me.'

'Why didn't you tell me this before?' I demanded, shaken.

'I did!'

'Not that she called you by name.' My head was spinning. This was no random opportunist snatch of a child. Well – opportunist, maybe, but certainly not random. Molly had been deliberately targeted. 'You should have said, Molly. It's very important.'

'I *did* say . . .' Molly's lip wobbled. She bent her head, pleating folds into the front of her T-shirt. 'I want to go home, Mummy!' she wailed. And she finally burst into uncontrollable tears.

It was past lunchtime before I pulled on to the drive, worried half to death and with none of the Saturday shopping I'd set out to buy. Molly had stopped crying, but she was very quiet.

'Did you get your transfers?' I asked. She nodded. 'Well, why don't you go and fix one of them while I get you something to eat,' I suggested, trying for some semblance of normality. I didn't want Molly to think about what had happened more than she had to. Something like this could traumatize her, and that was the last thing I wanted.

I unlocked the door and we went in. The house felt safe, but very empty. Molly must have felt it too. She paused at the foot of the stairs, the packet of tattoo transfers in her hand, and looked back at me.

'Oh, Mummy, I wish Daddy was here.'

'So do I, baby. Oh, so do I!'

The words came from the very bottom of my heart.

* * *

I made lunch from what I had left in the house – a tin of corned beef and a couple of jacket potatoes that I had to scrape the sprouting eyes out of before I could put them in the microwave. The only tomato left in the fridge was going soft and there was no fresh salad left, so I opened a can of sweetcorn and defrosted some frozen peas. It was a far cry from the meal I'd planned – fresh salmon fillets, new potatoes, broccoli and courgettes – but I wasn't hungry myself, and Molly liked corned beef so long as it was lathered in tomato ketchup. Well – actually, Molly liked most things as long as she got the ketchup too.

As I went through the motions my mind was racing. The last twenty-four hours felt like a never-ending nightmare. My ex-perience last night, the fact that Adam seemed to be missing, and now – worst of all – a woman attempting to abduct Molly. What the hell was going on? Had I somehow stumbled into an alternative universe where everything was distorted and disturbing? Or were all the separate events connected in some way?

No, that was crazy – they couldn't be. But why had I, usually so level-headed, been so sure I had been being followed that I had been panicked into crashing my car if there was nothing in it? Where was Adam? And why had a strange woman approached Molly, called her by her name, and tried to persuade her, with horrible untruths, to get into her car? None of it made any sense at all. But I was fright-ened enough to feel as if the next disaster was looming like a great black thundercloud gathering overhead, and a feeling of apprehension crept in the pit of my stomach, unidentifi-able beneath the morass of my whirling thoughts, my confu-sion and my anger, yet inescapable.

'Mummy – look at me!' Molly's voice cut into my thoughts. I turned to see her in the doorway. She had changed into a strappy little sleeveless top we'd bought in readiness for summer and she was teetering on the sandals Adam had given her, holding out her left arm to display a little rose tattoo just above her elbow. My heart turned over. She looked so pretty and so vulnerable.

And this morning I had almost lost her . . .

'I wanted it on my shoulder, but I couldn't reach,' she said. 'Will you do one for me?'

'After lunch,' I promised. 'It's just about ready now. Go and put a sweatshirt on now or you'll get cold, and then we'll eat.'

'OK.' Molly kicked off the sandals, leaving them lying in the middle of the kitchen floor, and skipped off upstairs.

She seemed to have forgotten the traumatic events of the morning, I thought, relieved. But I could not forget so easily. Something very strange and threatening was going on and somehow I had to get to the bottom of it.

When I'd cleared away the lunch things and Molly was settled in front of the television watching *Snow White*, I phoned Anna. We'd have to go out later, to the supermarket, to buy all the store cupboard essentials that I'd never got around to buying this morning, but right now, buying provisions was way below my daughter's safety on my list of priorities.

Dave himself answered the phone. 'Sorry, Jo – Anna's not here at the moment,' he said when he heard my voice. 'She's taken the kids up to the farm to see the lambs.'

'Actually it was you I wanted to speak to,' I told him. 'I'm really worried, and I want your advice.'

I went on to relate the morning's events, including the fact that since making the original report I'd learned that the woman had called Molly by name.

'Well, to start with, I think you should speak to the officer again and give him that additional information,' Dave said.

'I'm not sure he'd be interested,' I said. 'I don't think he believed any of it happened at all. But I know my own child. Molly would never make up something like that.'

'Nevertheless, you should report it.' Dave sounded very serious, very official, quite unlike the easy-going man I knew. He had slipped into policeman mode, I realized. 'Who was the officer, do you know?'

'I don't know his name, but his number was 1289,' I said. 'He was a smallish chap, receding hairline, not very pleasant.'

'Bob Cheeseman,' Dave said. 'He can be a bit of a bastard, but he's an old hand and a good copper. Give him a ring.'

'He won't believe me,' I said. 'He'll just think it's an embellishment Molly's dreamed up. The police force isn't scoring very highly in my book at the moment. Adam Garratt seems to have gone missing – Alison is worried to death about him – but when she reported it they dismissed that too. I was going to have a word with you about it, but quite honestly in the light of what happened to Molly this morning, Adam Garratt is the least of my worries.'

'He's *missing*, you say?'

'Well, it seems so.' I went on to repeat what Alison had told me about the unused bank accounts. Dave listened.

'Hmm, it does sound a bit suspicious,' he said when I'd finished. 'Especially given Adam's dubious associates.'

'You know about them?' I asked, surprised. I hadn't yet got around to mentioning that part.

'It's our business to know that sort of thing, and I have to admit it's something that's made me uneasy, what with Michael having been Adam's partner.' He sounded a little awkward, as if it was something he would have preferred not to have had to say. 'Look, leave it with me, Jo,' he went on. 'I'm off for a few days now, but when I go back I'll see if I can get a Misper raised for Adam – a Missing Person report, you know? And maybe I'll make a few enquiries myself.'

'But what about Molly?' I said. 'I'm really worried, Dave. It was bad enough when I thought it was just some opportunist child snatch, but when she told me the woman knew her name . . . well, it puts a whole different light on it, doesn't it? Molly didn't know her. So, how the hell did she know Molly? I can't help feeling she spotted Molly outside the shop when she was getting her sweets from the automated parrot and followed her inside. But I just don't understand why.'

Dave was silent for a moment, thinking. Then: 'Describe her to me again, Jo.'

I did. 'Hmm.' Another silence, then he said: 'Flashy, you'd say then. Money no object. Kind of *Footballers' Wives*.'

'Well . . . yes.'

'I've got alarm bells ringing. It sounds far-fetched, I know, but that's the way the Whites are.'

'The Whites.' Almost imperceptibly, my stomach had begun to tremble again. 'You mean . . . ?'

'I don't know what I mean really. Except that you're

concerned that something has happened to Adam – Adam is associated with the Whites – Michael was Adam's partner – Molly is Michael's daughter – and a woman who sounds like she might belong in their circle tries to talk her into her car. I don't recognize her from the description, it's true, but then I wouldn't necessarily. It's not my patch. Look – I don't want to frighten you unnecessarily, Jo, but I think it would be a good idea for you to keep a close eye on Molly for the time being.'

'Don't worry, I will be!' I said emphatically. 'But Dave – this is all crazy! Why would anyone connected with the Whites want to abduct Molly?'

'I don't know, Jo, and there's probably no connection at all. But I don't like coincidences, and one thing is for very sure – your friend Alison was right about those people. They are a tricky, unscrupulous lot. Best not take any chances.'

I felt as if I was drowning, suddenly. I'd rung Dave for comfort and advice and he'd actually made me feel worse.

It was only when I'd put the phone down that I realized I hadn't mentioned my own suspicion that someone had been watching the house, and the feeling that I was being followed when I'd run my car into the bank last night. But I wasn't going to ring him back now and say so. He might start trying to link that in, too, and I could do without being alarmed any more than I already was. Besides, I now knew there had been nothing sinister about the car that I'd thought was the one tailing me.

I thought of Tom Bradshaw, who had rescued me from the predicament I'd got myself into, and the fact that I'd arranged to go out with him next Friday evening. Well, that was out now. There was no way I was going to leave Molly, even if she was being baby-sat by a girl I knew and trusted. Apart from when she was in school I wouldn't let her out of my sight. I wasn't even keen on leaving her there and I thought I might have a word with her teacher – tell her to be wary of anyone who turned up at school claiming to have been sent by me. She'd think I was being petty, of course, and perhaps I was, but a woman who could lie to Molly about me having been taken ill could lie about anything, and I was taking no chances. No, I'd have to call Tom on the number he'd given me and tell him I couldn't make Friday.

In spite of everything, I was aware of a dart of disappointment. But that did nothing to change my mind. Molly was the most important person in my life. Her safety was paramount. And until this was sorted out my social life simply did not figure.

Mentally I squared my shoulders and fought back to some semblance of normality. I went into the living room where Molly was curled up watching her DVD.

'Come on, Molly. We have to go to the supermarket.'

'Oh, Mummy – can't I stay here? This is the best part of the film.' Molly's eyes never left the screen.

'No, Molly, you have to come with me, I'm afraid.'

With a deep sigh, Molly reached for the remote control and switched off the TV.

When we left the house the street looked as normal and peaceful as it usually did. No strange cars. Nothing in the least out of the ordinary. I might have imagined that our world was suddenly a more dangerous place. Except that I knew I had not.

I called in at the garage on the way to get my repaired tyre and found them closed – I suppose they call it a day at lunchtime on a Saturday – but though I was annoyed to have missed them, I wasn't overly concerned. I didn't plan on going anywhere over the weekend.

We whizzed round the supermarket as fast as possible. I felt sure there'd be things I'd forgotten – usually I take my time to look at the shelves as a reminder of anything I might have left off my list, but today I just wanted to be done and dusted and home again. Once there, I'd pull up the drawbridge, metaphorically speaking, and hunker down with Molly in the safety of our own castle.

Molly had returned to her DVD and I was just putting away the last of the shopping when the phone rang. I was up on a chair, trying to rearrange the top shelf of the cupboard to make room for the bag of sugar I'd bought unnecessarily – there was already a spare packet occupying the space I kept for it – and it took me a minute or so to juggle the items, climb down, and find the phone.

'Hello – Jo Lansdale.'

Nobody answered. There was nothing but silence from the other end of the line.

'Hello?' I said again.

Still nothing. I flipped the disconnection button twice, but still there was no one there, just the dialling tone interspersed with the beep that told me I had messages. Damn, I'd missed it. Whoever was phoning must have thought I wasn't going to answer and hung up. Yet I had the strangest feeling that someone *had* been there when I'd first picked up the phone.

Perhaps the answering service had cut it, I thought. I waited a moment to give my caller time to leave their message, then dialled 1571. Sure enough, the echoey automated voice I knew so well informed me I had two new messages and one caller who had left no message. I pressed 'one' as instructed and wandered to the window as I waited, the phone pressed against my ear.

The first call, timed at 12.45, was from the garage, informing me my tyre was ready but that they would be closing for the weekend in about a quarter of an hour. *Oh well, tell me something I didn't already know.* I pressed three to delete the message and waited.

The second call had been received at three o'clock, whilst I was still out at the supermarket. My heart did a silly skip when I heard a voice, remembered from last night.

'Jo. It's Tom Bradshaw. I just thought I'd give you a call to make sure you made it home safely last night. I'm sure you did – and I expect you're out now. I'll call again later in the week to confirm arrangements for Friday.'

'To save the message, press two. To delete it, press three,' the electronic voice intoned. Without even thinking about it, I pressed two.

'Your message will be saved for twenty-eight days.'

Twenty-eight days. I could listen later to that lovely dark brown voice again – as often as I liked for twenty-eight days. The thought was oddly pleasurable, a little oasis of something to look forward to in a world gone mad. Except that I had to call him anyway – tell him I would have to cancel Friday. Or at least postpone until things got back to normal . . .

Well, clearly whoever had rung me a minute ago had left

no message. I dialled 1471, hoping to find out who it was, but of course I'd dialled 1571 in between and the number the electronic voice quoted to me was my own. I put the phone back in its cradle and was about to climb back on my chair when it rang again.

'Hello – Jo Lansdale.'

'Jo. It's me – Anna.'

'Anna! Did you try to get me just now?'

'No. I've only just this minute got in from taking the children up to the farm. Why?'

'I missed a call. It doesn't matter.' I wished it had been Anna, though. The mystery would have been solved and I could stop wondering about it.

'Jo – Dave tells me someone tried to snatch Molly this morning. Is she all right? Are *you* all right?'

'No, not really,' I admitted. 'I'm pretty shaken up by it actually.'

'I should think you are! Do you want me to come over?'

'No – no – I'll be fine. We're here now, and Molly's watching *Snow White* and . . .'

'Well, I'll come this evening,' Anna said decisively.

'You can't do that,' I protested.

'Indeed I can. And I shall. Dave's here – once the children are in bed I'll hop in the car. No, I won't hear any arguments, Jo Lansdale. You need someone to talk to. As if last night wasn't bad enough . . . We'll have a glass of wine and a nice long girly chat.'

'You have to drive,' I protested weakly.

'I'll drink orange juice and lemonade, then. You can have the wine. I should think you need it.'

'Oh, Anna . . . I have to admit the company would be nice . . .'

'I'll be there as soon after eight as I can make it. And just take care, do you hear me?'

'I hear you. And thanks.'

I was smiling as I replaced the receiver. I was very lucky to have such a good friend as Anna, even if she did intimidate me sometimes with her bossiness. Already I was looking forward to seeing her. I'd feel a lot better when we'd had a heart-to-heart. I felt better already!

I'd almost forgotten about the mystery caller who'd left no message and who I'd thought for a fleeting second was still there when I answered the telephone. It had probably just been a wrong number or someone trying to sell me a conservatory or double glazing. Nothing important at all.

Determined to stop imagining problems where none existed, I went back to sorting out my cupboard.

Six

A nna's car pulled in to my drive a few minutes after eight. I hurried to the door to greet her.

'Jo – you poor thing!' She enveloped me in a bear hug that almost squeezed the breath from my body. Anna is a girl of what you might call generous proportions, and as I was enveloped by her amble bosom I felt for a moment I was almost a child again, nestling into my mother.

'Oh, Anna – thanks for coming. I am so pleased to see you!' I said, and felt suddenly as if I was about to burst into tears. 'Let's go in and have a drink.'

I'd already squeezed the oranges – Molly had helped me before going to bed – and I popped half-a-dozen ice cubes into a tall glass and filled it with juice. Then I opened a bottle of Rioja, poured myself a generous glass, and took a quick, needy slurp.

'Oh, I was dying for that!'

'I'm sure you were. So tell your Auntie Anna all about it.' Anna sank into an easy chair and I sat on the sofa, my legs curled up beneath me, and related everything that had happened.

'It's like a nightmare, Anna,' I finished. 'One thing after another. I just don't know what's going to happen next.'

'Nothing, probably.' Anna popped a honey-roasted nut into her mouth. 'Troubles are like buses – they all come at once until you think you can't take any more, and then – bingo! Everything's back to normal again.'

'Well, I certainly hope you're right,' I said. 'But I have this awful feeling there's more to come. Like when you're on a roller coaster and you can't get off and you're dreading the next big dip.'

'Rubbish,' Anna said forcefully. 'You feel like that because you had a bad experience last night and got scared. Look at it logically – there's no link. There can't be. You imagined someone was watching the house, so you panicked and had a bit of an accident. Adam has taken it into his head to go walkabout for some reason known only to him – which he's perfectly entitled to do.'

'With no money?'

'You don't know that. Knowing Adam he has plenty of cash stashed away in accounts Alison knows nothing about. He wouldn't go short – not he.'

'And the woman who tried to abduct Molly?' I said tautly. 'Dave seemed to think she sounded like someone who might be to do with the local mafia.'

'Dave's been in the job too long,' Anna said bluntly. 'Don't let him worry you, Jo.'

'How do you explain her then?'

'Well, I can't really.' Anna took a long pull of her orange juice. 'Some nutcase, maybe, who's lost a child of her own and took a fancy to Molly. She's a very pretty little girl, just the sort someone like that might want to take home.'

'But she knew Molly's name,' I pointed out.

Anna thought for a moment. 'Wasn't her photograph in the local paper a few weeks back? When she passed her ballet exam?'

'Oh, yes – it was!' Relief flooded through me. 'You're right, Anna. There were only five in her group and their names were listed underneath.'

'There you are then. Problem solved.' Anna tilted her glass of juice at me in a toast. 'Now all you have to worry about is this good Samaritan you've agreed to go out with. What did you say his name was?'

'Tom Bradshaw.' I swirled the wine in my glass. 'He phoned this morning when I was out and left a message saying he'd ring again to firm up arrangements. I was going to ring him back and tell him I'd have to call it off.'

'Why?' Anna asked – no, demanded. 'You seemed pretty keen on him when we spoke earlier.'

'That was before this Molly business,' I said. 'I don't want to leave her, Anna.'

'Well, that is a shame, if he's nice.' Anna had certainly

changed her tune. 'You could do with some fun in your life, my girl.'

'Not at the expense of my daughter's safety,' I stated firmly.

'You're being paranoid again, Jo Lansdale.' Anna eyed me quizzically. 'Did you save the message?' I nodded. 'Well, let's listen to it,' she said. 'I want to hear what he sounds like.'

'Oh, Anna!' But I got up anyway, fetched the phone and handed it to her. 'It's one-four-seven-one and then press one . . .'

'I know.' She pressed the relevant buttons and listened, raising an approving eyebrow at me as she did so. 'Lovely voice,' she commented, handing the phone back to me. 'Is he as hunky as he sounds?'

'Well . . . yes, actually.' To my annoyance I felt myself blushing.

'You've got to go then.' Anna was going even further into bossy mode. 'You can't pass up a chance like that when it's offered on a plate.'

I toyed with my glass, torn apart by indecision. Part of me wanted to see him again very badly, but the other part, the part that had thought I'd lost Molly this morning, was holding back.

'Suppose you're wrong about everything that has happened being coincidence,' I said. 'Suppose there's something sinister going on . . . I can't take that chance, Anna. I wouldn't enjoy myself, anyway. I'd be worrying the whole time and I'd be dreadful company. I mean, I know Maria is very good with Molly – I do trust her – but she's very young. If anything happened – something she couldn't handle – I'd never forgive myself.'

Anna was silent for a moment, then she set down her glass and sat back in her chair, looking straight at me. 'So how about she comes to me for the night? You don't think Dave and I would let anything happen to her, do you?'

A glimmer of hope. Certainly Molly would be safe with Anna and Dave. But I couldn't impose on Anna's good nature.

'Oh, Anna, thanks a million for offering, but you can't do that. You've got three children of your own to look after. And you haven't the room.'

68

'Compared to my three, Molly is an angel – no trouble at all,' Anna said roundly. 'As for sleeping arrangements, she can have one of the boys' rooms. They can all go in together. They'll love that. A sleeping bag on the blow-up mattress will be just like camping for them – a real treat. Now look . . .' She held up a finger, wagging it at me. 'No more arguments. Not another word. Molly comes to me next Friday for a sleep-over and you get your date with the man with the gorgeous sexy voice – so that's settled, right?'

I nodded. 'Right. You're a real friend, Anna.'

'And don't you forget it!'

'I won't.' I pulled a wry face. 'After all that he probably won't turn up. He'll have second thoughts – decide a neurotic woman with a seven-year-old daughter is not that great a bet.'

Anna smirked. 'From that phone call, Jo – I don't think so.'

To be honest, neither did I. I reached for the wine bottle and topped up my glass. Whether it was the effect of the alcohol or simply Anna's company, I was definitely feeling a hundred per cent better. The storm clouds had receded and for the first time since Molly's attempted abduction I didn't feel that everything I held dear was under threat. Things were definitely looking up.

Sure enough, over the next few days everything seemed to fall back into a normal, even pattern, and I began to think that Anna was right and I had lost all sense of proportion regarding the disturbing events of the weekend.

True, I was still protective of Molly, dropping her at the school gates, then watching until she was safely inside the building, and ensuring I was there five full minutes before school was out to collect her. True, I couldn't stop myself from checking the road for any strange cars when I drew the curtains at night. And true, Alison had still had no word from Adam. But I told myself that was not my problem. I'd done what I'd promised – had a word with Dave – and he was going to get the local police to record Adam as a Misper – a missing person. It was now up to them to do whatever they thought fit – though to be honest, I was coming around to the view that their original response was probably the right one. Adam was an adult man who was free to opt out of his everyday life for a while if he felt like it, and there was always the possibility he would not be best pleased at having his privacy invaded. He valued that so highly, and if he had decided to take a break from his responsibilities, he wouldn't thank Alison for raising a hue and cry to find him.

Though surely he should have anticipated that . . .? No! I was going to stop worrying about it.

The days sped by, full and busy as always. Tom Bradshaw called again as he had promised, confirming our arrangements. Then, before I knew it, it was Friday.

My stomach was full of butterflies as I drove Molly to Anna's.

'I'm really out of practice with this lark,' I confessed to her as Molly went skipping off with the boys, who were eager to show her a tree house Dave had built for them at the bottom of the garden.

'You'll be fine,' Anna reassured me. 'Go home, have a glass of wine and a nice long bath, and get your glad rags on. Then just forget everything and everybody and enjoy yourself.'

'I'm too nervous to enjoy myself,' I said. 'It's more than ten years since I went on a date, Anna! What the hell do you do? What do you say? Do I ask him in for a coffee when he brings me home? And what if he takes that as an invitation for something more? He's not going to end up in my bed, that's for very sure.'

'Stop worrying!' Anna scolded. 'Just behave naturally. Do and say whatever feels right. You're a grown woman, Jo, not a kid on a first date.'

'Well – I feel like one!'

'Relax!' She touched my hand. 'But just remember, if you need anything you know where I am. And Dave too. He's on nights tonight – ten pm till six am, you know. If this Tom Bradshaw should start making a nuisance of himself – which I doubt – all you have to do is call and provided Dave isn't dealing with something serious, he'd be with you in no time flat, with the twos and blues going.'

'Thanks,' I said, giggling. 'Police sirens are all I need to make my night the perfect date.'

'It won't happen,' Anna said. 'I'm sure the good Samaritan is also the perfect gentleman. And maybe your Knight in Shining Armour too. So just go off and enjoy yourself, Jo Lansdale. And be sure to tell me all about it tomorrow.'

I hugged her. 'And you will take good care of Molly?'

'What do *you* think? Of course I will. Go on now, or you won't be ready when he calls for you.'

The butterflies fluttered again. 'Everything Molly needs is in her bag. I don't think I've forgotten anything.'

'If you have, she'll survive. Stop fussing and go, Jo!'

'I'm on my way.'

I went into the garden to kiss Molly goodnight, but she was far too interested in the boys' tree house to spare me more than a brief hug. And then I was in my car, driving away; the nerves knotting my stomach now had nothing to do with the disturbing events of last weekend and everything to do with the fact that in an hour or so I was going out with a man I knew nothing whatever about, but who made me tingle with excitement whenever I thought about him.

I need not have worried.

It's strange, isn't it, how you can sometimes feel totally comfortable, at ease, in the company of someone who is almost a complete stranger? As if you've known them all your life. That was how it was with Tom, and it seemed all the more surprising to me given that I had been so afraid of him in those first moments when he'd stopped to help me.

I glanced at his profile as we drove, craggy, very attractive, and not in the least threatening, and wondered how on earth I could have suspected even for a moment that this man could be a danger to me. He was wearing a dark blue shirt, open at the neck, under a light tweed jacket, with light tan chinos – the ultimate in smart casual, understated yet eminently respectable. Even the fact that his car was a dark blue saloon didn't worry me any more. Since last weekend I'd noticed how many similar ones there were on the road. And in any case, the very idea that he might have been staking me out and following me seemed ludicrous now.

'I've booked a table at the Tolbrook Arms,' he told me,

turning out of town towards the country. 'I'm reliably informed it's pretty good.'

'So I've heard.' The Tolbrook Arms was an old coaching inn turned hotel and restaurant, and it certainly had a glowing reputation locally. I'd never been there, though – it had been too expensive for Michael and me in the early days of our marriage, and once Molly came alone we'd gone out only rarely. I was glad of that – I wouldn't have wanted to go anywhere that held too many memories.

The Tolbrook Arms was on the main street of the tiny village of Tolbrook. We found a space to park and walked through an archway into a cobbled courtyard. The main building, reeking of history, was to the left, on the right of the courtyard an old barn had been converted into a bar, busy with casually dressed locals who had clearly just popped in to what was the only public house in the village, as well as smartly attired diners enjoying a pre-dinner drink.

Tom got a gin and tonic for me and a pint of locally brewed beer for himself, and we'd hardly settled at one of the rustic tables when a man I assumed was the maitre d' brought us menus to peruse. We studied them for a while in silence and I was impressed by the large and imaginative selection of fresh fish dishes.

'I love fish!' I enthused. 'Goodness me, I'm spoilt for choice!'

'No such problem for me.' Tom closed the menu and put it down on the table. 'When I see the words "braised lamb shanks" the decision is made. And I'm going to start with the carrot and coriander soup.' He took a long pull of his beer. 'This is pretty good, too. It seems this place's reputation is well earned.'

'You haven't been here before either then?' I asked, trying to decide between 'simply grilled lemon sole' and halibut with a delicious sounding sauce.

'I haven't, no. I've not been in this part of the world long, and as I'm living in Bristol, I've used restaurants in the city when I've eaten out.'

I was a little surprised by this piece of information. Laverham was a good fifteen miles from Bristol, and I wondered why Tom had been out this way last week, but also that he'd bother-ed to drive all that distance to take me out. Bristol must be overflowing with single girls, a great deal more sassy than me, and without the encumbrance of a seven-year-old daughter.

'So what do you do in Bristol?' I asked. 'Something really interesting, I expect.'

He pulled a face. 'Sorry. 'Fraid not. I work for an insurance company. They have their HQ here, very modern, very imposing. One of those all-singing, all-dancing edifices to high finance. I was in London before I came here, and I must say I think it was a good move. Bristol is a lovely city.' His eyes met mine. 'How about you? What do you do when you're not at home looking after . . . what is your daughter's name?'

'Molly. Well, I was trained as a primary school teacher, but at the moment I'm working at a nursery . . .' To my amazement, I found myself chatting easily, telling Tom about my circumstances, my life, and not for one moment getting the feeling I was boring him. He seemed genuinely interested – a huge relief to me, since I have the horrible feeling I talk far too much. But clearly we complemented one another. I was the chatterbox. Tom was happy to listen. It was a pretty good combination.

The meal, when the maitre d' came to lead us across the courtyard to the restaurant, was every bit as good as it had sounded on the menu. I enjoyed every mouthful of the scallops I'd chosen as a starter, followed by the grilled sole, but it was that instant rapport with Tom that made the evening so special. He didn't talk a great deal, as I've already mentioned, but what he did say was interesting and he also had the ability to make me laugh, something that been sadly lacking in my life for a long time. The ease between us made me feel relaxed and content. And every time I looked at him I felt a little frisson of excitement shooting in my veins. I thought of the flip remark I'd made to Anna about sharing my bed with him and smiled inwardly. I certainly wouldn't be doing that tonight, but the prospect was far from an unpleasant one.

However much I was enjoying myself, however, Molly was never far from my thoughts. When we had finished our meal and returned to the big open barn for coffee, I reached into my bag, fingering my mobile.

'Would you mind if I gave my friend Anna a quick ring? I'd just like to make sure Molly is all right.'

'Go right ahead.'

Predictably, Anna was cross with me.

'Of course she's all right, Jo! Absolutely fine. She tired herself out, I think, playing with the boys and she went to bed without a murmur. She's fast asleep with that teddy bear with sunglasses that Adam gave her propped up on the bedside table beside her and her furry monkey cuddled up with her under the duvet. I know because I looked in on her just a few minutes ago.'

'Oh, good. That's all right then,' I said, feeling a little foolish.

'Now you are to stop worrying, Jo Lansdale. You are supposed to be enjoying yourself.' A tiny pause, then she couldn't resist. 'How is it going?'

'Fine,' I said briefly. I was hardly going to go into detail with Tom sitting just across the table from me. 'I'll see you first thing in the morning. And thanks again, Anna.'

'All well?' Tom asked as I slipped the mobile back into my bag.

'Fine. She's in bed and asleep. Anna was annoyed with me for ringing, but I can't help worrying.'

'That's only natural,' he said easily. 'I'm sure if I had a seven-year-old daughter I'd feel exactly the same, especially if I were solely responsible for her.'

So – he had no children. Or at least it didn't sound as if he did. I realized just how little I still knew about him. But for the moment, Molly was uppermost in my mind.

'I'm being a bit over-protective at the moment, I know,' I said apologetically. I hadn't had the slightest intention of telling him about the attempted abduction last Saturday – it was hardly the sort of small talk I'd expect to make on a first date. But the easy rapport between us had changed all that. Suddenly it seemed quite acceptable – more, I *wanted* to tell him. 'She gave me a bit of a fright a few days ago . . .' I began, and before I knew it I'd related the whole incident, though not of course about the other factors that had combined to make it seem even more sinister.

74

'I'm not surprised you're concerned to know she's safely where she's supposed to be,' Tom said when I'd finished.

'To be honest, I very nearly rang you to cancel tonight,' I admitted. 'I didn't feel like leaving her at all. But I'm sure she's safe with Anna. Besides being my best friend, her husband is a policeman. Molly couldn't be in better hands.'

'It was certainly a peculiar thing to happen,' Tom said, draining his coffee cup. 'You tell children to be wary of strange men – but a woman . . .'

'Anna thought she might have lost a child of her own and become mentally disturbed,' I said. I had no intention of going down the road of telling him what Dave had said.

'Hmm.' He looked unconvinced. 'Your late husband – he was Molly's father, was he?'

'Of course he was,' I said, a little taken aback. 'Why? What's that got to do with it?'

'I was just thinking that if she was the result of a relationship that had broken up and her father had been denied access it might be his way of trying to get to her. But if your husband was Molly's father, and he's dead, then clearly it isn't that.'

'Molly was certainly Michael's.' For the first time there was a hint of awkwardness between us. Anxious to dispel it, I said: 'Let's not talk about it any more. I've scarcely thought of anything else for the past week and I'd rather forget it.'

'So tell me about Molly,' he said, letting the subject of the attempted abduction drop. 'What's she into – ballet – ponies? That's what most little girls her age are into, isn't it?'

'Ballet, certainly,' I said. 'She's just passed her grade one with distinction. Her teacher called her a "little star".' A faint colour rose in my cheeks. I was so proud of Molly, but the last thing I wanted to be was a boasting mother. 'I think she'd like to learn to ride too,' I went on quickly, 'but there isn't the time – or the money – to do everything.'

'I'm sure she doesn't want for anything,' Tom said, and I felt his gaze warm on me. 'Do you want another coffee?'

'Better not. Too much caffeine and I'll never sleep.' I glanced at the foil-wrapped mint chocolate that he'd removed from his saucer and laid in the middle of the table – mine had been eaten long ago. 'I'll have your mint, though, if you don't want it,' I said cheekily. That I had the nerve to ask was a measure of the ease between us, restored once again after that brief hiccup.

Tom pushed it across the table in my direction. 'Be my guest. And I'm going to have another coffee even if you're not – I never have trouble sleeping – and you can have the mint that comes with that one too if you like.'

'Oh, no – I'll get as fat as a house!' But I was pleased anyway, not so much about the chocolate as the fact that he was going to order another coffee so we wouldn't be leaving just yet. I just didn't want the evening to end!

It had to, of course. Tom drove me home through the velvety black night and I thought I couldn't remember the last time I'd felt this way.

'I hope we can do this again,' he said.

I giggled, high on the pleasurable feelings I was experiencing as well as the gin and tonics and the wine I'd drunk. 'Too many meals at the Tolbrook Arms and I really would get fat.'

'Not necessarily the Tolbrook Arms. Doesn't even have to be a meal, if you'd prefer not. But I want to see you again, Jo.'

Yes, I thought. *And I want to see you . . .*

'Why don't you come to me sometime?' I suggested. 'It won't be up to the standard of the Tolbrook Arms, but I'm not a bad cook. I'll make you supper, or – what about lunch on Sunday? I won't have to worry about baby-sitters, and you can meet Molly too.'

Even as I said it I knew it was a risk. Perhaps I should wait until we knew each other better before introducing him to Molly. It could be a disaster even suggesting it. Yet somehow I felt deep down that Tom was going to be around for a long time. *Do and say whatever seems right,* Anna had advised me. And this felt right.

'That sounds like an offer I can't refuse,' Tom said, and any lingering doubts I might have had disappeared like April snow in the sunshine that follows.

'Really?' I said. 'You'll drive all the way from Bristol for a plate of roast beef?'

'You bet. I'd drive all the way to John O'Groats for that. And the company . . .' His hand snaked over to cover mine.

We were in my road now, pulling up at the kerb outside my house. Time to say goodnight – but also something to look forward to.

'Thank you. I've really enjoyed it,' I said.

'So have I.'

And he leaned over and kissed me. I'd been a bit worried about this part, but now it seemed the most natural thing in the world. He didn't pressure me at all, he wasn't all over me, it was quite a light kiss really, but I felt something sharp and sweet twist within me and found myself kissing him back before my natural caution returned me to reality.

'I must go,' I said. 'I have to be up early in the morning.'

'I'll see you on Sunday then. What time do you want me?'

As soon as you like. Preferably now . . .

'Oh, midday-ish?' My tone was casual, not for one moment betraying my fast-beating heart.

'Midday it is, then.' He kissed me again, a little more deeply than before. And then I was out of the car and he'd started the engine, waiting whilst I went up the path and unlocked the door. Only then, when I'd switched on the light and waved to him did he pull away.

I closed the door and leaned against it for a moment. I felt light-headed and happier than I'd felt in ages. I kicked off my shoes and felt more like a skittish teenager than a widowed mother of a seven-year-old girl.

'Tom,' I said aloud, and even the sound of his name sounded good. The whole world suddenly seemed full of promise.

There was a smile playing on my lips as I picked up my shoes and headed for bed. And for the moment every one of the events that had worried me so this last week were quite forgotten.

The insistent ringing of the telephone woke me. For a moment I lay dazed and thick-headed and then I was wide awake, trembling all over as you do when rudely woken from a deep sleep. Then I snapped on the light. The clock said three fifteen a.m.

I don't have a telephone by my bed; I had to run down

the stairs to the one in the hall, afraid it would stop ringing before I got there, wondering anxiously who it could be calling in the middle of the night, my heart pounding with the terrible conviction that something had happened to Molly.

I grabbed the receiver. 'Hello?'

'Jo.' Just as I'd feared, it was Anna, and I could tell at once from her voice that something was dreadfully wrong.

'What is it? Oh God . . . Molly . . .'

'No – no, Molly's fine. She's still in bed and asleep.' Relief flooded me, made my knees go weak. 'I'm really sorry to ring you, Jo, but I thought I should,' Anna went on. 'I have to go to the hospital, and I didn't think I should leave Molly without telling you, even if there is a policewoman here . . .'

Hospital? Policewoman? 'What the hell are you talking about, Anna?'

'It's Dave.' Anna's voice cracked; I could tell she was beside herself. 'He's had an accident. A hit-and-run driver has knocked him off his motorbike. They've just come to tell me. I have to go to him, Jo.'

My blood was running cold; I was experiencing déjà vu. The knock at the door in the middle of the night. The uniformed officer, grim-faced, on the doorstep . . .

'Oh my God, Anna!' I whispered.

The nightmare was back. I'd hoped it was over, but it wasn't. Brief respite there might have been, but now it had begun again. I don't think I have ever felt more frightened and helpless than I did at that moment.

Seven

I got to Anna's as soon as I could, which was, given the circumstances, not nearly as quickly as I would have wished. I didn't dare risk driving myself – now I was cursing the volume of wine I'd so happily consumed a few hours ago, not to mention the gin and tonic I'd had for Dutch courage while I was getting ready to go out and the second one in the bar of the Tolbrook Arms. I must be way over the limit, I knew. But getting a taxi in a small country town in the middle of the night is no easy task and I was so fuzzy and panicked that it took me ages to even find the numbers of the local operators let alone get hold of one willing to come out and take me to Little Ryedale. Then I threw on the first clothes that came to hand – jogging pants, sweat-shirt and my trusty fleece – and watched anxiously at the window for headlights turning into our road.

By the time I arrived at Anna's cottage she had already left for the hospital. The door was opened to me by a police-woman. She was much older than the one who'd come to the office last week when I'd reported Molly's attempted abduction; with a square, almost motherly figure and short-cropped hair peppered with grey.

'You must be Molly's mother,' she greeted me. 'I'm PC Stone – Gwenda. Don't worry, the children are fine – I've not heard a peep out of any of them.'

In spite of her reassurance, my first instinct was to run upstairs and check on Molly, but somehow I contained myself. The last thing I wanted to do was disturb her or the boys.

'The kettle's on the boil,' PC Stone said. 'Shall I make you a cup of tea?'

'Black coffee,' I said against the thumping of my head. 'That's what I need.'

'You've got it.'

She disappeared into the kitchen and I paced the long, low living room that ran the full length of the house. Everything looked just as it always did – perfectly normal – a few toys spilling out of the toy box in the alcove beneath the window, a glossy magazine open on the coffee table, a rosy glow still visible through the glass doors of the wood-burning stove, the curtains drawn against the darkness outside. But everything was not normal – far from it – so that there was something almost sinister about the cozy charade of everyday living.

PC Stone returned with two mugs of coffee, flattened out the magazine and set them both down on it. One was Dave's Chelsea FC mug – though he is West Country born and bred he has, for some reason, been a Chelsea supporter since he was knee high to a grasshopper – and seeing it, filled with coffee for someone else, gave me a sharp sick pang. I couldn't bring myself to use it; I picked up the other one – some anonymous geometric design – and sipped the coffee so hot that it seared my lips. Then, as it hit my stomach, I asked the question that was uppermost in my mind, but which I was almost afraid to hear the answer to.

'How is Dave? Is he badly hurt?'

'He's not good.' Gwenda Stone's plain but pleasant face was serious. 'He's certainly got a compound fracture to one leg and a suspected broken collar bone. But the really worrying thing is he was also unconscious when they took him to hospital.'

A head injury. I felt sick.

'What happened?' I asked. 'Anna said something about a hit and run.'

'That's right. The driver didn't stop. Drunk, probably, or else it was joy riders in a stolen car. Or then again, maybe someone just panicked when they realized they'd hit a policeman. One thing you can be very sure of though – we shall pull out all the stops to track down the bastard.'

They would, too, I felt sure. Dave was one of their own.

'Where did it happen?' I asked. 'Was it in town?'

'No, on the Midsley Road. You know there's a junction right on a bend just before you get into the built-up area?

80

Dave was on the main road and whoever hit him came out of the minor one – or so we think. But it could have been that they took the bend too fast and strayed on to his side of the road. We won't know until the accident investigators have had a chance to make a thorough examination of the scene, and his bike too. And at the moment, Dave's not been able to tell us anything.'

'No, he wouldn't . . .' Details of what had happened were not really important at this stage anyway. What mattered was Dave regaining consciousness, being all right. And yet . . .

I couldn't help feeling there had been far too many accidents. Michael's – never, to my mind, satisfactorily explained; my own last week – minor enough, but it could have been very different – and now Dave. Dave was a really experienced motorcyclist, a class one advanced police rider. He'd been in the job for years – there was a photograph on a shelf beside the wood-burning stove showing him and the other outriders with Princess Diana when they'd escorted her in the days when she was still HRH The Princess of Wales. He was safer on two wheels than most people would be in an armoured tank.

But a motorcycle could never be really safe, I reminded myself. It wasn't only up to Dave or anyone else, but all the other idiots on the road. And the motorcyclist was the vulnerable one. I finished my coffee and collected myself.

'Look – now that I'm here there's no need for you to stay,' I told Gwenda, though, truth to tell, I was glad of her reassuringly solid and sensible company.

'Are you sure?' She was looking at me closely, weighing me up and, once again, I was aware of the measure of care that was afforded by the police force to one of their own.

'Perfectly. I'll be fine.' I wished I felt as calm as I sounded.

Gwenda unclipped her personal radio. 'I'll have to call for someone to come and collect me. My colleague took Anna to the hospital in our patrol car,' she explained.

It was some twenty minutes before a police car arrived and Gwenda left. I have to admit my heart sank as the door closed after her. I had never felt more abandoned or alone, and the happy time I'd spent with Tom earlier this evening – yesterday! – seemed to belong in another lifetime. I left a light burning and went softly up the stairs. I simply could not bear not seeing Molly for another moment. If I woke her it didn't matter. I had to make certain she was safe and well. But in the event, Molly was sleeping so soundly it would probably have taken an army marching through her room to waken her.

I sat down on the floor beside her bed, not daring to touch her, however much I longed to, just looking at her in the soft glow of the little night light on the bedside table and watching her sleep. It was a long time before I went back downstairs, armed with a blanket, and made myself up a bed on the sofa. Then I lay down with my head against a bank of cushions and the blanket pulled up to my chin.

And lay sleepless, staring into the darkness, praying for Dave and wondering why on earth my life and the lives of everyone around me had suddenly turned upside down.

I must have fallen asleep eventually from sheer exhaustion, for I came to with a start to hear what sounded like the front door being closed and movement in the tiny hallway. A moment later Anna came into the room.

'Jo!' she exclaimed in surprise. 'What are you doing here?'

'I told you I'd come over,' I mumbled groggily.

'But on the sofa . . .' She looked distracted, haggard, her usually rosy face pale, her eyes dark-rimmed.

'How is Dave?' I asked, sitting up and wrapping the blanket round me like a shawl.

'Critical.' Her tone was flat, emotionless, but I detected the little tremor. 'Stable – but still critical.'

'Has he regained consciousness?'

She shook her head, still standing there with her hands deep in the pockets of her trench coat. 'No. Oh, Jo, it's so terrible, seeing him just lying there, with tubes everywhere . . .'

I went to her and hugged her; she stood stiff and rigid like a statue. Then, without any warning, she burst into tears.

'Oh, Anna, I'm so sorry . . . I feel for you, really I do.' Her whole body was shaking with sobs and I held her, stroking her hair, massaging her shoulder.

'You would. You know what it's like. Oh, Jo, how did you cope with it? If Dave . . . I couldn't go on. I really couldn't.'

'Dave will be fine,' I said with more conviction than I was feeling. 'And you will cope. You're strong, much stronger than you know.'

She fumbled in her pocket for a handkerchief and blew her nose.

'I'm sorry, Jo . . .'

'Don't talk rubbish,' I said crisply. 'You've always been there for me, and I shall be here for you. Now you sit down and I am going to make you a cup of tea. The children are still fast asleep, and you are going to dry those tears, calm down and think positive. They'll only be frightened if they wake up and see you like this.'

I helped her off with her coat, sat her down and went to make the tea. I felt shaky and thick-headed and physically sick. And I hoped with all my heart that my best friend was not going to have to go through what I had been through.

I had every intention of staying as long as Anna needed me, to look after the children whilst she went back to the hospital, cook meals, and do whatever was necessary to support her. But Anna told me she had phoned her parents from the hospital and they would be here in the time it took them to pack a bag and drive the thirty or so miles from their home in the Cotswolds.

Sure enough, by the time I had got breakfast, their car was pulling up outside.

Anna's mother, Heather, was very much an older version of Anna, plump, warm and bursting with energy, whilst her father, Maurice, was a wiry man with a shock of snow-white hair and a quiet but confidence-inspiring manner. The boys, who had been dreadfully subdued since waking up to the news that their father was in hospital, were obviously delighted to see them and I had no reservations about going home and leaving Heather and Maurice in charge. I wanted to ring for a taxi, but Maurice insisted on driving Molly and me, and after assuring Anna that she had only to call if she needed me and I'd be there, and extracting a promise that she would let me know if there was any change in Dave's condition, we set off.

As we approached the outskirts of Laverham, Molly, who

was in the back seat of Maurice's Renault, suddenly squealed so loudly I jerked round in alarm to see what was wrong. 'Mummy! That's the car!'

'What?' I had been having a conversation with Maurice, taking no notice of passing traffic, and for a stupid moment I thought she meant the car that had hit Dave. 'What are you talking about, Molly?'

'The lady! Last Saturday! With the red car . . .'

'Where?'

'There! It just passed us!'

I craned over the headrest and saw a red convertible disappearing around a bend in the road.

'Are you sure?' I asked.

'Yes! Well . . . it was just like it . . .'

My thoughts raced. Molly could be wrong, of course, but she is a very observant little girl. If I had been driving myself I would have found somewhere to turn and hurtled off in pursuit. But I couldn't ask Maurice to do that. I was already indebted to him for taking me home; I couldn't get him haring about after a car that might, or might not, be being driven by Molly's attempted abductress and which we might not be able to catch now anyway. Maurice needed to get back to Anna and the children as soon as possible, and in any case I couldn't burden him with a lengthy explanation of my own troubles. As it was, he didn't seem to have clocked what Molly had said at all – and why should he? He knew nothing about the events of a week ago.

'It's OK, Molly, it's gone now,' I said, trying to sound both reassuring for her benefit and nonchalant for Maurice's.

'But Mummy . . .'

'Leave it, Molly.'

But I made up my mind to keep a good look out for a red convertible in future. If it was the same car, it meant the woman lived in, or had connections with, the district. But if she was local, I was surprised that PC 1289 or indeed Dave hadn't recognized the description. There couldn't be that many red convertibles about here, surely. And it was the kind of car you would notice.

Maurice pulled up outside my house. I thanked him again,

reiterated my readiness to be on call should the need arise, and took Molly inside.

As was only to be expected, given my disturbed night, I felt lousy, thick-headed and totally lacking in energy as well as upset and worried. And I had so much to do! Perhaps under the circumstances it would be wisest to postpone the Sunday lunch I had promised to cook Tom tomorrow, I thought, regretfully.

I called him on his mobile number, but it was switched off. I left a message asking him to call me at home, then realized I'd shot myself in the foot. I'd have to stay here in case he returned my call, and I really needed to get into town to do the necessary shopping.

I made myself a coffee and decided to have a shower. Not only did I feel in desperate need of one but it might restore some of my energy too. I left Molly watching a DVD and headed for the bathroom, but no sooner was I undressed and in the shower than Molly came in, carrying the walkabout phone.

'Mummy – phone for you.'

I emerged from the shower cabinet, covered in foam and dripping. I reached for my towelling robe, slipped it on and took the phone from Molly.

'Good morning.' The dark brown voice made my tummy tip. 'You called me?'

'Oh, Tom. Thanks for calling back. I was in the shower.'

'So I gathered.' He sounded amused. 'That was Molly, I take it. She sounds like a great little girl.'

'She is.' Molly had disappeared already, hurrying back to her DVD, I imagined. 'Tom – I've got a problem.'

I outlined what had happened. 'The thing is, I'm worried about tomorrow,' I finished.

'You want to call it off?' Tom asked.

'I don't *want* to.' Just talking to him, hearing his voice, was making me feel better. More than anything I wanted to see him again. 'I'm just not sure whether Anna might need me. Or what sort of company I'll be.'

'Well, there's no need to worry about that,' Tom said lightly. 'With all this going on I wouldn't expect you to be

85

full of the joys of spring. And your friend Anna – her parents are with her, you say?'

'Yes, but if anything happened to Dave . . .'

'Look, we'll call it off if you'd rather. But why don't we just put a final decision on hold for the moment? It's understandable you're upset at the moment. Let's wait and see how things pan out. If you need to call me tomorrow and cancel, I'll understand.'

'Are you sure that wouldn't be messing you about?'

'Not nearly as much as if you cancel that roast beef I'm so looking forward to and there's no need.'

As I switched off the phone, shrugged out of my bathrobe and back under the shower, I was actually smiling. Tom certainly had the ability to lift my mood! It was a very long time since there had been anyone in my life who could do that so easily.

The remainder of the day passed in a sort of haze. Molly and I went to the shops and I bought the biggest piece of sirloin I could afford at my favourite butcher's shop – one of those lovely places where they wear straw boaters and striped aprons and cut your joint right there in front of your eyes. At the greengrocer's I bought parsnips for roasting, carrots and cauliflower, plus some Bramley apples to make a pie. I'd get a readymade dessert at the supermarket too, I decided, as a back-up in case I was too tired to make pastry, or circumstances prevented me, but I really wanted to put on the sort of old-fashioned home-cooked meal I thought Tom was looking forward to if I possibly could.

As we passed Michael's old office I glanced in and saw Alison arranging details of a house on one of the display boards. I didn't really want to stop this morning – I had too much to do – but she'd seen me, so I felt duty bound to pop my head round the door and say hello.

'Any news of Adam?'

'Oh – Jo! No, nothing. Look – I'm sorry – don't think me rude, but I'm rushed off my feet. Claire's not in this morning – she's called in with a migraine, though I suspect a hangover is more like it. I'm on the phone with a client and . . .'

86

'Don't worry, I get the picture. I'll catch up with you again when you're not so busy.'

'I'm really sorry, but if you only knew . . .' Alison looked really flustered, which was very unlike her. Normally she was the very essence of efficiency. This Adam business was really getting to her. But I was relieved not to be held up when I had so much to get done and I had enough on my mind without being dragged into the Adam saga again. Neither did I want to be forced to think again about the woman who had attempted to abduct Molly. Maybe, given that Molly had thought she'd seen her this morning, I should. Maybe I was just burying my head in the sand. But my emotions and my thoughts had gone into overdrive and for the moment I just didn't think I could take any more.

'Don't worry about it,' I said, and made a hasty exit.

It was only as I was walking along the street that it struck me. Alison had said she had a client on the phone, yet she'd been arranging details on the display boards when I'd first seen her. Strange! Had she had some reason for not wanting to talk to me today and used the client as an excuse? Surely not. In all probability she just really was run off her feet and had over-egged the pudding in the cause of getting rid of me.

I put Alison and Adam firmly out of my mind. But it wasn't so easy to forget about Dave, lying unconscious in a hospital bed. He was constantly on my mind, an inescapable niggle of anxiety as I finished my shopping and headed for home.

Once there, I picked up the phone to ring Anna and ask if there was any news, then put it down again. There were no messages on my answering service and Anna had promised to let me know if there were any developments. She had enough on her plate without me bothering her. I'd wait until she rang me – for the moment at least.

I made lunch and when we'd eaten it and cleared away I forced myself to find the energy to make an apple pie. Then I cleaned and tidied all the areas of the house that would be on show to Tom tomorrow – provided our planned lunch went ahead. After all that I was flagging badly. I flopped in front of the TV to watch *Dr Who* with Molly, and when she went to bed, I decided to have an early night too.

I called Anna, in case she should ring me after I'd gone to bed, and spoke to Heather. Anna had gone back to the hospital and wasn't home yet. As far as Heather knew, there was nothing new to report.

Exhausted, I locked up, went upstairs and got undressed. Then I fell into bed, almost weeping from the relief of it. I don't remember much after that. The moment I switched off my light, I was out for the count.

I'd just begun peeling potatoes and parsnips and the beef was in the pan ready to go into the oven when Anna phoned. I could tell at once from her tone of voice that she was feeling more cheerful, and her first words confirmed it.

'Dave's regained consciousness.'

'Oh, thank God!' I felt like skipping around the kitchen.

'He's not out of the woods yet, but the signs are good.'

'That is the most wonderful news!' I told her. 'And thank you so much for letting me know.'

'I feel like telling the world,' Anna said. 'But you are top of my list, Jo. Thanks for being there when I needed you.'

'You're always there for me,' I reminded her. 'And so is Dave. I'd like to go and see him when he's fit for visitors.'

'I'm sure he'd be pleased to see you,' Anna said. 'You know what it's like in hospital. The days seem endless. It's too early yet, of course, but when he's up to it I'll let you know. How did your date go, by the way? With the gorgeous-voiced Tom?'

'Very well.' I felt a warm glow. 'He really is rather gorgeous – not just his voice. Actually he's coming for lunch today. If you don't need me, that is.'

'Oh, my Lord – watch this space!' That sounded almost like the old Anna. 'No, you forget about me and enjoy the moment, Jo. It's time you had some good luck. If anyone deserves it, you do.'

'It has been a bit tough lately,' I agreed.

'Not just lately. It's been tough for you for the last two years. You could do with some light relief. And that's just

88

for starters. You need someone in your life, Jo. You're still a young woman.'

'Who sometimes feels about ninety.'

'Exactly.' Anna was getting into her stride and it made me smile. If anything could convince me the news about Dave was optimistic, it was Anna returning to bossy mode. 'Molly is going to grow up and need you less and less,' she went on. 'And you don't want to be left all alone.'

'Steady on – that's years off yet!' I said. But she was right, I knew. Although no one would ever take the special place that Michael still occupied in my heart it was time to move on. I needed companionship and someone to be there for me. I needed love. The last few days had shown me that – and shown me that feelings I had thought belonged only in the past could be reawakened. Perhaps I was ready to begin to live again. And maybe Tom was the one to show me the way.

My heart quickened a beat. Outside the sun was shining, bathing the garden in that clear light that is peculiar to spring-time. It made the trees look a softer, yet more vivid, shade of green, and against them a forsythia bush was a blaze of golden yellow. There was a blackbird on the lawn, head cocked as it waited patiently for a worm. The may was out in the hedges, a cloud of white. Spring was turning into early summer and it seemed to me to be a symbol of hope.

'I have to go now,' Anna said. 'But keep me posted.'

'You too. And love to Dave.'

'Will do. Speak to you later.'

I clicked off the phone and went back to peeling potatoes feeling happier than I had done in a very long time.

Tom arrived on the dot of twelve. Punctuality, it seemed, was another of his attributes.

'Something smells good,' he said, sniffing appreciatively.

'I hope you're hungry. I've cooked enough to feed the five thousand.'

He held out a couple of bottles of wine. 'A small contribution.' I glanced at the labels – a Chablis and what looked like a very good Rioja. Not so small! 'I know you said beef, but you were drinking white on Friday night . . .'

'I adore Chablis! Am I allowed one now, to help the cooking process? And what about you? What would you like to drink? I remembered Friday, too, and got some beer.'

'In that case I'd love one.'

I handed him the corkscrew and fetched the beer from the fridge.

'How is your friend?' he asked, pulling the cork of the Chablis.

'He's regained consciousness, thankfully. It looks like he's turned the corner.'

'I'm glad to hear that.' Tom set the opened bottle down on the counter, took the beer from me and popped the seal. 'Has he been able to shed any light on how the accident happened?'

To be frank, I was surprised by that. Such details seemed supremely unimportant compared to Dave's recovery.

'I didn't ask. I shouldn't think so. They won't bother him, surely, until he's a good deal stronger, will they?'

A small sound from the doorway. Molly was there, peeping in.

'Molly!' I said. 'Come and say hello to Tom.'

I'd explained to her a friend of mine was coming for lunch and she'd been quite blasé about it. Now, though, I could see she was having a shy moment. She hung back in the doorway, twisting one of her bunches round towards her mouth and sucking the tail of it.

'Don't do that, Molly,' I chastised her, then turned to Tom. 'This is my daughter.'

'The one I spoke to on the phone. Hi again, Molly.'

She didn't answer, just regarded him with big serious eyes, then turned and disappeared into the hall. I heard her foot-steps on the stairs and the slam of her bedroom door.

'She gets a bit self-conscious with people she doesn't know,' I said, feeling a little awkward. 'She'll come round before long.'

'Don't worry about it.'

Tom really was the easiest person in the world to get on with. Not to mention drop-dead hunky . . .

He remained in the kitchen with me whilst I kept an eye on the progress of the cooking, heated the fat for the Yorkshire puddings and popped them in the oven. It would have been easier, I suppose, to have made a casserole, something that needed less last-minute attention, but I'd wanted to do a roast, and there was something very cosy about cooking with Tom there, leaning casually against the sink, glass in hand. It felt very right.

When everything was ready I called Molly, hoping she'd overcome her shyness. She came down a little hesitantly, not running as she usually did, but there was a sheet of paper in her hand and she went straight to Tom. 'This is for you.'

He took it and I glanced over his shoulder. Molly had drawn a picture of a street scene – Laverham High Street on Farmers' Market Day, by the look of the stalls with their brightly striped awnings, one displaying cheeses, another cakes and biscuits, a third stacked with trays of bedding plants. A family of ducks were waddling in line beside the river railings, and an assortment of figures, fat and thin, jostled with baskets on their arms.

'Molly, that is lovely!' Tom said. 'You're quite an artist, aren't you?'

'She certainly is,' I confirmed. Not only was I proud of Molly's talent, I was also touched that she should have done this picture for Tom. It was a good sign and boded well for her acceptance of him.

Just one thing was bothering me. Amongst the cars in the background of the picture, all carefully drawn, one stood out – to me at least. A red car with a black soft top.

Molly might give the impression of having got over her fright of a week ago, but it was still playing on her mind.

And it was playing on my mind too.

With all my heart I hoped it had been a bizarre one-off. That the woman had simply been a deranged opportunist and that she wouldn't figure in our lives again.

But I couldn't get away from the sick fear that it was more than that. That something was happening in our lives that I didn't understand. And it was not over yet.

Eight

It was a lovely day. Lunch was perfect – in spite of the fact that the cook had been merrily sipping Chablis throughout the last hour of preparation – and both Tom and Molly did the food full justice. I was especially gratified to see Molly's clean plate – she'd even had seconds of everything – and I made up my mind to cook more proper roasts. When it was only the two of us a joint was rather daunting and I tended to buy chops and chicken breasts. But Molly had enjoyed it so much I resolved to do it again soon, whether Tom was here or not. And hopefully he would be . . . sometimes, at least . . .

For the space of a few hours I was able to put all my worries behind me.

Once we'd cleared away the lunch things – Tom insisted on helping though I assured him there was no need – we all went out for a walk. Molly had lost all traces of her shyness now, it never lasted long, and seemed to really take to Tom, skipping along beside him and chattering to him as if she'd known him all her life. We did a round trip taking in a small holding where we stopped to watch a couple of dozen baby goats gambolling in their enclosure, across an open field to a hidden lake, and home around the lanes, heavy with burgeoning early summer greenery.

We had tea – scones with thickly clotted cream and strawberry jam. Shop-bought, I admit, but I resolved next time to make my own as I'd used to. Baking was something else I'd once enjoyed but which had gone by the board lately.

'I expect you're ready to kick me out,' Tom said when it was time for Molly to go to bed.

'Not necessarily,' I said. I didn't want him to go, I realized.

I put Molly to bed and went back downstairs to find him comfortably ensconced watching television. It felt cosy and right, as if we'd been together for years instead of a few days. But when I sat down on the sofa beside him and he put an arm around me it was anything but commonplace. I was suddenly so aware of him that every particle of my body seemed to be drawn to him like iron filings to a magnet. I was trembling with a desire that I'd almost forgotten. I sat perfectly still, staggered by the strength of it, feeling almost that I was in a parallel world, alone with Tom. My muscles seemed paralysed, it was almost as if I had stopped breathing. I wanted to stay there forever in the circle of his arm, and yet at the same time I wanted more, much more.

'All right, Jo?' he asked softly in my ear.

And then he kissed me.

The kiss was gentle at first, as it had been on Friday night, warm and chaste, yet setting me on fire. And then it became deeper, exploring my mouth, and I opened up to him, kissing him back with a hunger that seemed to come from my very soul. My arms were around him now too – I could feel the hard muscles in his shoulders and back. I clung to him as his hands moved over my own body, luxuriating in every touch, wanting him – wanting him so badly that I was nothing but a vacuum of desire.

And then, quite suddenly, with his mouth in the hollow between my breasts, reality came crashing in. I have no idea what triggered it, maybe the sudden realization of where we were headed, but it was just as if someone had turned a hosepipe of freezing water on to me.

I drew back, pushing him away. 'No!'

'What is it?' One arm was still around me; he looked at me questioningly and I could see the desire I had felt a few moments ago mirrored in his eyes. 'What's wrong?'

'I can't. I'm sorry, Tom.'

'OK.' He released me; sat back. I wondered if he was angry. I felt guilty, a tease. But he didn't look angry, he looked more regretful. And he didn't sound angry either. 'You want me to go now?'

'No!' I didn't know what I wanted, except that I wasn't

ready for this. 'No – but I don't want things to get out of hand either. I'm sorry.'

'It's all right, I understand.' But I wasn't sure he did, especially when he went on to ask: 'Are you sure there's something you're not telling me, Jo?'

I stared at him, puzzled. 'What do you mean?'

'I just get the feeling . . . is there someone else?'

'No!' I hesitated, and knew that wasn't quite true. Michael. He might have been dead for more than two years, but in many ways he was still here with me. He was in my heart and my soul; my body still remembered him. There had been no one but him for the best part of ten years and the thought of intimacy with anyone else was a huge bridge to cross. It seemed like a betrayal. As long as Michael was the last person to have made love to me, I still belonged to him. Moving on meant leaving him behind, pushing him out. Not forgetting him exactly, but consigning him to the past. And I couldn't do it. Not yet. Perhaps never.

'Well, actually there is,' I said hesitantly. 'My husband.'

Tom's eyes narrowed. 'I thought your husband was dead.'

I lowered my gaze. 'He is, but . . . in some ways, he's not. Tom, I'd really rather not talk about it.' I moved away from him, uncomfortable for the first time in his company, and stood up. 'Would you like a drink?'

'Better not. I have to drive.'

'A soft drink, then? Or a cup of tea?'

'All right. I'll have an orange juice if you've got one. Or a can of coke.'

'With a child in the house, I have both.'

I poured him an orange juice and added plenty of ice, but I felt in need of something stronger myself and mixed a gin and tonic. I shouldn't really – I'd already had quite a lot to drink today – but what the heck?

Tom stayed for another hour or so but the slight awkwardness was still there between us. When he got up, saying it was time he went, I felt a bolt of panic. Had I ruined everything?

'Will I see you again?' I blurted.

Tom grinned. 'You didn't think you could get rid of me that easily, did you? Especially since you cook such a mean roast beef.'

I pulled a wry face though inside my heart had lifted. 'Just as long as I know what it is you want me for.'

'You underestimate yourself, Jo.' He slipped on his jacket, which had been hanging draped over the back of a chair, and looking for all the world as if it belonged there. At the door he kissed me, just a light touch of his lips on my forehead.

'I'll phone you. Or you can phone me. You've got my number.'

And then he was gone and I was alone. A little confused still, a little unsettled, but happy.

The phone rang as I was tidying up. I hurried to answer it thinking it was probably Anna. To my surprise, however, it was Alison.

'Jo – I hope I haven't called at an inconvenient moment.'

'Not at all.' I could only think of one reason, though, why Alison might ring me on a Sunday evening. 'Have you heard from Adam?'

'No. But Jo, there is something very strange going on. I've been doing some investigating as I said I would and I think I know who the woman in the red car was – the one who tried to take Molly last Saturday.'

Instantly I was alert. 'Who?'

There was a slight pause, then: 'I'd rather not say at the moment. There's someone I need to talk to first.'

I frowned, frustrated and a little annoyed. 'What's the point of phoning me with half a story?' I asked bluntly. 'If you think you know who it was, I want to know too.'

'I'm sorry, I can't.' Alison sounded flustered. 'And that wasn't the reason I phoned, Jo.' She hesitated. 'I don't know how to ask you this, but I have to . . .'

'What?'

I almost heard her take a deep breath. 'How sure are you that Michael is really dead?'

'*What?*' Nothing she could have said could have shocked or dumbfounded me more. I could not find the words to describe how I felt in that moment. I scarcely even know how I felt myself beyond the fact that I couldn't believe Alison should have asked me such a thing.

'What sort of a question is that?' I demanded, my voice shaking. 'My husband, as you very well know, has been dead for two years. Good heavens, you attended his funeral.'

'That's not what I asked, Jo,' Alison persisted. 'Oh, God, this is awful, but . . . could it have been someone else in the car that night? Is it possible it wasn't Michael at all?'

'I think you've taken leave of your senses, Alison,' I raged. 'I don't know what this is about but . . .'

'There's never been anything to make you suspect he might still be alive?'

Suddenly I couldn't take any more. 'I am not having this conversation,' I grated out. 'Goodbye, Alison.' And I slammed down the phone.

I was really badly shaken, trembling all over, and close to tears too. How could Alison have asked me such a thing – and why? I had no idea. I was incapable of stringing two thoughts together.

The phone was ringing again. I stared at it, my hands clenched. If that was Alison again, ringing back to explain or apologize, I wasn't going to speak to her. I couldn't just at the moment. I wasn't sure I wanted to speak to her ever again.

I let it ring and ring and eventually it stopped. The answering service would have cut in, I knew. I gave it a few minutes, pouring myself another stiff gin and tonic and gulping at it as if it were a lifeline, then I returned to the phone, my hand hovering over the receiver. Should I pick it up and see if there was a message? If it was Alison, I didn't want to hear it. But it might not have been Alison. It might have been Anna. Maybe she needed me and . . . oh, God, I needed her!

I picked up, dialled the numbers for the answering service, poised to hit delete if it was Alison. It was. But somehow, in spite of myself, I felt compelled to hear what she had to say.

'Jo – I'm really, really sorry. I didn't mean to upset you. Well, I knew I would, of course, but there are things I've found out and I had to ask. And warn you, really. Please forgive me. I'm only trying . . .' Her voice tailed off as if she, too, was in tears. Then she went on: 'I wish I'd never started this, believe me. But now that I have I can't just leave it. I've got to find out what's going on. Get to the bottom of it all. I'll be in touch – if you ever want to speak to me again. And I am truly, truly sorry.'

End of message. I put the phone down. I was trembling all over again as the initial shock wore off and the questions came tumbling in.

What on earth had made Alison ask me such a question? And what did she mean by 'things I've found out . . . I had to ask. I'd known she was going to try to do some investigation into Adam's disappearance, but what did that have to do with Michael's death? Were they connected in some way? And was the connection this local gangster Kenny White? Alison had suggested he might be behind Adam's disappearance – and Michael had been with him on the night he died. Both she and Dave had said he was a dangerous man to know. Could it possibly be that there had been more to Michael's crash than a straightforward accident? That Kenny White had been involved in some way? It had never been satisfactorily explained as far as I was concerned. Michael, my careful Michael, driving so recklessly that he'd run off the road, crashed into a tree with such impact that the car had burst into flames.

But it still didn't explain why Alison should ask me if I was really sure that Michael was dead. And why had she posed the question almost in the same breath as saying she thought she knew who the woman was who had tried to abduct Molly? There could be a link back to Kenny White again. Dave had said the woman sounded like someone who might be part of his circle. *But why ask me if I was sure Michael was dead?* Unless . . .

The most appalling thought occurred to me and the realization of what Alison had been implying hit me with the force of a hammer blow. She was suggesting that it had not been Michael at all who had been killed that terrible night. That it had been someone else entirely whose remains had been recovered from the burned-out wreck of his car. And that the woman who had tried to get Molly into her car had been doing it on behalf of Michael, because he wanted to see his daughter.

97

It was a preposterous idea, and yet it was the only explanation for the bizarre conversation I'd had with Alison and her garbled apology. Surely she couldn't honestly believe such a thing? What in the world could have given her such an idea?

Strictly speaking, I supposed, it would be possible to hypothesize that Michael's identity had not been proved beyond doubt. Though he had been burned beyond recognition, the question that it could be anyone but him had never arisen. It was his car, in which he had left the golf club that night. He had not come home. The man in the car had been wearing Michael's wedding ring, watch and neck chain. Put all together it had been enough to provide identification. As far as I knew, no other tests had been deemed necessary, and certainly it had been enough for me.

Now I felt sick to my stomach that anyone, particularly a friend and colleague like Alison, could entertain for even a moment the idea that Michael might collude in faking his own death. He had been my husband, I had loved him dearly, and he had loved me. He was Molly's father, and he had adored her. There was no way he would have put us through something so terrible, even if he had been the crookedest crook in Kenny White's gang, which I knew he wasn't. Michael was the most honourable man I'd ever met. That Alison could suspect him of this made me furious.

I picked up the phone again, intent on ringing her and telling her exactly what I thought of her and her sick insinuations. Normally, I'd run a mile from a row – just now I was too fired up to even hesitate. But the phone simply rang and rang. Either Alison didn't want to answer or she'd gone out and not switched her answering machine on. Frustrated, I banged down the receiver.

I thought about ringing Anna – I desperately wanted to talk to her. But I restrained myself. Anna had enough troubles of her own without me inflicting mine on her.

Trying to get a grip on my shot nerves, I went back to tidying up. But I was still all over the place when I went to bed. It was a long time before I went to sleep and when I did it was to the most confused and disturbing dreams. All involving Michael. In one, he was getting out of a red convertible, holding his arms out to Molly. 'I've missed you, sweetheart,' he said. But he was looking straight through me, as if I wasn't there at all. And Tom was there too, and he was telling me to forget Michael, that he just wasn't worth grieving for. And Alison was watching from the shadows. I knew she was there, though I couldn't see her. I woke up, and my face was wet with tears.

I tried to put it all out of my mind. I had to – allowing myself to dwell on it was driving me crazy. But for all my resolution it was still there, a cloud I couldn't escape, pervading my senses, colouring my emotions and creeping into my conscious thoughts.

It was impacting on my feelings about Tom and my recollection of the happy day we'd spent together too. The attraction he held for me was as strong as ever – I could still close my eyes and feel my tummy tip when I pictured his strong-featured face and his smile, still experience a momentary warm glow and a frisson of excitement, but it was hemmed in by a sense of something like guilt.

I'd physically pulled away when I'd thought our relationship was moving into too intimate territory last night; now I also stepped back emotionally from the edge of the abyss too.

It was almost as if some unacknowledged part of me did believe that Michael was still alive and I was betraying him. I immediately took myself to task. The way I'd reacted last night had been perfectly natural. I simply wasn't ready to take the next big – and irretrievable – step in our budding relationship. It was the echo of my response then that was colouring the way I felt now. It had nothing whatever to do with Alison's preposterous theory, which was quite ridiculous as well as upsetting.

I'd known my husband through and through. I had followed his coffin. And though my last goodbyes had had to be made by kissing the closed oak lid and laying a rose there, on the brass name plate, I had not had the slightest doubt but that the remains I'd wept over were Michael's. Gradually these guilty feelings would fade. And sooner or later some if not all of the mysteries that were dominating my life at the moment would be solved. Things would return to normal and this whole disturbing chapter of events would slip into the past. I had to believe that or go crazy.

Take one moment at a time, I told myself. Stop worrying. But the overwhelming unease and the apprehensive feeling that it was not over yet would not quite go away.

Four days went by with no developments on any front. There were no further calls from Alison and Tom had not rung either. I was glad of the first but slightly anxious about the second. I hoped he had not come to the conclusion that I was carrying too much baggage to make a relationship with me worth pursuing. Well, if he had, there was nothing I could do about it. But knowing that didn't stop me feeling regretful – or checking my answering service regularly in case I'd missed his call.

The bright spot was that Dave was still making good progress, and Anna suggested I might go with her to visit him.

'It would make a change for him to see a different face,' she said. 'He must be sick to death of mine.'

'You know that's not true,' I said with confidence. Anna and Dave were devoted to one another – a refreshing change from all the couples I knew who had grown apart or whose marriages had broken up and ended in divorce.

'Oh, I'm sure it is,' Anna said cheerfully and I thought how good it was to hear her sounding cheerful again. 'In any case, it may help him to get his memory back,' she went on, more seriously. 'He knows me and the children, thank God, but he still has these huge gaps. Anything that might help jog him into remembering bits and pieces to fill in the blanks can only be good.'

'It will come back eventually though, won't it?' I asked.

Anna shrugged helplessly. 'I don't know, Jo. No one can say for certain. He's OK with things that happened years ago. It's the recent past – the last few weeks especially – that he's having trouble with. Anyway – will you come with me one day? He'd be so pleased, I know.'

'Of course I will. How about Thursday? Molly has art club after school, so I don't have to pick her up until five thirty, and if I can arrange to have an afternoon off that will give us plenty of time.'

'Sounds good to me,' Anna said, and we made the necessary arrangements. She'd pick me up and we'd go together – parking was always at a premium at the hospital – then she'd get me back in good time to collect Molly from school.

It was about half past two when we arrived at the hospital and took the lift up to the unit where Dave was being cared for.

I really don't like hospitals – but then, who does? I hate the bleakness, which somehow seems only to be exacerbated by the forced, bustling cheeriness of the nurses and the bunches of flowers that sit in an assortment of unsuitable and unlovely vases. I hate the smell of antiseptic and food trolleys and sickness. I hate the feeling of being trapped in a time capsule that has nothing to do with normality, the peculiar routines, the clanking trolleys, the depressing sight of terribly ill patients hooked up to their life-saving paraphernalia and obviously out of it, and the not-so-sick ones who can barely disguise their desperation to get home. But at the same time I'm jolly glad they're there when we need them and full of admiration for the nurses and doctors who work their miracles with cheery good humour under such grim conditions.

Dave was in a side ward – a little room to himself with a glass-panelled door. As we approached we could see that there was someone with him – obviously not a member of the hospital staff, as he was wearing police uniform.

'Oh, blimey,' Anna muttered, 'looks like the top brass have come visiting. Bunter Williams. Dave's superintendent.'

She opened the door. I hung back, concerned there might be rules forbidding more than two visitors at a patient's bedside, but she motioned a little impatiently for me to follow her.

Superintendent Williams rose from the chair he had been sitting in beside Dave's bed. It was easy to see where he had got the nickname Bunter, though it was not very flattering and I didn't suppose anyone called him that to his face now that he had a crown on each shoulder. He was a big man, well over six foot tall, and broad with it. He had a huge bald spot over which long strands of jet-black hair from the remaining fringe had been artfully trailed and secured with gel, heavy jowls and a high colour which made me think he might be a little too fond of the bottle.

'Mrs Smart,' he greeted Anna.

'Mr Williams.' Her tone was formal, clipped. Either she was in awe of the superintendent, which, knowing Anna, seemed unlikely, or she didn't like him much. I suspected it was the latter. 'How good of you to come to visit Dave.'

'Least I could do, considering he was injured in the call of duty.' His voice was fruity, his tone almost avuncular. False bonhomie, I thought. He's here because he thinks he should be, but he'd far rather be on the golf course – or giving some hapless probationer a roasting. 'Good to see your husband looking so much better.'

'It certainly is,' Anna agreed.

If this was 'better', how on earth had poor Dave looked before? I wondered. He still looked dreadful to me. Anna went to his side and kissed him. He made a feeble attempt to respond, taking her hand with fingers that were as slow and clumsy as an old man's.

'Dave,' I said from the end of the bed. 'How are you?'

'A damned sight better than I was.' His voice lacked its usual vigour and authority, but he made an effort to smile. 'Good to see you, Jo.'

'Well, it's time I was going.' Bunter Williams reached for his uniform cap which he had parked on Dave's locker amongst the get well cards. 'Keep up the progress, Smart. And let's hope you soon get that memory back. It might help us to nail the swine that did this to you.'

'You aren't any closer to finding out who it was then?' Anna asked.

'Unfortunately no.' The superintendent moved toward the door. 'We have the paint samples of the offending vehicle but as yet nothing to match them to. No stolen car abandoned damaged or burned out, no garage reporting anything likely being brought in for bodywork repairs. Unless your husband can recall something about the vehicle that hit him, it's a little like looking for a needle in a haystack, I'm afraid. And the culprit goes scot free.'

'The important thing is that Dave is left in peace to get well,' Anna said fiercely. 'I don't want him badgered. What's done is done and much as I'd like to see the bastard caught and punished, I don't want Dave to have any harassment that might set back his recovery.'

'Quite – quite. None of us wants that,' Williams hastened to agree. I personally wouldn't mind betting a pound to a penny he'd been quizzing Dave before our arrival. 'Well, I've asked your doctor to keep me posted as to your progress, Smart. I hope you'll go ahead now in leaps and bounds. And rest assured you are in the thoughts of each and every one of your colleagues.'

'Thank you, sir,' Dave managed. 'And thank you for coming.'

'Windbag!' Anna exploded as the door closed after him. 'Pompous bloody windbag!'

'Forget him.' Dave was still holding Anna's hand.

'Look who's talking! All the stuff you can't remember, but you still know your superintendent when you see him!'

Dave grinned, but it was a parody of his usual ready smile. 'I know. Once seen, never forgotten.'

'Does that go for me, too?' I joked. 'You knew who I was too.'

'Ah, yes. The girl I might have married if Anna hadn't seen me first.'

'Charming!' But she was laughing, secure in the knowledge of Dave's love.

'You're jogging something, Jo, but I don't know what.' Dave was looking at me intently. 'I was doing something for you, wasn't I? Something you asked me to find out . . . or sort . . .'

Anna and I exchanged glances. All my troubles were the last thing Dave needed to be worrying about now.

'It was nothing important,' I said. 'As your superintendent said, all you need to concentrate on is getting well. He may be a windbag, but he's right there.'

As Anna perched on the edge of the bed, I took the chair Bunter Williams had vacated. An orderly came in to offer us all a cup of tea, and we settled down to the ritual of hospital visiting.

*   *   *

103

I'd been home an hour or so when the phone rang. I'd collected Molly from her art club and now she was eating baked beans and sausages at the kitchen table with the latest edition of her ballet magazine open beside her plate. It had been waiting for her when we got home – I'd taken out a subscription, so it always came by post – and Molly had fallen upon it eagerly. Now she barely raised her nose from the page as I hurried to answer the phone. Might it be Tom this time? I wasn't expecting anyone else.

It was. We exchanged a few pleasantries, me trying to conceal my relief that he'd called at last, but aware that there was something a little stilted about his conversation, as if there was something he had to say that he wasn't keen on getting to. As the impression grew stronger, I began to feel apprehensive. Was he going to end by saying he didn't think we should see each other again? At last I could bear it no longer.

'Is something wrong, Tom?' I asked.

There was the slightest hesitation. Then: 'You haven't seen the local paper this evening, I take it.'

'No.' The *Evening Chronicle* wasn't a paper I was in the habit of buying. 'Why?'

'There was something in it that . . .' Another hesitation. 'Garratt Properties in the high street – that's the estate agents your husband was with, isn't it?'

I was very alert suddenly, every nerve ending tingling and I had gone cold with dread. Something had happened to Adam just as Alison had suspected. Something dreadful – and it was in the local evening paper.

'What about it?' I said. 'Oh, God – is it Adam?'

'Adam?' Tom sounded vaguely puzzled.

'Adam Garratt. Garratt Properties,' I said shortly.

'Oh, yes. I mean – no. That's not who the story is about.'

'Who then?' I asked, genuinely puzzled.

'It's the office manager. Alison . . .' He paused, as if checking the report.

'Alison Singer,' I supplied. 'What about her?'

Tom's reply shook me to the core.

'It seems she's dead, Jo,' he said.

104

Nine

'What did you say?' The words came out on a taut breath of disbelief. *'Alison? Dead?'*

'Yes. She was discovered at her home. Police broke in when her colleague became concerned because she'd failed to turn up for work. From the way the report is worded, it sounds as if she committed suicide.'

'Suicide?' I was incapable of words beyond inanely repeating Tom's. And then the inevitable question. 'But how? How did she do it?'

'The report didn't say. It's too early to jump to conclusions, I suppose. But if she was found at home I'd imagine she took something – pills or a prescription drug. She wouldn't have suffered, Jo. She'd just have gone to sleep.' If he was intending to comfort me it didn't work. That lovely bubbly girl, so depressed she wanted to end it all. Dying alone.

'Oh, my God, Alison. Poor Alison . . .'

'I've given you a shock. I'm sorry.' Tom sounded more his usual self now that he'd broken the news he'd obviously been dreading having to impart. 'Are you all right? Do you want me to come over?'

'No – no, I'll be fine.' I was far from fine, but it sounded wimpish to admit it. 'It's not as if she's a close friend or anything – but oh . . . it's just such a shock. Poor Alison! What on earth possessed her? I was only speaking to her a few days ago. She was worried, I know, because Adam seems to have disappeared. But suicidal . . . I just can't believe it! She didn't say anything to lead me to believe . . . Oh, it's awful! Just awful!'

'I *am* coming over,' Tom said decisively.

'No . . . really . . .'

'Yes. You're clearly upset. I'll be with you in – well, say in about an hour. No more arguments now. I'm not listening. I'll see you soon.'

'OK,' I said meekly. And realized how good it was to have someone make a decision for me. Since Michael's death I'd had to make them all for myself – and for Molly – alone. At this moment, with the world going mad around me, I had never felt more in need of support.

It was actually more like an hour and a half before Tom's car drew up on my drive and he came in, looking anxious.

'Sorry – the traffic was really bad.'

'It would be at this time of night,' I said. 'I should have warned you.'

'And I should have known.' He took me by the arms. 'How are you?'

'Still in a state of shock.'

He glanced over my shoulder and spoke quietly. 'Does Molly know?'

I nodded. I'd broken the news to her as gently as I could and she'd bitten her lip and looked at me with big serious eyes.

'You mean she's gone to heaven like Daddy?' she'd asked.

'I'm afraid so, Molly.'

She'd chewed her lip some more, then gone off upstairs to her room. She'd been there ever since, drawing, no doubt. It was what she usually did when something had upset her and she needed to sort herself out.

Alone I'd done some thinking of my own, and plenty of it. I'd gone over and over that last conversation I'd had with Alison and, bizarre as it had been, I couldn't see that Alison had shown the slightest sign of being suicidal. Quite the opposite. She'd been full of determination to get to the bottom of what had happened to Adam and all the other unexplained things that had occurred – and from what she had said she had already made some headway in that direction. Even if she had taken some wrong turnings, such as her suspicion that it was not Michael who had died in his blazing car.

I wished with all my heart she'd never said that, and now not only because I found it offensive to Michael's memory,

106

but because it had caused us to fall out. It was horrible to think that the last words I'd spoken to her had been in anger, and I felt bitterly regretful for that. Was it possible she'd been balanced on a knife edge and our quarrel had been the last straw?

I dismissed that idea as quickly as it occurred to me. Alison must have known what my reaction was likely to be and she'd said what she said all the same. We weren't close enough for her to take it to heart to the extent that she would take her own life. And in any case she wasn't an emotional, highly-strung personality who might be pushed over the edge by something like that. She was an efficient, level-headed career girl with her own car and flat.

Could it have been an accident, then? Too many paracetamols or aspirin for a raging migraine or toothache or something? Or a too pure batch of a recreational drug? But you'd have to make one hell of a miscalculation to take enough paracetamol or aspirin to kill you, and I couldn't imagine Alison doing drugs, not the kind that you take alone at home, anyway. Cannabis or Ecstasy at a party, maybe, but not the hard stuff. She was no addict, I'd stake my life on it. But she wasn't the suicidal type either. I just couldn't see her doing something like that. At all. For any reason whatever. Any more than I could see Adam doing it.

Which left the unthinkable.

Alison had been worried that the Kenny White gang were behind Adam's disappearance. Dangerous, she'd called them – ruthless – and Dave had confirmed that. Adam had been mixed up with them in some way – and perhaps Michael too – and Alison had been investigating that connection, trying to find out exactly what was going on. Dave had been investigating too, though probably from quite a different angle. Now Dave was in hospital, knocked from his police motorcycle by a hit-and-run driver and left for dead, and Alison had apparently taken her own life. But I didn't believe it for a second, and quite suddenly I didn't believe that Dave's crash had been an accident either. Both of them had probed the Kenny White connection and both had been dealt with.

I was certain, as certain as I could be, that if Alison had died of an overdose of some drug or other that it had not been self-administered. Somehow, someone had forced a lethal dose into her. Murdered her and made it look like suicide.

Though the whole scenario seemed like something out of crime fiction or one of the more far-fetched police dramas on TV, I was suddenly quite certain that all the sinister events were somehow connected – perhaps even the accident that had robbed me of my husband two years ago. And I was afraid, more afraid than I had ever been in my life. I didn't know what was happening, but I had the horrible feeling that if I went down the same road as Alison by trying to find out I too could very well end up on a mortuary slab. What would happen to Molly then?

But I couldn't just let it all go on without doing something. Someone had already tried to abduct Molly, though I had not the faintest idea why. Was she in danger? How the hell could I protect her? I couldn't be with her every minute of the day, couldn't wrap her up in cotton wool and turn her into a frightened little rabbit. I wasn't even sure that given the reputation of the people I would be dealing with that I would be able to keep her safe myself. But I didn't know who I could turn to for help. The police, it seemed, weren't interested. Maybe some of them were even in the pockets of the White gang, if Alison was to be believed – though to be honest I couldn't imagine that their involvement would go so far as to condone harm to an innocent child. The one policeman I trusted implicitly was still seriously ill in hospital. Who could I turn to for help? Who would even believe me?

All this had been running around in my head for the past hour and I was no closer to reaching a solution. Now, looking at Tom's concerned face, I realized that the one person who would not think I had taken leave of my senses was right here in front of me.

'Oh, Tom, I'm so frightened!' I said.

And burst into tears.

I sobbed for a few moments into his shoulder, and it felt so good, so solid and safe. Then I got myself together and levered away.

'I'm sorry. I just feel so . . . overwhelmed. I don't know what's going on. I don't know which way to turn.'

Tom fished a handkerchief out of his pocket and gave it to me. That was comforting too. A real handkerchief, man-size, not a silly little tissue. As a child when I was ill or upset I always wanted one of my father's handkerchiefs – it had smelled faintly of tobacco and lighter fuel and Daddy. And when Michael had died I'd cried out some of my grief into his handkerchiefs. Now they were laundered and stacked in a neat pile in a dressing-table drawer. It was a long time since I'd had a man's handkerchief as a comfort blanket.

Tom waited as I wiped my eyes and blew my nose. Then he asked: 'So what *is* going on, Jo?'

'It's so complicated. I don't know where to begin . . .'

'Let's get you a drink and we'll sit down quietly. It sounds to me as if you need to talk.'

I fought the tears that were threatening to start flowing again.

'Oh, I do! Believe me, I do!'

I told him everything, keeping my voice low in case Molly should come downstairs and overhear me. He listened, asking questions sometimes but mainly just letting me relate all the disturbing events in my own way.

'I've come to the conclusion they're all linked in some way,' I finished. 'And the connection seems to be this character Kenny White.'

Tom was silent for a few moments, deep in thought.

'You thought someone was watching your house,' he said at last. 'That was the start of it all.'

'Yes. That was why I panicked the night we met. I thought I was being followed. I thought *you* were following me.'

'But you don't think that any more?'

'No, of course not. I wouldn't be confiding in you now if I did. But it could be that someone else had me under surveillance.'

Tom frowned. 'That's an odd way to put it.'

'Oh, you know what I mean. That was how it felt. At the time I told myself I must have been imagining it, but now I'm not so sure. What I don't understand is – why would anyone do that? It doesn't make any sense at all. And why would the woman in the red car try to abduct Molly? There was something else, too,' I said, remembering suddenly. 'I got a telephone call and when I answered it no one was there. I didn't think anything of it at the time but . . . supposing it was someone checking up on me? Trying to find out if I was at home or not?'

'Now you are being paranoid,' Tom said. 'Cold-calling centres do that all the time – multi-dial numbers and then when one replies, cut off all the others.'

'I suppose . . . but it didn't feel like that. There was someone on the other end when I answered, I'm sure there was. But they just hung up.'

Tom was silent again for a moment. Then he said: 'Alison told you she'd been doing some digging and then she asked you if you were sure Michael died in the accident two years ago. Is that right?'

All my distress and anger at Alison bubbled up again. For the moment I quite forgot that she, too, was now dead.

'I can't believe she could have suggested such a thing! It's just outrageous! How dare she?'

'Jo.' Tom leaned over, covering my hand with his. 'Looked at logically it has to be considered as a possibility.'

I tore my hand away. 'No! God – you're as bad as she is!'

'Take it easy, Jo. I'm just trying to understand why she should have suggested it. Someone watching the house. Phoning you but not speaking when you answered. Trying to abduct Molly. She might very well have thought it could be Michael.'

'She didn't know about the phone call.' I grabbed my drink – a stiff gin and tonic – and gulped it, glaring at him over the rim of the glass.

'OK, I accept that. But if she was doing some investigation, then it's possible that something she turned up led her to believe that Michael was still alive.'

'Michael is dead. He'd never put me through this. God, Tom, do you think I didn't know my own husband?' I was losing it again.

'Sometimes we don't know people nearly as well as we think we do,' Tom said gently.

'Well, I knew Michael!' I said fiercely. 'You didn't, and neither did Alison if she could suspect him of such a thing. And what about all the rest of it? Adam's disappearance, to start with. Dave's accident . . . Alison's death. Are you suggesting they all came to this ridiculous conclusion and Michael – my Michael – bumped them all off, or tried to, in order to keep secret the fact that he was actually still alive?'

'Of course not,' Tom said. 'Just try and calm down, Jo.'

'Calm down!' I banged my glass down hard on the coffee table in front of me. 'You're coming out with all this terrible nonsense and you tell me to calm down!'

'Jo – Jo – Jo . . . stop it! You asked me to help you get to the bottom of this, and I'm trying to look at it logically.'

'By suggesting my husband, who is not here to defend himself, is not only a cruel fraudster but a murderer!' I blazed.

'No, I'm not. We don't know that Alison's death was anything other than an accidental overdose or suicide. It sounds from the newspaper report that the police are satisfied on that score.'

'The police! Huh!' I snorted scornfully. 'The same police who refused to accept Adam was missing and tried to tell me Molly had invented the woman in the red car so she wouldn't get into trouble for wandering off. And who can't find out who knocked Dave off his motorbike and left him for dead. One of their own – and they still can't find out who did that to him. Or won't.'

'Hit and runs are always notoriously difficult to deal with. Especially if there are no witnesses . . .'

I cut across Tom as if he had not spoken.

'And there's something else you've omitted to mention. You're suggesting it wasn't Michael in his car that night. Well then – who was it? Someone died. There's no disputing that. To follow your preposterous theory to its logical conclusion, Michael must have murdered him too. He's killed three people – four almost, except that Dave survived. That's what you're suggesting. It's crazy! Crazy . . .' And I was in tears again.

'Jo . . .' Tom reached for me; I pushed him away. He had become the enemy now. I'd turned to him for help and he had just made things worse.

111

'Leave me alone!' I sobbed. 'Just leave me alone!'

'OK.' He stood up. 'If that's what you want.'

I didn't answer. He crossed to the door. And suddenly I knew it wasn't what I wanted at all. He might have upset me all over again, but for all that he was a rock in a stormy sea. And maybe more. I wanted him. Without a single conscious thought I knew it with every fibre of my being. I couldn't just let him walk out the door.

'Tom . . .' He turned and looked at me. I couldn't read the expression on his face. 'Please . . . don't go.'

I didn't need to say any more. Didn't need to explain myself in any way. He came back, sat down beside me, took my hands in his.

'I thought you were going to shoot the messenger,' he said.

I shook my head. 'I'm sorry . . . I'm just beside myself. I don't know what to think. Except that I know Michael would never do something so terrible . . .'

'I believe you.'

'And I don't know what to do . . .'

'I think you should go to the police. I know they haven't been much help so far, but I don't think you have any choice, Jo. Tell them everything you've told me.'

'Perhaps I should . . .'

'You must. For your own safety. And Molly's.'

Molly! I looked at the clock; it was way past her bedtime. And she had school in the morning.

'I must get Molly to bed.'

I got up, checked my appearance in the mirror, rubbing smears of mascara from under my eyes and tweaking my hair back to some sort of order. Then I went to the kitchen, warmed a cup of milk to make a drinking chocolate and took it upstairs.

I pushed open the door to her room, then stopped, surprised. The curtains were closed and Molly was in bed, the clothes she had been wearing folded in a neat pile on a chair, the teddy in sunglasses that Adam had given her sitting cheekily on top. I crept over to the bed. Molly was fast asleep, her hair spread across the pillow, Monkey tucked in beside her. Molly had got herself to bed without a word from me. My little girl was growing up.

My heart twisted as I looked down at her, the most precious thing in my life. Whatever else was going on, I still had Molly. And I would do anything in the world to keep her safe.

'OK?' Tom asked when I went back downstairs.

'She's fast asleep.'

'And you – are you OK?'

I grinned feebly. 'Not really. Too many terrible things have happened and I don't understand any of them.'

Tom put my drink in my hand. 'Sit down – try to unwind a bit – and let's go over it again.'

'I've gone over and over it and I'm still no further on.' I did as he said, though. I sat on the sofa, but perched on the edge, tense still. Tom sat down beside me.

'That's not quite true. You've come to the conclusion the White gang is the link.'

'Well – yes. And it scares me to death. But I don't see what it could be, or why . . . I can't understand how Adam came to be involved with them, let alone Michael.'

'Could the connection be Spain or Tenerife?' Tom suggested. 'Adam owns property there, you say. And it's a magnet for a lot of British criminals.'

'Are you saying Adam is a criminal?' I said, bristling a bit.

'Not necessarily.' Tom ignored my implied protest, his eyes narrowed in thought. 'It was the Whites I was thinking about. Though it has to be said – Adam owns an estate agency business and a lot of the money being made in Spain and Tenerife is through dodgy property sales, so there's a possibility there of a connection. Tenerife is rife with people making fortunes from the crooked side of the timeshare business. Take John Palmer, for instance. "Gold finger", as they called him.'

'But he was involved in disposing of the gold from the Brink's-Mat robbery, surely?' I said.

'He was acquitted. They got him in the end for fleecing would-be buyers out of fortunes through phoney property deals in Tenerife. But the scams didn't stop – far from it. The scratch card merchants are still out there on the streets enticing holidaymakers into their offices with promises of jackpot prizes and then conning them into shelling out for worthless schemes.'

'That is awful. But I can't believe that Adam . . .'

'You just never know. People can be seduced by big money, Jo. But if he is involved in something like that, it's a murky world. And when partners in crime fall out violence usually follows. Beatings. Killings. Retribution. That's why the big boys live behind electronic security gates with Rotweillers patrolling the grounds. And almost certainly there's trouble in the camp amongst the timeshare barons in Tenerife. Do you remember the story that was in all the papers back in January? The Robinsons, who were murdered on their way home from a dinner out in Playa de las Americas? They had been employees of John Palmer – she'd been his secretary I think – and they'd set up their own business out there. That was clearly some sort of revenge attack – it certainly wasn't robbery, anyway. Mr Robinson was still wearing a gold watch worth one hundred thousand euros when he was found, and Mrs Robinson's diamond earrings were still in her ears. No, they queered someone else's pitch and paid for it with their lives.'

'Oh my God. You don't think . . . ?' My mouth had gone dry.

'I don't think anything. I'm just suggesting possibilities. This Kenny White is known to have made a lot of money – and not from any legitimate business source. He's friendly with Adam. Adam has homes in Spain and Tenerife, not to mention a property business. Adam has disappeared. I don't want to frighten you, Jo. I'm just trying to impress on you that you could be way out of your depth here.'

'Even if that were the case, I just don't see what any of this has to do with me!' I protested, helplessly.

'If Michael were involved too . . .'

'Michael would never get involved with something like that. And Michael is dead.' I said it decisively.

Tom did not argue with me. 'I still think what you should do is go to the police and tell them everything you've told me. However you might feel about the way they've handled matters so far, even if someone is lining his pocket by turning a blind eye to a few local shenanigans, the whole of the local force can't be corrupt. And they should be put in the picture. And you believe there was something suspicious about Alison's death too. That you think she was murdered and it was made to look like suicide. Then they'll look at it again, more thoroughly.'

I chewed on a fingernail. He was right, I knew. But I could just imagine the response I'd get. *'I know it's hard to believe a relative or friend could be in that state of mind and we don't know about it . . . we hear it all the time . . . but there were no suspicious circumstances, Mrs Lansdale. If there had been we'd have been on to it . . .'* I shuddered at the prospect of being treated like an imaginative hysteric again. But I had to try.

'OK,' I said. 'They'll think I'm crazy, I expect. Even *I* think I'm crazy. Things like this don't happen in real life. I keep thinking I'm having a bad dream. That I'll wake up and everything will be normal. But it just goes on and on . . . Will it ever end?'

'Of course it will.' Tom pulled me close, stroking my hair as if I were a child. I burrowed into his chest, my head still echoing with the unbelievability of it all, every muscle aching with tension and an ache of anxiety making me feel a bit sick.

Gradually I felt myself beginning to relax, taking comfort in the solid, safe feel of his arms around me and his heart beating next to mine. A quiver of desire ran through me, darting like quicksilver, teasing me, making me aware of Tom as a man, not just a confessor for all my fears. Instinctively I wriggled closer. His lips were on mine, his hand on my breast, and a sense of urgency was overwhelming me. He pulled away slightly, raising an eyebrow at me in an unspoken question. For answer I pulled him close to me again. This time I was not going to tell him no.

We made love and it was frantic and all-consuming, a catharsis. For those timeless minutes I forgot everything – all my doubt and anxiety and the guilt of being with another man who was not my husband. And when it was over I snuggled against him, lazy, replete.

Often in the long dark nights after Michael's death I had

115

lain awake remembering the passion and the peace, wrapping my arms around myself and aching for what I had believed was lost to me forever. Now, in spite of everything, I was experiencing it again. And in spite of everything I was, on the deepest level, content.

The telephone was ringing, jarring on my mood. We'd made love again, more slowly, more gently, and I'd relaxed to a point where all my fears and confusion seemed to belong in a parallel universe. Now the feeling of apprehension hovered around me again like a cloud obliterating the sun. I'd answered the telephone as automatically as drawing breath; now, my senses primed for the next shock, I felt nothing but dread.

'It's probably Anna,' I said, easing myself out of Tom's embrace and getting up to answer it.

'Don't be too long, sweetheart,' he murmured lazily.

The endearment warmed me. I went into the kitchen and lifted the receiver, fully expecting it to be Anna. 'Hello?'

But it wasn't Anna. The voice at the other end of the line was totally unfamiliar. A man's voice, with a North Country accent.

'Could I speak to Mr Lansdale, please? Mr Michael Lansdale?'

Instantly I was tight as a drum, shock waves reverberating in my veins and the pit of my stomach.

'No,' I said abruptly. 'Who is this?'

The man did not identify himself. Instead, he asked: 'I have got the right number, have I?'

'This is Mrs Lansdale,' I said. I could hear the tremor in my voice. 'What do you want?'

There was a slight pause, as if the caller was a little taken aback by my aggression. 'I was just ringing to let him know I found his passport,' he said.

I'd misheard. I must have.

'I beg your pardon?'

'His passport. I picked it up when we were in Spain. It was just lying on the ground. I said to my missus – eh up, somebody'll be in trouble here. I 'anded it in, of course, but I thought I'd just make sure he knew it were safe.'

This was crazy – insane. 'When was this?' I asked, dazed.

'A couple of weeks ago. We just got home today ourselves and I said to the missus, I'm going to give that man a ring. It's all sorted out by now, mebbe, but I know how long these things can take with the red tape and all that, and I thought if he knew where it were he could take steps . . .'

'There's some mistake,' I said.

'Well, I were sure I took down the details right.' The man was beginning to sound offended. 'But if it's all sorted, I won't take up any more of your time.' And he rang off.

For a moment I stood frozen, then clicked buttons furiously as if I could reconnect with him by magic. There was so much I wanted to ask him, and it was too late. I was on the point of ringing 1471 to see if I could access his number when Tom's voice from the doorway made me swing round as if I'd been stung.

'Jo?'

'You made me jump.'

'Sorry.' He looked at me narrowly. 'Is everything all right?'

I was in a total daze. 'That was . . .' I broke off. I couldn't bring myself to repeat the bizarre conversation I'd just had with an unknown man with a North Country accent. In spite of the fact that I'd told Tom everything else, despite our newfound closeness in the loving we had just shared – perhaps because of it – I simply couldn't. Without thinking, without stopping to try and work out the reason why, I blurted: 'It was just someone trying to sell me a conservatory.'

'At this time of night?' He was looking at me narrowly, as if he didn't believe me.

'Oh, you know what these cold-callers are like . . .'

'Jo, you are still in one hell of a state.' He went to put his arm round me; I drew back. What had felt so right a few minutes ago suddenly felt quite wrong.

Tom pretended not to notice my withdrawal. Perhaps he didn't notice.

'If I'm going home, Jo, I ought to be making tracks.' He looked at me levelly. 'Unless you want me to stay?'

Something sharp and sweet twisted inside me.

'Better not.' It had occurred to me, when we'd been entwined in each other's arms, but my gut feeling was that it was too soon – not for me, but for Molly. It was best that she got used to Tom being around gradually. I didn't want her to wake in the morning to find him in her mother's bed, just like that.

But I had another reason now, too, for not wanting Tom to stay. I needed to be alone, to gather my thoughts, assess the maelstrom of emotion that was raging inside me.

'How would I explain to Molly?'

'I could sleep on the sofa if that would make it more acceptable,' he said easily. 'But kids are a good deal more adaptable than you give them credit for.'

How would you know? Stress was making me impatient. I didn't say it aloud, though.

'You're probably right,' I said instead. 'But all the same . . .'

'OK. Just as long as you're sure you're all right.'

'Honestly, I'm fine.'

I wasn't, of course. Everything was closing in on me again, a thick fog of terrible events that couldn't be explained. I was back in the nightmare. And when Tom had left and I locked the door after him, I was in it alone.

Correction. I'd been in it alone from the moment I'd lifted the receiver and heard a strange man's voice telling me he'd found Michael's passport in Spain. It was not something I could share yet with Tom – or anyone. I hadn't yet even wondered why. I only knew that for the moment at least it was something I had to work out for myself.

Ten

I got ready for bed, going through the motions automatically, but I knew I would not be able to sleep. Already the wonderful closeness I had shared with Tom seemed like a distant dream – an oasis of happiness that might never really have happened at all. My stomach churned and my mind seethed with questions, all of them unanswerable, so that I felt my head was going to explode.

Who was the man with the North Country accent who had telephoned? Was he an associate of Kenny White – was this the latest piece of strategy in the war of nerves that seemed to be being waged on me for some inexplicable reason? Or was he exactly who he had claimed to be – a holidaymaker who had found a passport in Michael's name, thought he would be worried about its loss, and called to set his mind at rest? And if so, what did it mean? Could it really be Michael's passport?

I racked my brains trying to remember if the passport had been amongst Michael's effects when I'd turned them out, and couldn't. But I was as sure as I could be that if it had been, grief stricken as I undoubtedly was, I would never have been so careless as to dispose of it where someone could find it and make fraudulent use of it. In fact, I was equally sure I wouldn't have disposed of it at all. A passport has sentimental value – a reminder of happy times shared. Our honeymoon in Goa, a skiing trip to France, carefree holidays in the sun. And Michael's photograph. Not the best or most flattering of likenesses – when are they ever? – but still Michael as he'd been then. I couldn't have brought myself to dump it, I was sure. But I couldn't remember seeing it either and having to face the decision to keep it or throw it away.

Distractedly I pulled on my dressing gown and made for the room which had been Michael's study and where I still kept all the documents that are the important minutiae of everyday life – insurance policies and birth certificates, savings accounts, receipted bills and a copy of my will. Everything connected with the winding up of Michael's estate was in an emerald green box file; I got it down and opened it, leafing through it hastily at first, then more thoroughly. There was no passport.

I pulled out the holiday file then, wondering if it might be there. I hadn't taken a proper holiday since Michael's death, apart from a week last year at Center Parks, for Molly's sake. My own passport was there in the wallet, but not Michael's. Frantic to find it, I pulled out every other file, however unlikely, emptying them and stuffing the contents back again, and all the while the knot of panic in my stomach was growing.

It wasn't here. I couldn't discount once and for all what the man on the other end of the phone had told me – that he'd found it in Spain. But if he'd been telling the truth, how had it got there? Who had been using Michael's passport? And how had they come by it?

I have to admit my first thought was Adam. Adam was a frequent visitor to Spain. He had helped me with the sorting out of Michael's estate for probate and could conceivably have come into possession of the passport. And he had gone missing. But it made no sense. Why would Adam want to use Michael's passport when he had one of his own? How would he be able to? Though they were both white males of roughly the same age, the resemblance ended there. Michael had been dark, while Adam was much fairer. Adam was several inches taller and a couple of collar sizes bigger and it showed in their faces. I couldn't believe that he'd think he could get away with it. He'd know that any self-respecting immigration official would query the photograph.

In any case it did not do anything to explain how Adam was managing for money if for some bizarre reason he had decided to use Michael's identity to disappear. It was the fact that he had drawn no money on any of his accounts that had worried Alison most, and she had hacked her way into all of them. But there was no way Adam would be able to obtain the wherewithal to live on through pretending to be Michael. All his affairs had been wound up two years ago, all his assets had been transferred to me. As an explanation for Adam's disappearance it just didn't hold water.

I sat back on my heels and realized that I'd actually been trying very hard to make a case for it being Adam. For one thing, it would mean he was safe and well in Spain. For another it would put a stop to this ridiculous notion that I'd refused even to consciously consider since the phone call, yet which was still there nagging at the periphery of my brain.

You have to think about it. However little you want to, you have to think about it. Even if only to knock it on the head once and for all . . .

I got up, leaving the contents of the last file scattered across the carpet, and perched on the edge of the big black leather office chair I'd given Michael the Christmas before he died and which he had loved. I wrapped my arms around myself and faced the possibility that I had so far shied away from.

Alison had intimated to me that she had found out something that had made her suspect that it had not been Michael who had died in his blazing car. Tom had argued the same possibility, although he'd withdrawn when he'd seen the effect the very suggestion was having on me. I'd been adamant that it was an outrageous idea, railing against it to both Alison and Tom. I'd been so certain that Michael would never put me through something so terrible, never willingly abandon me and Molly, and certainly never have been involved with what would have to be, at the very least, the suspicious death of another man.

But supposing I had not known him at all? Supposing our whole life together had been a charade – a cover for an entirely different life? Supposing Michael had deceived me from first to last?

Was it possible my husband was not dead at all?

There was absolutely no way I could go into work the following morning. I'd had virtually no sleep, my head was thumping, and I was in no fit state, either physically or emotionally, to cope with the demands of a group of pre-school age children.

Besides which, sometime during the long hours of the night, when the silence echoed inside my head like rolling thunder preceding a storm and the living room light I'd left on because I didn't want to be alone in the dark made my tired eyes burn, I'd come to a decision. Somehow I had to do some investigating of my own – try to learn the answers to at least some of the questions that buzzed incessantly in my brain. Perhaps I would be straying into dangerous territory – almost certainly I would be if the Whites were involved as I felt sure they were. But I'd been passive for far too long. Whatever the risks, I wasn't prepared to behave like a frightened rabbit caught in the glare of headlights any longer.

I would go to the police as I'd promised Tom, but I wanted, if possible, to have more to give them. What I had so far was no more than a series of accidents and events that could well be dismissed as unrelated. At best I'd sound like an imagin-ative hysteric who'd watched too many made-for-TV movies, at worst they'd think I needed locking up – and not in a police cell, either, but a job for the men in white coats. But if there was something, some firm nugget of information that could not be explained away as coincidence, then perhaps they would be more inclined to listen to me.

And there was something else, too, driving me now. The suggestion that Michael might still be alive.

I couldn't believe it. For all the reasons I'd cited both to Alison and Tom as well as to myself, I couldn't believe it. Yet there was an element of doubting now, bothering me like a splinter under a nail. Something Alison had discovered had prompted her to ask me that preposterous question – a question that had never been raised at the time of the accident. Nobody had doubted for a moment that it was Michael who had died that night in his blazing car – not the police, not the pathologist who'd carried out the post mortem on the pathetic remains, not the coroner. Yet something had made Alison question it. And now Alison was dead.

I couldn't live with even the smallest sliver of uncertainty. Even if this whole nightmare came to an end tomorrow and life returned to normal, that treacherous little doubt would still be there. I'd never be able to forget it completely. I had to know what had raised Alison's suspicions, put the idea in her head that Michael was not dead at all. I had to be sure that there wasn't a dark side to my husband that he'd kept hidden from me. I had to be absolutely certain that it was his coffin I'd walked behind.

How on earth I was going to prove it now, I had no idea. But I knew without a shadow of doubt that I had to try.

Doing any kind of investigation at the weekend, when Molly was around, would of course be impossible. It was another reason why I'd made up my mind not to go into work today.

The nursery opened its doors at seven thirty and I knew someone would be there, setting up, from seven onwards. I called in sick and Sandra, the leader, assured me I need not worry at all, they'd manage, and expressed her good wishes for my speedy recovery. For a moment I felt ridiculously guilty, knowing that whatever she might say my absence would make for extra work for all of them, and less personal attention for the children. But hey, I didn't make a habit of this and I really did have a thundering headache that was making me nauseous. Not to mention an emotional problem the size of Mount Everest.

Molly, touchingly, was quite concerned about me.

'You don't look very well, Mummy.'

'I don't feel great, Molly,' I agreed.

'I could walk to school if you want.'

'No, I'll take you.' There was no way on earth I was letting her out of my sight until she was safely inside the school gates.

Marooned in the strange unreal hinterland I was inhabiting, I waited while she went upstairs to gather her things together. When she came down, she was carrying the bear Adam had given her.

'Why have you got Manuel?' I asked.

'We're doing Spain in Geography. I said I'd take him in today because he's a real Spanish bear.'

Spain. Again. I couldn't seem to get away from it. It was haunting me.

'Right.' I swallowed a couple of aspirins with the remains of my cup of tea.

In the car, Molly insisted on belting Manuel into the back seat before climbing in beside me on her booster and fastening her own seat belt.

'Why did Tom come last night?' she asked as I pulled out of the drive.

Her question took me aback. But the truth was the easiest option. 'He knew I was upset about Alison. He was worried about me.'

'Good.' Molly's voice was serious. 'I'm glad.'

'What do you mean?' I asked, puzzled.

'I'm glad there's somebody to worry about you. I mean – you worry about me – there should be someone to worry about you too.'

'Oh, Molly!' I melted inside at her concern. 'I'm fine, really.'

'But you had Daddy, and now he's not here anymore.' A slight pause. 'Is Tom going to come and live with us?'

'Oh, Molly, I don't know about that. I've only just met him.'

'But you like him, don't you?'

'Yes,' I admitted.

'And so do I. He's really nice.' She was silent for a moment, then: 'I wouldn't mind if he lived with us. I wouldn't be horrid to him like Daisy was when her Uncle Graham came to live with them.' Daisy is one of Molly's school friends – her parents had split up a while ago and there was a new man in her mother's life. 'But Daisy's daddy wasn't dead. Mine is, isn't he?'

I nodded, swallowing hard at a lump in my throat. 'Yes, Molly.'

What on earth would it do to her if Michael had perpetrated a terrible deception on us? She'd never get over it. She had adored her father – and he had adored her. It was unthinkable. I couldn't believe I'd given it credence for a single moment. And yet . . .

Who was the woman who had tried to entice Molly into her car? Why had she attempted to abduct her? My thoughts churned relentlessly, my head throbbed. I thought I might be going to be sick.

I pulled up at Molly's school gates, managed to hold on to my stomach until she had skipped inside, then wrenched open my door and threw up in the gutter. When I straightened up, wiping my mouth and my streaming eyes, Molly had disappeared inside.

I sat for a moment, collecting myself, then put the car into gear. Time to go. Time to begin my investigation. There was so much I needed to find out and so little time to do it. The sooner I got started, the better.

I drove first to the outskirts of town, to the house I'd been told was the residence of Kenny White. I wanted to see if I could spot the red convertible the mystery woman had been driving. But although there were two vehicles parked on the gravel drive behind the electronically controlled gates – a big silver four-wheel drive and what looked like a Mercedes – I could see no sign of a car that answered the description Molly had given. That didn't mean it wasn't there, of course. A house like this one probably had a double garage at the very least and there was no way I could see what might be parked inside.

But the fact remained the policeman and woman who'd interviewed us on the day of the attempted abduction hadn't seemed to recognize the description at all, and I would have thought they would have done if it belonged to the most notori-ous criminal on their patch or his lady friend. As Tom had said, the entire police force couldn't be taking back-handers from the local villain, and surely one or the other officers would have shown at least a glimmer of recognition. But it had still been driving round the district last weekend – unless Molly had been mistaken when she'd identified the car that had passed us on the road home from Anna's as the one the woman had tried to get her into.

I sat for a few minutes watching the house in the vain hope that someone might come out. But no one did – perhaps it was too early in the day for them to be up and about. People like them were night hawks, I imagined. And to be honest I didn't know what I would do if anyone did appear. I couldn't challenge them and if they drove off and I followed it would most likely turn out to be a fruitless wild goose chase. No, I still couldn't tie the woman's car to Kenny White and his cronies, so I might as well give up for the time being and go on to Plan B.

I went back into town, parked, and walked through the arcade to Michael's old office. Given what had happened to Alison, I did wonder whether I would find it all shut up, which would mean I was up against yet another brick wall, but as I approached I could see that the fluorescent lights were on.

It was a really odd horrible feeling, pushing open the door and stepping inside. Not so long ago it had been a busy office and either Michael, Adam or Alison would have been calling a greeting the moment I stepped inside. Now they were all gone. There was only Claire, the junior assistant, sitting at her desk and doing nothing at all. She had never been the most dynamic of girls – Alison had complained that she needed chivvying up the whole time – but this morning I couldn't find it in me to blame her. Her world was falling apart around her too.

'Oh, Jo – it's you.' There was obvious relief in her voice. She'd been worried I was a client, I guess, and had not known how to cope. 'Have you heard about Alison? Isn't it terrible?'

Her face, framed by a fall of thick brown hair tied loosely into a single bunch, was pinched and her eyes were red and dark-rimmed with mascara smudges.

'Yes, it is terrible,' I said.

'I just can't take it in!' Claire sounded close to tears again. 'They say she killed herself! Why would she do something like that? She didn't say anything about being depressed or upset, though I knew she was worried about Adam. She just seemed normal. In fact, I got the impression she was going out on a date that night. She didn't actually tell me so – she wouldn't, she never talked to me about her boyfriends or anything – but she seemed kind of excited. And she went home a bit early because she said she had things to do – left me to lock up. I thought she was going to get her nails done, or her legs waxed or something. Or she just wanted time to make herself look nice. And all the time . . . oh, it's just too awful to think about. Oh, poor Alison!'

'Have the police been to talk to you?' I asked.

'Oh, yes. They were here for ages. I had to make a statement and everything. Well – it was me who raised the alarm when she didn't come in for work. I'm just so glad I didn't go round to her house myself. If I'd been the one to find her, I don't know what I'd have done. If I'd opened the door and found her hanging there . . .'

'*Hanging?*' I repeated, shocked. 'I imagined she'd taken an overdose or something.' Claire shook her head wordlessly, obviously unable to bring herself to go into details. 'Oh my God!' I whispered. Somehow it was infinitely more terrible than swallowing an overdose of pills with a bottle of whisky, or whatever it is people do when they feel they can't go on. And more than ever I was convinced that Alison had not done this herself. Far-fetched as it seemed, I was convinced that someone else was responsible, and they had been clever enough to make it look like suicide.

'They think she'd taken pills of some kind first,' Claire offered. 'Perhaps they weren't working quickly enough and she got impatient.'

I shook my head, trying to clear it of the terrible images, regrouping the questions I needed to answer.

'Claire – what was Alison doing in the days before her death?' I asked.

'What do you mean?' Claire looked puzzled.

'Was she working as normal, or pursuing some project of her own?'

Claire shook her head. 'I wouldn't know about that. She just gets on with things – whatever needs to be done. She did seem to be spending more time than usual on the computer in her office, but I assume it was work connected. She's never been one to waste time playing Solitaire or FreeCell.'

'And she seemed . . . normal . . . to you?'

'Yes. I said. She was worried about Adam, which made her a bit short-tempered, but otherwise . . .' She chewed on a knuckle, eyes brimming. 'I just don't know what to do, Jo. I've never had to run the office – I'm just a dogsbody. I know it's really not your problem any more, but please . . . can you help me out here?'

'Oh, Claire . . .' I felt really sorry for her – she was scarcely out of school, and totally out of her depth. But extra responsibility was the last thing I needed. And in any case . . . 'I don't know any more about running this place than you do,' I said truthfully. 'I think the best thing would be to get help from one of the other estate agents in town. I'll speak to Richard Nelson at Town and Country Properties.'

Adam wouldn't be best pleased to find his door opened to the opposition when – if! – he ever came back. But quite honestly I couldn't come up with any other solution. Presumably there were negotiations in progress, properties on the books, clients waiting for news, and Claire clearly wasn't up to dealing with them.

'I think for the moment, though, the best thing would be for you to go home. You're in no fit state to be here.'

'Oh, Jo . . .' She was almost weeping with gratitude.

'Go on,' I urged her. 'Get your coat and give me the key. I'll ring you later and let you know what I've arranged.'

'Are you sure?'

'Quite sure.' I wasn't being as magnanimous as she thought – I needed the office to myself.

'And you'll ring me?'

'Yes.'

When she had gone I locked the door and disconnected the telephone. Then I went into the office and switched on both computers.

Whilst I waited for the computers to boot up I had a look around for the old diary which Alison had said Adam had used to record the passwords for his personal accounts. If she had been using it recently I imagined it would still be to hand and sure enough I found it quite quickly in the top-right hand drawer of Adam's desk – a blue bound desk diary with 2003 embossed in cold on the cover. The passwords were jotted down on the fly leaf with no attempt to conceal them. Adam had not been very security conscious, I thought, but then I suppose he had had no real reason to be. Alison was the only other person to use this inner sanctum and he had trusted her implicitly. Even so, it seemed a little careless if he had anything to hide.

I settled myself in Adam's office chair, then laid the diary open at the relevant page, on the desk top, and went online. The moment the connection went through an electronic voice

128

informed me – Adam! – that I had e-mail, and the little flashing envelope on the tool bar showed the mind-blowing figure of 167. And most of them junk, I thought, and decided to leave investigating the e-mails until later. Instead I clicked on Adam's 'Favourite Places' and before long, with the aid of the list of passwords, I was tracing the same route Alison had taken, trawling through Adam's bank statements.

I was a little surprised at the size of some of the amounts that were detailed, though, knowing Adam and his lifestyle, I suppose I shouldn't have been. But Alison had been absolutely correct in saying there had not been a single withdrawal since Adam's disappearance. The only entries in the right hand column were direct debits and standing orders. On the credit side, payments from the business which presumably were the salary he paid himself had gone in – they were transferred automatically from the business account, I assumed – and the fact that he had not drawn on them recently went some way to explaining the healthy credit balance.

Next I looked at the business accounts. They were a good deal more complicated – they covered not only the estate agency but also an insurance agency that Adam had set up as a sideline when things had been quiet and kept up afterwards for the quick turnover it provided. Before long my head was throbbing more insistently than ever. But the accounts appeared to be in perfect order and more or less exactly as I'd have expected them to be, if ever I'd given such a thing a moment's thought. I found the staff salaries and was a little shocked at how little Alison and Claire were paid, but the amount Adam paid himself coincided exactly with the sums that had shown up in the credit column of his own personal statement.

Just one thing struck me as slightly odd. Far less money had gone through the books in the last few weeks, particularly in cash transactions. But I had heard Michael say there were always quiet periods followed by peaks of crazy activity and with Adam not on the scene it was possible Alison had not had time to chase outstanding accounts. Really there was nothing here that could give rise to the suspicion that anything untoward was going on at all.

Frustrated, I pushed the button to put the computer into

'sleep' mode and went to make myself a cup of coffee. Somehow I needed to get inside Alison's head, follow her line of thinking. As it was I hadn't a clue what it was I was looking for, let alone how to find it.

When I returned to Adam's desk with my coffee I yanked the drawer open again looking for a coaster of some relatively unimportant paperwork that I could stand my cup on while I investigated further. And saw, staring up at me, something I had not noticed when I'd pulled out the diary. A sheet of paper that looked like the print out of a web page dominated by pictures of holiday scenes – a photograph of a sculpted swimming pool with a backdrop of luxurious balconied apartments – a smiling couple raising glasses to one another with an azure sea in the background – a water-skier being towed behind a speedboat on the same blue sea. And headed with a banner: 'Best Sun – Your Holiday Solution'.

I'm honestly not sure what it was that started alarm bells jangling. Perhaps it was because, according to the blurb, the company was based in Tenerife – and Tenerife and Spain seemed to be the common link between everything that had happened and was still happening. Perhaps it was because I couldn't see why Adam would be interested in holiday literature when he owned his own homes in the sun. Perhaps it was because I was remembering what Tom had said about crooks and timeshares. Whatever, I studied the page, wondering whether Adam had left the page in his desk drawer for some reason, or whether Alison had printed it off in the course of her investigations. Then I typed the website address into the computer and clicked on 'Go'.

The home page, when it loaded, was an exact replica of the hard copy on the desk at my elbow – an indication, I thought, that it had been printed off quite recently. There were the glossy enticing pictures in all their glory, the same statements – 'Holiday Clubs – International Travel Services – The Vacation System of the Future' and, intriguingly, an advertisement block for Independent Marketing Partners, whatever that might mean. I set about working methodically through the site, which was clear and professional, but told me nothing beyond what I would have expected.

Best Sun is your doorway to a lifetime of dream holidays. The cream of luxury apartments in exotic settings all over the world are available to you via the click of a computer mouse or, if you prefer, by telephoning one of our friendly agents. If you already own a timeshare, we will find buyers for you at top prices, to enable you to move into our scheme and enjoy our 5-star facilities. But we know you will be unwilling to wait to take advantage of our fantastic offer. Join Best Sun today – and enjoy all the benefits we can offer. This year, next year, every year. You know you deserve nothing less!

A scam, without a doubt, I thought. A scam dressed up to entice gullible punters to sign over their existing timeshare to this 'Best Sun' and probably pay a hefty administration charge into the bargain. On top of that they'd be persuaded into parting with a few thousand more to become members and take advantage of the new scheme. They'd eagerly anticipate their holidays in apartments which may not even exist, and by the time they realized they'd been duped the company would have moved offices and disappeared or simply declared themselves 'in administration'.

And the worst of it was that the people targeted would often be those who could least afford to lose their hard-earned savings – families with young children, or middle-aged or even elderly couples looking for relaxation in the sun in their retirement. Certainly it echoed the case Tom had cited of John Palmer. He might have been sent to prison for the con he'd been working, but his victims had never recovered the thousands of pounds they'd handed over with such hope and enthusiasm.

Surely – surely Adam couldn't be mixed up in something so immoral?

I returned to the home page and ran the cursor along the banners that headed it. 'The Company' one read. I clicked on it and immediately the screen was filled with the image of a smiling, sun bronzed man. But it was the name alongside the photograph that made my heart lurch.

Managing Director: Barrymore White.

131

White. Not the most uncommon of surnames, but all the same – *White.* I read on.

> Barrymore White hails from the West of England. A born entrepreneur, he was already running his own music bar for young people by the time he left school, and soon expanded into a string of clubs, bars and other entertainment venues. Barrymore formulated the idea of Best Sun in 1998, and moved to Tenerife where the HQ is now situated. The business expanded rapidly, providing an umbrella for corporate partners as well as providing a much needed service for the more discerning holiday home owner. His vision means that complete flexibility and unparalleled luxury are within the reach of anyone who chooses to join the ever-growing number of satisfied owners who make up the family that is Best Sun.

It was just the sort of hype I'd expect, but at least it confirmed that Barrymore White hailed from the West Country. Our part of the world. And I had a feeling there was a music bar in Laverham where local groups played gigs. I hadn't a clue who had started it or who ran it now – it was the sort of place that catered for youngsters, not harassed mothers like me – but it could very well have been Barrymore's first venture.

At the foot of the blurb there was another link tab: 'Our Other Directors'. I clicked on it, wondering whether the name I was looking for would be on the list.

It was. Kenneth White, Barrymore's brother, was listed. But it wasn't that which was turning my stomach to water and numbing me with shock, but the two names that leaped out at me from the four or five listed.

Adam Garratt. And Michael Lansdale.

Eleven

I stared at the computer screen paralysed with disbelief. I'd been half-prepared, I think, to see Adam's name on that list, though I hadn't wanted to believe he could be involved with such a dubious outfit. His connections with Spain and Tenerife, the homepage printout on his desk, and his association with Kenny White, a known criminal, had all pointed to it. But to see my own husband's name – that was not something I had been prepared for at all.

Michael – a director of this Best Sun? He'd never so much as mentioned the company to me, or any company, if it came to that, beyond Garratt Properties. When Adam had offered him the partnership he'd talked it over with me before accepting – now I was stunned that he should have become a director elsewhere and not even mentioned it. Stunned, too, that he could ever have contemplated being a part of what I was sure was an immoral, if not illegal, operation. But that, of course, would be the reason he *hadn't* mentioned it. He'd known I would be horrified at the very suggestion.

'Oh, Michael!' I said aloud. 'Whatever possessed you?'

It must have been the lure of making a fast buck, I supposed, but really that wasn't the Michael I knew – or thought I knew. My Michael had had principles. He wouldn't have traded on the gullibility of others, got rich at their expense. He'd been vulnerable, of course. I knew how inadequate he'd felt when he'd been made redundant and been unable to keep us in the lifestyle we'd enjoyed previously – though it had been through no fault of his own, he'd considered himself a failure. Had he been tempted into this money-making scheme to ensure we never went short again? Had he perhaps had more debts and commitments then he'd ever let on to me? It was possible. I'd been glad enough to allow

133

Adam to do all that was necessary to wind up his estate. If there had been loans or debts to be paid he might well have kept it from me to save me more worry and stress, and in any case Michael's life insurance would have covered them, just as the mortgage protection had covered the mortgage. I'd never questioned the lump sum that was credited to my account or wondered how the figure had been arrived at. I'd simply gratefully accepted the windfall that would mean I had no worries on the financial front at least.

But to think that I was benefiting at the expense of people who had been defrauded by what I felt sure was a horrible scam . . . I felt sick all over again.

Something else was bothering me too. It was two years since Michael had died. Why was his name still on the list of directors? Surely the website would have been updated since then? Several times, I wouldn't wonder. So why was his name still there? Why hadn't it been removed?

Was *this* what Alison had discovered? Was *this* the reason she had asked me if I was quite sure that Michael was really dead? Or was there something else – something even more compelling – even more damning?

I pressed my fingers to my aching head and closed my eyes, desperately trying to avoid the awful doubts and suspicions that were beginning to assail me. But when I opened them, Michael's name as a director of Best Sun was still glaring at me from the screen of Adam's computer.

I was in turmoil, adrift in a sea of uncertainty. The very foundations of my world had been shaken; everything I had accepted without question was suddenly shifting. And all the terrible things that had happened swam around me like sharks waiting to devour me.

I had trusted Michael implicitly – in life and in death. Now I no longer knew what to believe. It was a total nightmare, black and inescapable, because whatever the truth behind all this, the danger was all too real. Someone had tried to abduct Molly. Adam was missing. Alison was dead. Dave lay badly injured in hospital. And someone had died in the blazing wreck of Michael's car, whether I could still bring myself to believe it was Michael or not.

Without a doubt, though, the connection was this company

– Best Sun. Adam and Michael had somehow got mixed up in it through the local arch villain Kenny White, whose brother had set it up and who was the front man. But something had gone terribly wrong. Perhaps a turf war of some kind was taking place. I had no idea – the whole thing was totally outside my experience, and beyond my comprehension. And there was absolutely no way I could hope to sort it out on my own. I had to do as I'd promised Tom and go to the police. But even that could place me in greater danger if there were bent policemen involved. Dave was an officer of the law himself, but it had not saved him.

My mind raced in wild circles and I felt utterly trapped by panic and indecision. The computer screen was black now – it had gone automatically into sleep mode as I sat there, wondering what the hell to do. I moved the mouse over the mouse mat and the list of directors of Best Sun came into focus once more. I read it again, looking at the other names – the first time I had been so startled to see Michael and Adam's names I hadn't taken in any of the others. Now I wanted to see if I recognized any of them, but they meant nothing to me at all. John Clarke, Edward Docherty, Kelvin Dewar. They could be anybody. They could be police officers for all I knew. Except that I didn't suppose that if there were police officers involved with this decidedly dodgy company they would allow their names to appear openly on the website. Either they would use an alias or they'd simply lurk in the background, taking substantial backhanders for looking after the health of Kenny White and turning a blind eye to whatever crimes he might commit or have committed on his behalf.

But as Tom had said, it wasn't the entire police force that was bent. There could only be one or two bad apples in the barrel at most. I just had to hope and trust that the one I spoke to wasn't one of them. And somehow I had to make them take notice of what I said. I had to convince them I wasn't completely round the bend. I had to make them believe me.

I stared again at Michael's name there, mocking me from the computer screen, and trembled with dread at what I might have to face if I went through with this. But I had no options

135

left. My own safety and the safety of those around me – and whom I cared for most – was under threat. And even if it hadn't been, if my perception of that danger was all an illusion, nothing more than a series of disastrous coincidences, if life went back to normal tomorrow and nothing dreadful happened ever again, I still had to pursue this. There was no way I could live with the doubts and uncertainties that were tormenting me now.

One way or another I had to learn the truth. And find a way to deal with it.

On the point of shutting down the computer I remembered I'd only skipped briefly over Adam's e-mails. At that first cursory glance nothing had leaped out at me, but then why should it have? If Best Sun had been the subject of one of the plethora of unopened correspondence I wouldn't have given it a second glance. I'd simply have thought it was junk mail from a holiday company. Similarly the names of the men I now knew to be Adam – and Michael's – co-directors would have meant nothing to me. Perhaps it would be worth having another look now that I was in possession of this further information.

I pulled up Adam's e-mail inbox again, daunted once more by the list of unread messages but determined, none the less. The most recent ones, those that had come in over the last few days, were a motley mix, but once I'd worked through and discarded all of them, my task became a little easier. Clearly Alison had been checking the mail on a regular basis whilst she was still at work, and dealing with anything connected with the legitimate business of Garratt Properties. I also suspected she had deleted the junk mail and any spam that had slipped through the filter. Might it also mean that she had saved any personal communications to Adam's personal folder? If she had, of course, it wasn't likely it contained anything telling, or she would have picked up on it at the time. But was it possible that something which might, on the face of it, seem innocuous could be interpreted quite differently in the light of what I now knew? Was it possible Alison herself had later realized the significance of something she had previously dismissed as nothing out of the ordinary?

When I tried to open the folder, however, I hit a snag. A box popped up asking for a password. I tried all the ones jotted in Adam's diary and drew blanks with all of them. I chewed on a fingernail, frustrated. The password box was a very little one and most of the passwords I had successfully used so far were quite complicated – combinations of letters and numbers – the reason Adam had felt the need to record them for his own convenience, presumably. It might be that this one was something incredibly simple and easily remembered. Something personal to Adam. I'd read somewhere that pets' names were popular as passwords, but Adam didn't own a cat or a dog, and if he'd had one as a child I'd never heard him speak of it. He didn't have a wife or even a regular girlfriend as far as I knew. Or a nickname. Had Alison known this password? If not, she could have saved these incoming e-mails to Adam's personal folder and then not been able to access them again. There could well be something there that even she had missed.

My head was throbbing unbearably again but I had become obsessed with accessing that information. I tried everything I could think of – the make of Adam's car, his hobbies including golf, his favourite drinks and food, all without success. I tried Molly. And then, without the slightest hope I typed in Manuel, the name Adam had insisted Molly call the bear he had given to her. And the folder opened.

Manuel. What on earth had possessed Adam to use Manuel as a password? Spain and Tenerife again, I thought. Everything came back to Spain and Tenerife.

There were half a dozen files in Adam's personal folder and one was titled Other Business. My senses tingling, I clicked on it.

Five e-mails were listed – I was surprised there weren't more. Two pre-dated Adam's disappearance and three were more recent, the latest ten days ago. I pulled those up first. All were from Kenny White asking Adam to get in touch, and each one in more forceful language than the one before. Did that mean that the local arch villain was no wiser than the rest of us as to Adam's whereabouts? Or was it a double bluff? Was that exactly the impression he intended to give? I opened the earlier e-mails. One was from Kenny White

137

requesting a meeting, the other was Adam's reply, confirming the arrangement. The date of both was, as far as I could remember, a day or two days before Adam went missing.

Had Adam kept that appointment? Had something dreadful happened to him? I was now way past believing such a thing was too far fetched to warrant consideration. The world as I knew it had turned upside down and, in this new frightening universe I was inhabiting, anything was possible.

I checked the other folders, but found nothing of any consequence. I was about to go offline and close down the computer when another box caught my eye. *E-mail waiting to be sent.* I pulled it up, and stared in total disbelief. The e-mail was addressed to me. The date was the same as the correspondence between Adam and Kenny White, the time during the day, when I would have been at work.

Jo,
Could you give me a call? On my mobile if needs be.
I have to talk to you face to face as soon as . . .

The message ended there – presumably Adam had been interrupted. Never finished it. Never sent it.

I read and re-read it, that message I had never received. For some reason Adam had wanted to talk to me urgently. Not over the telephone. Face to face. Whatever he had been going to say he had wanted to say it in person. I felt my stomach contracting again. My skin crawling.

A loud rattling noise suddenly made me almost cry out with fright, so wound up was I. What the hell was that?

It came again, metallic and insistent, and this time I recognized it for what it was. Someone was trying to open the outer door, the one I'd locked to ensure I wasn't interrupted by clients coming in to ask for house details or use the financial facilities. Surely they could see the office was closed?

I pushed back Adam's chair, got up, and, keeping well back behind the inner door so that whoever it was wouldn't see me and realize someone was there, peeked out to see who was making such a racket. And froze.

138

The big frame of the man was clearly visible through the plate glass door. Tall. Broad. Huge head with short-cropped hair. Flattened nose. Thick neck. In spite of the warm weather he was wearing a dark overcoat, white shirt, black tie. As I watched he pushed at the door again with an angry movement, slammed the glass with the flat of his hand and turned abruptly away.

My heart was in my mouth. Though I'd set eyes on him only once before, and briefly, I knew who it was.

The man whose e-mails I'd just been reading; the man at the heart of this whole terrible business.

Kenny White.

I don't know what came over me then. For days – weeks! – I'd been frightened out of my wits; now, suddenly, practically face to face with the man I was almost certain was behind everything that had happened, I wasn't frightened any more but angry. Well, maybe I was frightened, but the rush of fury and determination to get to the bottom of this whole business was so strong that it overwhelmed me, making me oblivious to danger, and throw caution to the winds.

Without a second thought I flew through the outer office to the door. My hands were shaking, all fingers and thumbs, and I wasted precious seconds fumbling with the key and the bolt. By the time I had the main door open and was out in the street the man in the black overcoat was a hundred yards or so away, crossing one of the bridges over the river that linked the precinct with the main high street. I darted out on to the paved walkway, leaving the door wide open behind me. I could think of nothing but catching up with Kenny White and demanding some answers. He was on the other side of the river now, heading away from the office in the direction of the top end of town. I began to run after him.

And then I saw the red soft-top car, parked in a space reserved for taxis. And at the same moment turned my ankle on the edge of a paving stone and went sprawling.

Briefly the shock of falling blanked my mind. From my hands and knees I saw Kenny White getting into the passenger side of the red car.

'Hey – you all right?'

A gang of youths with skateboards surrounded me. With their hoodies and ripped jeans they were the last ones you might expect to stop and help me, but they looked genuinely concerned – all but one who scooted in an idle circle around his friends and me.

'Yes – I'm fine . . .' I was struggling to my feet, scarcely noticing my stinging hands or the burning pain in my knee where I'd snagged an ugly tear in my best linen trousers and skinned the flesh beneath.

Over the shoulder of one of the lads I saw the red car driving past down the high street. The bulky figure of Kenny White was in the passenger seat. I couldn't see who was driving. The traffic lights at the end of the one-way system were green; the car sailed through and turned left – the direction for Kenny White's home – and disappeared from view. I'd lost him. Damn, damn, damn – I'd lost him.

I dusted off my hands, very aware now that I'd grazed them quite badly, and saw the blood mingling with the dirt and torn fibres at the knee of my trousers. The boys grunted a bit more concern then rattled away on their skateboards and I limped back to the office.

A young couple were inside, the woman scrutinizing one of the display boards of properties for sale, the man pacing expectantly. They'd arrived in the few minutes the door had been open.

'I'm sorry,' I said, 'but we're closed.'

The man frowned, the woman turned indignantly. 'The door was open.' Her tone was aggressive. 'We want to enquire about property in the area.'

I was not in the mood to argue. 'We're closed,' I said again. 'I'm not an estate agent. I'm sorry, I can't help you.'

'Well, we won't be coming back here again, that's for sure!' The woman flounced out; her partner, aiming a look of total bewilderment at me, followed. I slammed the door after them, locked and bolted it again. Then I went into the tiny cloakroom to try and repair the damage I'd done to myself.

By the time I'd cleaned up the rush of adrenalin that had driven me to run after Kenny White had subsided and I'd realized just how recklessly I'd behaved. Not that he would have been likely to attack me in Laverham High Street in full view of passers-by, but I would have drawn attention to myself and without doubt turned up the heat. Given the terrible things that had happened to everyone else who had tried to find out what was going on I wouldn't give much for my chances of escaping unscathed if he realized I was on his tail. Perhaps my fall had been fortuitous – not only had it wrecked any chance of me catching up with Kenny White before he drove off, but also the gaggle of lads who had surrounded me had probably prevented him from seeing me at all. And at least I'd come out of it with a little more information. I now knew for certain that Kenny White either owned, or had connections with someone who owned, a red convertible car exactly as Molly had described the one the mystery woman had tried to entice her into.

Time to go to the police. But I couldn't do it in filthy torn trousers. Well – perhaps I could, but I didn't want to. When I walked into the police station and started demanding that someone pay attention to me I needed all the confidence and composure I could muster. And that meant looking more like a smartly turned out woman of the world and less like a bedraggled tramp. I gathered my things together, locked up the office and headed for my car – and home.

An hour later, looking more respectable but feeling sore and bruised, I turned into the car park of the police station.

During normal working hours the reception desk was manned by a civilian clerk, a cheerful efficient woman of about my own age. She rose from her desk as I pushed open the swing doors, came to the glass partition that separated us, and slid it open.

'Can I help you?'

'I need to talk to a policeman.' I didn't want to have to repeat my long, complicated and frankly unbelievable story twice. I called on my sketchy knowledge of the workings of the police force, gained mostly from TV cop shows. 'Probably someone from CID.'

She frowned. 'Can you give me some idea what it's about?'

'A number of things. Alison Singer's death for one.'

141

'Ah. Well, that's not a CID matter. PC Cheeseman is dealing . . .'

PC Cheeseman. Number 1289. The one who had dealt – or *not* dealt – with Molly's attempted abduction. I certainly didn't want to have to face his scepticism again.

'I really don't think . . .'

And then I got a break. I was due one for heaven's sake! Over the reception clerk's shoulder I saw a uniformed figure I recognized come into the office, a sheaf of papers in her hand. A square, rock-solid figure with short-cropped peppered grey hair. The policewoman whom I'd met at Anna's house on the evening of Dave's accident.

'Perhaps I could speak to . . .' I struggled to remember her name, failed. She had placed the papers on the clerk's desk and was turning to leave again. I pointed at her urgently. 'That policewoman!'

The clerk glanced over her shoulder. 'PC Stone? She's not dealing with . . .'

'Yes. Please.'

'Gwenda?' the clerk called after her. 'Can you . . . ? This lady . . . ?'

Gwenda Stone crossed to the window. When she saw me recognition flared in her eyes though she said nothing. Perhaps she couldn't remember where it was we'd met before.

'I really need to talk to you,' I said.

'OK, just a second and I'll let you through.'

Entry to the police station was by way of a toughened glass door that was opened from the inside by some sort of security code device. Gwenda Stone admitted me and the door shut behind me again.

'We'll go to the interview room.' She led me along a passage to a small room furnished only with a table and three or four chairs. 'You're a friend of Dave Smart's wife, aren't you?' she said, indicating that I should sit down.

So she had recognized me. 'Yes.'

'How is he?'

'Well, he's not completely recovered yet, but the prognosis is pretty good.'

'I'm glad. Dave's a nice chap.' She sat down opposite me. 'So, what can I do for you?'

I sucked in my breath. 'I hardly know where to begin. And it all sounds so far fetched . . . but you have to listen to me, please. You have to believe me.'

'OK,' Gwenda Stone said. 'Try me.'

Twelve

B y the time I got out of the police station it was almost time to collect Molly from school. It had taken long enough to tell Gwenda Stone the whole unbelievable story, and then she'd fetched someone from CID – a Detective Sergeant Mowatt – and I'd had to go through it all again. But it was such a relief to actually be taken seriously that I would have willingly repeated myself a dozen times.

'You are going to have to leave this with us, Mrs Lansdale,' the DS said when I'd finished. He was young, serious and very articulate, the sort of policeman who was probably being fast-tracked from Bramshill College through the ranks to high office. 'Some of the allegations you have made are very serious ones. They'll have to be investigated thoroughly, along with the people you've identified as being involved. It may well be that we shall need to talk to you again. If we do, we'll be in touch. And of course I'll let you know the result of my enquiries.'

Gwenda Stone had come with me to the security operated door to let me out.

'I suppose it's going to be quite a long job,' I said, trying to sound sane and reasonable after all the seemingly insane and unreasonable allegations I'd just made.

'It is pretty complicated,' she agreed, 'but Sean won't let the grass grow under his feet.'

I sighed. 'I certainly hope not. This is all a complete nightmare.'

'I'm sure it is.' She punched in the security code and opened the door. 'You take care.'

'I will.' But I honestly didn't know how. I experienced a moment's panic. I wished they'd said they'd give Molly and me police protection, but I supposed they had no proof as yet that I wasn't a complete nutcase with a vivid imagination and in any case I wasn't sure I'd warrant such a drastic measure given that no attempt had been made on *my* life. Wasn't sure I'd want it even, though I felt horribly vulnerable leaving the safe environment of the police station. But I had a daughter who had to be collected from school – a daughter who had already been targeted by someone who wanted to abduct her. Molly was my number one priority. Somehow I had to buffer her from everything that was going on.

Now, as I sat outside the gates waiting for the eager surge of children to erupt out of school at the end of another week, I found myself constantly scanning the road for a red convertible. There wasn't one, of course; just the usual assortment of small family cars and big four-wheel drives, and a gaggle of waiting mothers, some with younger children in buggies. And it wasn't likely there would be. Whoever it was who had tried to take Molly was too clever to try to snatch her from outside her school in full view of dozens of parents and teachers. But it was little comfort. I saw danger now everywhere I looked, shimmering like a miasma in the bright sunshine, lurking in the shadows just around the corner. I was primed like a gun waiting to go off, or a wildebeest at a water hole ready to take flight at the first scent of a marauding lion.

I was ready for anything. Or so I thought.

Six o'clock. I'd made Molly tea – fish fingers, baked beans and oven baked potato faces – not the healthiest of meals, not the sort of nutritious food I liked to feed her, but I didn't feel up to cooking. She was eating in front of the television, another thing I didn't really approve of, but I couldn't face food myself. It wouldn't hurt her just this once. At least she was safe in her own house with both front and back doors locked. By comparison any other concerns about her welfare seemed trivial and unimportant.

The phone rang. I jumped as if I'd been bitten. 'Hello?'

'Jo? Are you all right?'

Anna. I felt myself relax.

'Yes, fine.' I couldn't burden her with all my problems.

'That's OK then. It didn't sound like you, that's all.'

Breathy. Tense. Terse. No, I didn't suppose it did sound like me. 'Well, it is. Just rushing around doing a million things at once, that's all.'

'I won't keep you then. I just wanted to share my good news. I've just got home from visiting Dave, and he is so much better. Really – a vast improvement. He's even getting his memory back.'

'Oh, I'm so glad, Anna! It's great to hear some good news for a change.'

'I know. The doctors are really pleased with him. They say he's a model patient. If everyone did as well as he has, their job would be a whole lot easier.'

'He's a model everything,' I said truthfully. Dave was one of the nicest men I knew.

'You'll have to come and visit him again,' Anna was saying. 'He was specifically asking after you. Several times, actually. If I didn't know different I might have thought there was something going on between the two of you.'

'Anna!' The tension was back in my voice. I could hear it myself, and so did Anna.

'It's OK, Jo, I'm only teasing.'

'I know you are.' It wasn't that I was upset by her remark. I knew very well that she wouldn't seriously think for a moment that Dave and I were having a fling. It was that I was wondering just why I'd been so much on his mind. His memory was returning, Anna had said. Was there something he'd found out prior to his accident, forgotten, along with practically everything else in the recent past, and was now remembering? And if so, what was it?

'I'll let you go then,' Anna said. 'Speak to you soon, Jo.'

'Yes. And I really am pleased, Anna,' I said. 'For both of you.'

I'd hardly put the phone down when it rang again. It gave me less of a shock this time and I answered it more normally.

'Hi, Jo. It's me. Tom.'

Warmth tingled in my veins, the warmth that came from just hearing his voice, before I remembered. I might not be free to fall in love with this man.

'Hi, Tom.'

'I wondered if you could use some company this evening.'

Until this was sorted out, I should tell him 'no'. Instead I heard myself say: 'Well, yes – if you're offering.'

'That's good, because I'm just around the corner. I'll be with you in five minutes.' He rang off.

My first thought was that I must look a wreck. I dashed to the mirror, slicked on some lipstick and tidied my hair. My second thought was Molly. I went into the front room where she'd finished her tea and was sprawled on the rug, chin resting on her cupped hands, watching a cartoon.

'Molly – Tom's coming round. He'll be here soon.' No response. 'Molly? Did you hear what I said? Tom . . .'

'Yes, Mummy, I heard you.'

'I just thought I should warn you.'

'Mummy.' She looked up at me, eyes wide, lips pursed in a studied expression of exasperation. 'I told you, Mummy. It's fine by me.'

But would it be fine by your father? The thought popped into my head before I could stop it. I gave myself a mental shake. Michael was dead. And if he wasn't . . .

If he wasn't, I owed him nothing. If I'd been wrong, wrong, wrong about him and he had deceived us, allowed us to grieve for him, walked out on us and let us think he was dead, then he'd forfeited any right to our love, let alone our fidelity to him. But I couldn't believe that. For all the doubts that had been raised in my mind, I couldn't bear to.

Michael was dead. He had been for two years. It was time for me to move on. Molly knew that, though she was only seven years old. Perhaps *because* she was only seven years old. Broken marriages, single parent families, were commonplace in her world. Plenty of her friends and classmates had parents who changed partners. Molly had loved her father dearly and still missed him. But she was perfectly ready to accept another man in her mother's life.

But was I? I heard a car on the drive, looked out of the window, felt the eager twist in my stomach as I saw him, couldn't wait for him to walk in the door. And knew I had my answer.

He kissed me, there in the kitchen, held me close for a

moment then held me away, looking at me with a very straight expression. 'Are you OK?'

I nodded. 'I am now.'

'And this isn't too early for you?' I shook my head. 'I figured it might be a good idea to get here before Molly went to bed. Rather than creeping around later as if we had something to hide.'

'Molly's fine with you.'

'She's a good kid. Shall I go and say hello to her?'

'Good idea. And I'll fix you a drink. What would you like?'

'A cup of tea would be nice.'

I could hear Molly chattering in the next room as I put on the kettle and got the milk from the fridge. Tom got far more response from Molly than I did when she was engrossed in a television programme, I thought ruefully.

The kettle had boiled by the time he came back and I was squashing tea bags in mugs.

'You aren't having a G and T?' he asked snidely.

'Oh, so you think I'm an alcoholic, do you?' I parried.

'You don't do so badly.' His tone was teasing.

'Just recently I've needed it!' I retorted. 'I've had a stinking headache all day though. It's on its way out now, thank goodness, but I think a cup of tea would do me more good.'

I pushed the mug towards him. He caught my hand, turning it over to reveal my grazed palm. 'What's this?'

'I fell down. I've got a lot to tell you, Tom. I've found out quite a bit more stuff. And I've been to the police . . .'

I pulled out a chair and sat down at the kitchen table. Tom sat opposite me. Under any other circumstances it might have felt like cosy domesticity. As it was, it was more like a council of war.

I brought Tom up to date with everything that had happened, including the fact that Michael was listed as a director of Best Sun, but I didn't mention the inner conflict I was suffering regarding his 'death'. It was still one step too far, something so deeply private I had to deal with it alone.

'And you had no idea?' Tom asked.

'I've never so much as heard of the company.' I twisted

148

my wedding ring round and round my finger. 'Michael never mentioned it – never mentioned anything to do with foreign properties at all.'

Tom looked at me narrowly. 'You think he knew himself?'

I frowned. 'Wouldn't he have to?'

'From my experience in the jiggery-pokery that goes on in dubious companies, anything is possible. There are plenty of wives, for instance, named as non-executive directors who know absolutely nothing about the business. "Board meetings in bed" they call it.'

'Well, we certainly didn't have any!'

'You aren't listed as a director.'

'True.' I was silent for a moment. 'I'm beginning to wonder if I knew Michael at all.'

'That's not an unknown scenario either.' He hesitated for a moment before he said it, yet his tone carried serious conviction.

We were getting back to the things I didn't want to talk about.

'Whichever, this Kenny White is in it up to his neck,' I said, changing the subject subtly to safer territory. 'Adam arranged a meeting with him just before he disappeared. Suppose he went to Kenny White's house and never came out again? The place is a fortress – security gates, a couple of acres of grounds – anything could go on in there and no one would ever know. Then Alison followed the trail and she—' I broke off, not even wanting to think about what might have happened to Alison, let alone put it into words. 'She was dealt with,' I finished lamely.

'Alison was found in her own home,' Tom reminded me.

'Well, yes, but perhaps they thought another disappearance would look too suspicious – attract attention, precipitate a search of the house and grounds, even. Given Kenny White's reputation and his connections with Adam and – by association, Alison.' I was thinking furiously now, cogs in my mind whirring round, clicking into place. 'They said she'd taken drugs before hanging herself. That's pretty odd, don't you think? I've never heard of it before. Why would she do that?'

'It's hard to explain the actions of someone who's reached

149

the point of committing suicide.' I had the feeling Tom was playing devil's advocate. 'The balance of their mind is disturbed, as the coroner often describes it.'

'Except that I don't believe Alison did commit suicide at all,' I said. 'I just don't believe it, Tom. She was cheerful and chipper, according to Claire. She'd gone to the hairdresser's or the beauty salon. Does that sound like someone contemplating suicide?'

'It's not unheard of for someone to want to make themselves look good one last time.' Tom was playing devil's advocate again. 'Take Marilyn Monroe – one of the reasons there is still so much speculation about her death not being suicide is because she'd always said she'd pretty herself up to do the deed – and she hadn't.'

I toyed with my mug of tea. 'Claire was under the impression Alison had a date. I think it's much more likely she wanted to look her best because she was meeting someone. She wanted to feel confident. I'm sorry, but I just don't buy this suicide theory at all. And I don't believe she took the drugs knowingly either. Perhaps whoever it was she was meeting with slipped them into her drink. And when she was woozy or even unconscious they took her home and killed her and made it look like suicide.'

'They'd be taking one hell of a chance, getting her out of a car and into her house without anyone seeing them,' Tom pointed out.

'Then perhaps they drugged her in her own home. Perhaps the meeting was there. Oh, I don't know! I'm just on a fishing expedition – trying to make some sense of all this. And I can't.'

'So,' Tom said. 'If Kenny White is behind both Adam's and Alison's demise, what was he doing at the office this morning? He'd have known that he wouldn't find either of them there.'

'But he wouldn't have known that I'd sent Claire home and locked up. Perhaps he wanted to get access to the computer, wipe off the evidence that Alison had uncovered.'

'In that case, surely he'd have had to get Claire out of the way first. Are you suggesting he intended to bump her off too? In a high street office in broad daylight?'

150

I chewed my fingernail. It did seem unlikely.

'Surely if that was his intention it would have been easier to break in at night when he'd know the office was empty. Or even this morning, when he thought no one was there.' Tom pressed home his point.

'And set off the burglar alarm?'

'Not necessarily. If he's as big a crook as you seem to think, he's probably got people working for him who could disable it without too much trouble. Or they could go in, snatch the computers and any relevant files and be gone out of a back window long before the police arrived with a key holder. Who is the key holder now, anyway? Presumably Adam and Alison were. Neither of them are now on the scene.'

'Claire has a key . . .'

'But is she registered as the key holder? If not, it would take some time to track her down.'

'Oh, I don't know.' My head was spinning again. Nothing made any sense at all.

'And I still don't see where the attempted abduction of Molly fits in,' Tom went on. 'Why in the world would Kenny White want to take Michael's child?'

His use of phraseology jarred on me. '*My* child.'

'And Michael's,' he pointed out. 'And Michael is the one involved with them.'

I could feel the panic gathering again, the fear for Molly's safety eclipsing everything else. Someone connected to the Whites had tried to snatch an innocent seven year old. Now that I'd positively identified the red car the woman had been driving it was the one thing I was certain of. And who was to say they wouldn't try it again? For whatever reason.

'Oh, why did he ever get mixed up with them?' I exploded. 'Why did he ever get mixed up with Adam? I had no idea Adam kept such unsavoury company. If I had, I'd have raised Cane before I'd have seen him involved in Adam's business. God, I'd rather have finished up on the streets! But Michael must have known. He must have! He couldn't have run the office and been unaware of it. And he was with them on the night of his accident. Why the hell did he go along with it?'

But I knew I had already answered my own question in

my hours of soul-searching. Michael had been devastated when he'd been made redundant. He'd lost his self-esteem, his identity almost. He'd been at his wits' end wondering how he was going to support us. Pay the bills. Meet the mortgage repayments. We wouldn't have starved, I suppose, but certainly our whole lifestyle had been in jeopardy. There would have been no more holidays in Italy or Spain, no weekends in Cornwall or the New Forest. Our smart cars would have had to be traded in for cheaper, older models – perhaps one of them would have had to go altogether. Molly would have had to make do with market-stall trainers instead of the brands that meant so much status-wise to her and her peers. We'd have had to think twice about buying a bottle of good wine or a piece of fillet steak. And worst of all, the house might have been repossessed. Our home, the one we'd built together. Goodness knows, I'd been worried enough myself about the distinctly bleak future we faced if Michael couldn't get another job with a similar salary to the one he'd lost when the redundancy money ran out, and I hadn't had the added burden of feeling it was my responsibility.

Michael had been low and vulnerable and along had come his old friend Adam with an offer that provided him with a lifeline. It probably never even crossed his mind to question who Adam was associated with before he accepted the job, and afterwards, when he found out, it would have been too late. He wouldn't have been able to bring himself to give notice and find himself back in the no-man's land of unemployment, this time without even a financial package to smooth the way. He'd have told himself he had no option but to accept that Adam kept questionable company, ran with a motley pack, and distance himself from them as far as possible.

Except that he hadn't distanced himself. He'd been drawn in up to his neck. All the excuses I was making for him were based on the character of the Michael I'd thought I'd known. And hadn't really known at all . . .

'I think,' Tom was saying, 'that the best thing you can do now is leave it to the police. You've given them everything you know – you must let them deal with it. They're the experts, after all.'

'But they said it could be a long job . . . Honestly, I don't know how much more of this I can take.'

'Jo.' He sat back, looking at me with an expression that was almost stern. 'There is nothing more you can do. And I don't want you taking risks. It's just not worth it.'

'Oh, I don't know . . .'

'I think,' he said, 'that what you need is a break. It's Saturday tomorrow. The weekend, right? The weather is good and the forecast better. I think we should take off for a couple of days.'

'Take off? Where?'

'Anywhere you like – within reason. The country. The coast. I won't suggest a timeshare in Spain or Tenerife . . .'

'What an awful thing to say!' I was blazing suddenly.

'Sorry. Just trying to lighten the mood.'

'Well, you didn't. It wasn't in the least funny.'

'I know. I'm a foot-in-mouth idiot. Do you forgive me? Enough to come away with me for the weekend?' He looked genuinely remorseful, like a little boy slapped down for a stupid prank.

'As long as you promise not to make any more crass remarks.'

'I can promise to try.'

I smiled faintly. Quite honestly I was too emotionally drained to sustain anger and though insensitive, I didn't think for one moment that he'd intended any offence.

'OK.'

'So what's it to be?'

'I don't mind. Anywhere that's not here.'

'Shall we ask Molly?'

'Good idea.'

Unsurprisingly Molly chose the seaside. Whilst I put her to bed – which took quite a long time, since she was now over-excited at the prospect of a weekend away and eager to pack her swimsuit, shorts and flip-flops into a wheeled Minnie Mouse suitcase herself – Tom searched for suitable accommodation by accessing the internet on my computer. He was still there, sitting at the desk in what had once been Michael's office, when I came back downstairs.

'Any luck?' I asked.

Tom switched off the computer. 'All sorted.'

I gesticulated at the blank screen. 'Aren't you going to show me?'

'No, you'll just have to wait and see.'

'Oh . . . all right then.' For a moment, in spite of everything, I felt almost light-hearted. I'd forgotten how pleasurable it could be, relinquishing responsibility, allowing someone else to organize things. 'When are we going?'

'Tomorrow. Of course.' He got up. 'I'll get off home and pack a few things while you do the same and I'll be back first thing in the morning. Or I could come back tonight. That way we could make an early start.'

'Sounds like a good plan.'

'OK. I'll need a couple of hours. Will you be all right?'

'I'll be fine.' We went into the hall. 'I'll give you my spare key, then you can let yourself back in.' I twisted it off its hook by the door, and he put it in his pocket. Another Rubicon crossed.

'See you later then.' And I was alone.

As I looked out suitable clothes, sorted toiletries and packed, I wondered about sleeping arrangements. I didn't know what accommodation Tom had reserved for the weekend, but even if it was a double room for us, I didn't feel ready to share my bed with him here, in my own home. Molly might be OK with him becoming part of our lives, but I didn't want her rushing into my room in the morning, eager to begin her weekend away, and finding him in my bed. Later, perhaps. In a different environment. But not here. Not in the bed that had been her Daddy's, the one where she'd squashed in between us on Christmas mornings to turn out her stocking and see what Santa had left for her, where we'd comforted her and got her back to sleep after she'd had a bad dream. The bed in the spare room was made up with clean sheets and pillow cases – he'd have to sleep there. I only hoped he'd understand.

But a tiny treacherous part of me was regretful. For myself, I'd have liked nothing better than to curl up in his arms, or against his broad back. In a frightening world-turned-upside-down, Tom made me feel safe. I thanked heaven for him.

*　　*　　*

154

Next morning as we loaded our cases into Tom's car it began to rain. I could scarcely believe it, after all the good weather we'd had. But Tom said he was certain it was only a storm and certainly the sky was far from completely overcast. 'If there's enough blue to make a pair of sailor's trousers it'll clear up, as my old grandmother used to say,' he prophesied.

'I'm sure you're right.' I was determined not to let a drop of rain spoil things, and determined too to put this whole nightmare out of my mind as far as I was able for a couple of days at least. For Tom's and Molly's sake – and for my own. There was no disguising the dark circles that sleepless nights and worry had etched under my eyes, no escaping the fact that I was stiff and sore from my tumble yesterday, no way I could completely ignore the ache of tension that was constantly niggling at me like a worrisome tooth. But I would hide it if it killed me. And perhaps I'd even manage to fool myself into pretending, for the next two days at least, that we were no different to any of the other parties of family and friends heading for a weekend break by the sea.

Molly skipped around excitedly as we packed the car and chattered incessantly throughout the entire journey to Devon. She had insisted on bringing both her Baby Annabel doll and Manuel, the bear Adam had given her. They sat one each side of her on the back seat, carefully strapped in with the spare seatbelts. I was happy enough that she had Annabel – the doll had gone everywhere with her ever since she was two years old. But I wished I could have persuaded her to leave Manuel at home. With his straw hat and sunglasses he was a poignant reminder of all I was trying to forget.

It was still only mid-morning when we arrived at the hotel Adam had booked – a lovely old house set in its own grounds on a hill that dog-legged up from the bay.

'I've reserved single rooms,' Tom said as we walked past neatly-kept rose beds and huge peony bushes, heavy with deep red blooms, to the main entrance. 'But we can try to change them for a double if you like.'

The tingle that was part warmth, part excitement, twisted inside me. I was grateful, too, for his consideration, the lack of pressure that might have panicked me and would certainly have made me feel trapped.

'Yes,' I said. 'Let's try. Just as long as Molly's not too far away.'

'You and she can have the double if you like.'

'No.' My mind was made up. 'Molly is quite big enough to be in a room of her own. And no woman in a red car or Kenny White or anyone else is likely to find her here.'

'OK, just as long as you're sure.'

'I'm sure.'

And I was. More sure, suddenly, than I was of anything.

Thirteen

It was a precious stolen hiatus, that weekend. If it had not been for the shadow that lurked, omnipresent, rumbling softly but insistently like a volcano preparing to explode, it would have been idyllic. We spent time on the beach with Molly, paddling with her in the shallows where the tide broke in lace-frilled flounces on the sand, watching her clambering with her little fishing net in the rock pools. Tom helped her build an impressive sand castle and bought her a paper flag to stick in the turret. We ate ice-creams and shrimps from little plastic pots and soaked up the warm sunshine.

In the evening we went into dinner early so that Molly could eat with us and secured a table in the big bay window that gave a view of the harbour far below.

'Can we go on a boat?' Molly asked, watching the activity there – white sails billowing, motor yachts manoeuvring, a speedboat skimming across the bay with a trail of foam in its wake like the vapour trail of an aeroplane.

'I'm not sure,' Tom said. 'It depends how long the trips are. But next time definitely.'

Next time. It sounded good. Something permanent in my life. Something to hold on to.

'I want to go *this* time!' Molly begged. 'Oh, can we go tomorrow? Please!'

'Molly, you know we have to go home tomorrow,' I said. And felt a tug of apprehension.

'But we only just got here! Couldn't we stay longer? Couldn't I miss school for just one day?'

I wish!

'No, you can't, young lady. And I have to go to work too. This was just a special treat. One night only.'

'Oh . . .' A long drawn out sigh of pure anguish.

'I told you, we'll do it again, for much longer,' Tom said. His eyes met mine over her head. 'If that's OK with your mother, anyway. But if you really want to go on a boat that much, we'll see if we can go on one for a quick flip round the bay. Would you like that?'

'Oh, yes! Oh, thank you, Tom!' She gave me a look, then beamed at Tom. There was no doubt which of us was flavour of the month and it wasn't me. But that didn't matter. Molly was safe and happy – and she liked Tom. Couldn't be better.

When she was finally tucked up in bed, in a pretty little room that was next door to ours, Tom and I adjourned to the small private bar. It was cosy and chintzy, but it seemed a shame to be indoors when the evening was so balmy – Tom had been quite right about the weather. We'd left the storms far behind us this morning and hardly seen so much as a single cloud since.

'Is there a terrace?' I asked.

'I'm sure there is.'

We took our drinks and went to investigate. On a paved area outside we found a couple of cast-iron tables, with chairs set around them facing the setting sun, but there was also a swing-seat in the middle of the lawn, canopied and inviting.

'Let's sit there,' I suggested.

'You're sure you won't get sea sick?' Tom joked.

'If I do, I'll know not to come on the boat tomorrow with you and Molly.'

We crossed the lawn and sat down. We might have been in our own private world. With no prying eyes it felt companionable and easy, yet at the same time electric with the magnetism that had sparked between us almost from the moment we had met. And my other world, where dark things happened, seemed very far away.

The sun was going down in a blaze of red and the dew had begun to rise in the manicured grass – I could feel it damp and cool between the straps of my sandals. Tom's arm was around my waist, my shoulder rested against his, and I wished we could stay there forever, cocooned against the world. Frissons of desire were darting deep within me, shivering over my skin, and I relished them, precursors of the

closeness we would share later yet unwilling yet to relin-
quish the delicious anticipation.

'Not sorry you came?' Tom asked softly.

'You must be joking! This is heaven.'

'There are things we ought to talk about though.'

His words jarred on me. 'Oh, don't spoil it, please!' I
begged. 'All I want to think about is you and me.'

'You know nothing about me.'

'I know all I need to know.' I nestled against him. 'You're
thoughtful and funny and you are marvellous with Molly.
And if that wasn't enough, you really turn me on.'

'I'm flattered. But all the same there are things . . .'

'I don't want to hear. What I want is for you to kiss me.'

I turned to him, seeking his mouth. For a moment it felt
as if he might be holding back, then he was kissing me too.
And my need for him was greater than my need for peace
and safety, so insistent it drove out conscious thought, and
I knew it was the same for him. The energy between us
burned bright as a comet there in the soft darkness and our
separate selves fused into one.

'Shall we go to bed?' Tom's voice was husky in my ear;
I could feel his breath on my cheek. For answer I took his
hand and started back across the dew wet lawn.

I woke early next morning and lay for a few minutes watching
him sleep. One arm was spread-eagled across the coverlet,
heavy on my stomach; his face in repose was almost child-
like and strangely vulnerable. I felt the warmth of his body;
it melted me. And I knew I loved him.

He stirred then, reaching for me, and we made love, not
the driven passion of the night before, but gentler, more
leisurely. And when it was over the contentment it brought
me was tinged with sweet yearning sadness. It had all been
over so soon. I wanted to spend more nights with him, making
love, falling asleep wrapped in his arms. I didn't want them
to be overshadowed by anxiety and confusion, I wanted them
to be . . . normal! But at the same time I wondered if it was
the traumatic effect of all that had happened that had height-
ened my senses, given an edge to every touch, imbued every
embrace with urgency.

Longing ached in me now and the sense of foreboding began to creep back. Time to move. Time to shower and dress and face the world again. Time, almost, to return to the nightmare which had become reality for me. But I felt strengthened now, refreshed, renewed. It couldn't last forever. And when it was over, the enigmas solved, the consequences dealt with, I would have Tom. That was what I would hold on to.

We made the most of that Sunday. Once we'd had breakfast we had wandered down to the harbour and, to Molly's delight, found a boat that was touting for business for hour-long trips round the bay. I'd plastered her in sun cream, knowing it was possible to get burned a good deal more easily on the water than on land, and we'd chosen our seats in the bow and then had waited for the boat to fill up.

It was quite a gentle, stately trip, and I think Molly was actually hankering after the speedboats that hurtled past us in great curving arcs, but I forestalled her: 'No way, Molly. Not until you're older!' – and she settled down to enjoy herself, watching for fish and dolphins, though I don't think she saw any of the first, and certainly none of the second!

We'd been back on dry land for about ten minutes and were heading back in the direction of the beach when Molly suddenly stopped short, eyes wide, an expression of horror on her face. 'Oh, no!'

'What's wrong, Molly?' I asked.

'Manuel! I haven't got him! Where is he?'

'Oh, Molly!' I hadn't wanted her to bring that wretched bear out with us this morning, but she had insisted.

'I've lost him! I can't lose Manuel!' Her voice was rising dramatically – in Molly's world, losing Manuel ranked as a crisis of the highest order and one that could very easily turn into a tragedy.

'When did you have him last?' I couldn't believe I hadn't missed him – the bear was big enough, for goodness sake.

'On the boat. I had him on the boat. He was sitting beside me.' Her eyes went even rounder. 'Oh, Mummy – you don't think he's fallen overboard, do you?'

'How could he do that?' I asked.

160

'When I was looking for dolphins. And I thought I saw one. I jumped up – don't you remember? I jumped up! Oh, no! Oh, poor Manuel . . .!'

'I'm sure he didn't fall overboard,' Tom said. 'We'd have noticed. You probably kicked him under the seat, that's all.'

'You mean he's still there? On the boat? Oh, quickly, quickly! We must get him!' She was tugging at my arm.

We began to retrace our steps.

'I hope somebody hasn't gone off with him,' I said softly to Tom.

'I wouldn't think so. Who'd take a toy bear?'

'Another child might. There was that family right across from us. And he is a very nice bear. He is pretty appealing, with his hat and sunglasses . . .'

'If we didn't notice him under the seat, then probably neither did they.' Tom was unfazed as ever. 'The worst thing that can happen is that the boat's filled up and gone off for another trip and we'll have to wait for it to come back.'

'I hope you're right,' I said. 'Molly thinks the world of that darned bear, even if the man who gave it to her isn't exactly my favourite person just at the moment.'

We were almost running now, dragged by an increasingly frantic Molly. To my enormous relief the boat – *The Pride of Devon* – was still tied up at the jetty. A small queue had formed beside the gangplank and a few people were already on board.

'Hurry – hurry! Oh, Mummy – come *on*!'

'You stay here,' Tom said to me.

He skirted the queue, going directly to a boy in shorts and flip flops who was taking the money. Molly went with him. I waited anxiously whilst he explained, oblivious to the outraged stares of the would-be trippers who clearly thought he was jumping the queue. I saw the boy nod and Tom went up the swaying walkway, Molly practically under his feet in her eagerness to look for her beloved Manuel.

A few minutes later they were back, Molly beaming from ear to ear and clutching her bear. Tom caught my eye, raising his eyebrows and shaking his head, but his smile told me he too was relieved. It would have been a shame if our weekend had been marred by the loss of a so-loved toy.

'I've got him! I've got him!' Molly came running up to me.

Manuel looked slightly bedraggled – his sunglasses awry, his fur wet from lying in the pool of water under the seat, his hat a little stained.

'I think we should take him straight back to the hotel,' I said.

'No – no!' Molly hugged him.

'Well, don't put him down again,' I told her. 'Next time he might be gone for good.'

'I won't put him down.' Molly straightened his sunglasses. 'Don't worry, Manuel, I'll look after you,' she told him solemnly.

I caught Tom's eye and smiled. The crisis was over. It was oddly comforting somehow to have had to deal with one that was so trivial in the great scheme of things. And so normal and ordinary!

The sun was low in the sky when we pulled on to my drive and Molly had fallen asleep in her booster seat with Manuel tucked under one arm and Baby Annabel under the other.

'If you open the door, I'll carry her straight upstairs,' Tom suggested.

I fished out my keys, went to the front door, fitted the Chubb key into the lock. But when I went to turn it, I encountered resistance. Odd. I took it out, reinserted it, tried again. Same result. What on earth . . .? I fiddled, turning the key the other way, and heard the lock click shut. Turned it back again – and it flipped open easily.

What? Surely I hadn't forgotten to lock the door when we left? Surely the house hadn't been left open the entire weekend whilst we were away? Oh, my God, how could I have been so stupid?

But I couldn't deny the evidence. I hadn't been unable to unlock the door in the first instance because it wasn't locked. Simple as that.

Tom was out of the car and bent double through the rear door getting Molly out of her seat belt.

'Tom. The house was unlocked.'

All my nerves were on edge again. I didn't want him

162

taking Molly into the house until we'd had a chance to make sure everything was all right. That the place hadn't been ransacked. That somebody wasn't inside. I think that even under normal circumstances I'd have been nervous, knowing that for two days my unoccupied house had been accessible to anyone who cared to open the door. As things were, I was really spooked. And cursing myself for never getting round to having a burglar alarm fitted.

Tom looked at me over his shoulder, frowning. 'Unlocked?'

'Yes. I can't believe I could have been so stupid! I suppose I was thinking about loading the car – whether we had everything we needed . . . But not to lock the door . . . !'

Tom straightened. Molly stirred but did not waken. Manuel fell out of her grasp on to the seat beside her.

'You want me to check it out?' Tom asked.

'Would you?'

I waited whilst he went inside, hovering between the house and the car. I was concerned to know if, through my own stupidity, I'd been burgled, but equally anxious to be able to reach Molly quickly if the need arose. I saw lights go on one by one at each of the windows as Tom went from room to room. Minutes, it seemed, ticked past. How could he be taking so long?

At last he emerged. 'I think you're OK.'

'You mean . . . ?'

'No obvious signs of burglary. No drawers tipped out or cupboards ransacked. And no bogeymen hiding in a wardrobe. Or under the bed.'

How could he treat it so lightly – making a joke of it?

'Tom – it's not funny!'

'I know.' He sounded contrite. 'But I'm sure everything's all right. Burglars would probably not have stopped to close the door, or gone out through the back where they'd be less conspicuous. And the back door is locked with the key on the inside. I don't suppose anyone realized the front door was open, Jo. You wouldn't, unless you tried it.'

Sound common sense again. But still . . . I couldn't quell the feeling of unease. When Tom had carried Molly upstairs and I had settled her in, tucking the duvet under her chin, propping her toys beside her, I found him waiting on the landing.

'I really have to go home tonight, Jo. Work in the morning
. . .'

'I know. Would you mind checking just once more?'

'For bogeymen under the bed?'

'Mmm.' I didn't snap back this time.

'OK, you come with me. To double check.'

I followed him around the house as he lifted bedspreads, opened curtains, even pulled a trunk out of an alcove.

'Satisfied?'

'I guess.' I felt slightly foolish. This nervous creature just wasn't me.

'And you'll be OK now?'

'Yes. You go.'

He kissed me. 'I'll see you soon. Take care, my love.'

'I will. And thank you for the weekend. It was – ' I wanted to say magic – 'great,' I finished lamely.

'Yes, it was good, wasn't it? Apart from the Manuel crisis.'

'Which turned out all right in the end.'

'Yep.'

He kissed me again and then he was gone. I locked the door after him and went back inside.

I'd unpacked, loaded the washing machine and got it going, and was just setting the table ready for breakfast in the morning when something made me jump and I turned round to see Molly in the doorway.

'Mummy, why am I in bed in my clothes?'

'You were fast asleep when we got home. I didn't want to wake you up. It's only your leggings and T-shirt, Molly.'

'And my vest and knickers.'

'They'll go in the wash tomorrow.'

'I want to put on my pyjamas. I don't like sleeping in my clothes.' She looked bleary, but wide awake.

'All right, we'll get you into your pyjamas.'

'I couldn't find them.'

'That's because they were in the case. You need clean ones.'

I went upstairs with her. The bedside light was on in her room; she'd clearly been hunting for her night attire. I fetched clean pyjamas from the airing cupboard, then went into her room.

'Where's Tom?' she asked.

'Gone home.'

'Will he be back tomorrow?' She was undressing, folding her clothes neatly.

'I don't know about tomorrow, but he will be back.'

'Mummy, why is my carpet all muddy?'

'What?'

'There – look!' She indicated a patch of dirt to the left of the foot of her bed between the window and the cupboard where her toys and games were stored. I frowned.

'I don't know, Molly. It looks like mud. Have you come upstairs with dirty shoes?' But even as I said it I was thinking she wouldn't have done that. Apart from yesterday morning's shower we hadn't had rain for ages and in any case I would have noticed it long before now.

'No! Of course I haven't!' She sounded indignant.

I crossed and went down on hands and knees. As I'd thought, it was dried mud – a small crumbling patch. I turned over my own feet one at a time to check the soles of my sandals though I knew perfectly well I hadn't been anywhere to collect mud and carry it in, and in any case the little heap on Molly's carpet looked as if it had been trodden in since it was deposited – random specks ground into the pile dribbled away in the direction of the window.

A frisson of alarm prickled my skin. I'd gone to the window to close the curtains when I'd put Molly to bed. Tom had come in to check the house. It could have been either of us who had squashed it flat and trod it in the direction of the window. But I was perfectly certain it hadn't been there when I'd made Molly's bed before leaving for Devon yesterday. The only person who could legitimately have brought it into the house was Tom, and as far as I was aware, he'd been nowhere to get muddy shoes any more than I had. In fact, I knew he hadn't. We'd walked on sand, yes. We'd walked on grass, yes. But not on mud. And in any case, this mud had been here long enough to dry out into powdery dirt. A day, at least. My heart thudded sickeningly suddenly as I remembered the storm of rain on Saturday morning. But that had been *after* we had left the house . . .

'I'll brush it up tomorrow,' I said, trying to conceal my

growing agitation from Molly. 'Come on – into bed now. It's way past the time you should be asleep, and you have to go to school in the morning.'

'OK, OK.' She rolled her eyes at me and climbed into bed. 'Night night, Mummy.'

'Night, darling.'

I closed her door, switched on the landing and hall lights and went down the stairs searching for any more traces of mud. There were a few crumbs on the bottom step and a few more just inside the front door. But they could have come from anywhere. I hadn't vacuumed since the middle of last week. The specks proved nothing.

I had a good look around the house checking to see if there was anything out of place – something that Tom wouldn't have noticed but I would. But I could find nothing untoward at all, nothing disturbed from how it should be. The kitchen scissors were in the wrong drawer, true, but they were always getting in the wrong place. I spent half my life looking for them. And the top was off the bread crock but again that was scarcely anything to get worked up about. I'd probably left it off myself in the hurry to get breakfast cleared so we could get away.

There was not a single shred of evidence that anyone had taken advantage of that open front door and nothing appeared to be missing. I could still scarcely believe I could have been so careless, but on the face of it, it seemed no harm had been done. As Tom had pointed out, no one would have known it wasn't locked unless they'd tried it, and no one but an opportunist thief would do that.

And yet . . . I couldn't shake the feeling that someone had been in the house whilst we had been away. Not just in the house – in Molly's bedroom.

The phone rang. It was Tom.

'Just to let you know I'm home safely.'

'Oh, good.'

'Are you OK?'

'I'm fine. Molly's fast asleep and I'm just going to bed myself.'

'Speak to you soon, then.' He hesitated. I felt something unsaid. Then: 'I love you, Jo. Remember that.'

I melted inside. 'Love you too.'

I put the phone down and warmth replaced my rekindled anxiety. Just hearing his voice made me feel better. I hadn't told him about the mud and my suspicion that someone had been in the house and I wasn't going to. He'd just think I was being paranoid, and perhaps I was.

Making certain the doors were securely locked and the windows fastened I switched off all the lights and went to bed.

Next day was a typical Monday, only more of a rush than usual since I normally sorted Molly's school uniform and made her lunch box on Sunday evening. There certainly wasn't time for sweeping up the pile of dirt on her bedroom carpet. It would just have to wait until this evening.

'The latest evidence for the prosecution,' I said to myself in an attempt to make light of my paranoia. But I was unable to raise a smile. Too many bad things had happened. Impossible things. And maybe somebody had been in Molly's room. Somebody who had no business being there . . .

Stop it. Just stop it! You will drive yourself insane . . .

With a huge mental effort I put the whole thing to the back of my mind. I took Molly to school and went to work myself.

The first thing I did when we got home, at about four, was to brush up the dried mud and throw it in the kitchen bin. The second was to ring Anna. It was some days since I'd spoken to her and I wanted to enquire about Dave's progress and also, if I'm honest, tell her about my weekend.

'Yes, Dave's still improving,' Anna said in answer to my question. She sounded a little guarded though, a little un-Anna-like.

'Getting his memory back at all?'

'Yes.' Still that guarded tone, as if she was holding something back. 'I've been trying to ring you. Where have you been?'

That was more like Anna, practically accusing me of daring to go off for a weekend without telling her.

'I've been to Devon. With Tom. And Molly, of course. We

167

had a lovely time. I really needed to get away and . . . Oh, Anna, you'll probably think I'm crazy, but he really is rather special. No . . .' I corrected. 'Very special.'

'You're falling for him. Be careful, Jo.'

I laughed. 'Wrong tense, I'm afraid. It's a bit late for warnings, Anna. I have fallen for him.'

'Oh, Jo . . .'

'You must stop worrying about me! He really is very nice, I promise you. And he's marvellous with Molly. She's accepted him much better than I could have hoped for. In fact, I think he's flavour of the month.'

'You mean it's getting serious.'

'I think so, yes. It's early days, of course, but yes . . . I do think we're pretty much an item.'

There was a small pregnant pause.

'Anna?' I said. 'Do you think it's too soon? Is that it?'

'No. Not for the right person. If Michael really is dead . . .'

Oh, no. She was at it now. 'Anna, I don't need this . . .'

'I know you don't, Jo.' Another pause, even more loaded than the last one. 'Jo, I really do need to talk to you. Are you home this evening? If I popped in on my way back from the hospital?'

'Yes, I'll be here.' Alarm bells were ringing. I could feel a lead weight suddenly in the pit of my stomach. What the hell did Anna want to talk to me about that couldn't be said over the phone? Was it something Dave had remembered? Oh – what now?

I controlled the rising panic. If Anna was going to tell me something that would make sense of all this, whatever it was it could only be a good thing. I wanted this nightmare sorted so that I could get on with my life.

'I'll see you about eight thirty then,' Anna said.

Fourteen

She was late. She was flustered. So was I. I'd spent the last few hours unable to concentrate on anything. Wondering what it was Anna wanted to say to me.

Tom had phoned and though we hadn't made any arrangement to meet tonight, spoke almost as though we had.

'I won't be able to get over this evening, Jo. I've got a hell of a lot of work I have to catch up on.'

'No problem. I wasn't expecting you. Anyway, Anna's coming over.'

'As long as you're all right . . .'

'I'm fine. I don't expect you to keep minding me, Tom.' But that he wanted to felt good. 'I'm a big girl.'

'I know.' Appreciatively. 'I'll see you tomorrow, shall I? Sevenish?'

'That would be nice.' But I wondered as I hung up how long he would be prepared to keep driving fifteen miles to see me. Sooner or later we'd have to come up with some other arrangement. It was early days yet, but if he suggested living together that would probably mean moving to Bristol since his work was there, and it would be unrealistic for me to expect him to commute every day. The complications nagged at me for a moment. Molly would have to change schools. I'd have to find another job. But that might be a plus. There were probably more opportunities for primary school teachers in the city.

But I really was putting the cart before the horse. I had too many things on my mind to start thinking about that yet. Time enough when all this was over. And when – if! – Tom asked me to move in with him . . .

Whilst I was waiting for Anna I tried to catch up on some ironing, and I'd more or less finished by the time I heard her car in the drive.

'Sorry I'm late, Jo,' Anna said, getting out of the car. 'I got held up. Calum wanted to come with me to see his daddy, so I had to take him home first instead of coming straight here as I'd planned. And George was awake and kicking off. He doesn't usually play his grandparents up, but I sure as heck don't want him to start. If Mum and Dad get fed up with being given the run around by three boisterous kids and decide to pack up and go home I'm not sure how I'd manage.'

'I'm sure your parents wouldn't leave you in the lurch whilst Dave is still in hospital,' I said.

'You're probably right. But I don't want them being taken advantage of.' Anna dumped her bag on a chair and ran a hand through her hair. As I mentioned before, she looked flustered. 'Any chance of a cup of tea?'

'I'll put the kettle on. I could use one myself.'

'Actually,' Anna said, 'I think you might need something stronger.'

A prickle of foreboding. I attempted levity.

'I'm getting quite a reputation as an old toper,' I joked. 'Tom fills my glass at every opportunity.'

At the mention of his name I saw a guarded expression cross her face and her eyes cut away from mine. I tried to ignore what I felt was a sudden awkwardness, though I couldn't understand why Anna had taken against Tom, particularly since she'd never met him, and in the beginning she had positively encouraged me to go out with him.

'If I don't want to end up in the Priory I think I'll stick to tea,' I said lightly.

'You'll have a drink.' Anna was going into bossy mode. 'Not G and T, though. Gin can be very lowering. That's why they call it mother's ruin. It depresses you. What you need is a whisky. Do you have any whisky in the house?'

'Yes, but I'm having a cup of tea.' I was determined not to be bullied. Often it was easier to do as Anna said rather than argue, but this time I was making a stand. 'So what is it you've come to talk to me about, Anna?'

'Make the tea first.'

'Oh, for heaven's sake!' I could feel my stomach tightening with apprehension. 'It's about Tom, I take it. You don't approve. Well, I like him. More than like him. He's the first

170

man I've had anything to do with in more than two years. And you know what? It feels good. It feels right . . .'

'But how much do you know about him?'

I glanced round sharply, the kettle in my hand. It was almost an echo of what Tom himself had said to me, and Anna was looking at me very oddly. Her cheeks had become flushed, her expression determined. But there was also something that might have been pity in her eyes.

'What do you mean – what do I know about him?' I flared defensively. 'I know he's kind and – old-fashioned as it might sound – a gentleman. I know he's great with Molly. And he seems to feel about me the way I feel about him. What more do you want?'

'Honesty, perhaps.' She must have seen my reaction to that; she raised a hand to me like a policeman stopping traffic. 'Please, Jo, don't go flying off the handle. Hear me out.'

'Are you trying to say . . . What are you trying to say, Anna?'

Anna took a couple of deep breaths, her hand spread out across her chest as if to help squeeze the air into her lungs. I'd noticed in the past that if she got upset about something she became a bit breathless, just as she did if she over-exerted herself. She really should try to lose a bit of weight. I caught myself. Why the hell was I thinking about Anna's weight problems when she was trying to tell me something detrimental about Tom? Because I didn't want to hear it, perhaps. Didn't want to listen . . .

'OK,' Anna said. 'What has he told you he does for a living?'

'He works for an insurance company in Bristol.'

'Doing what?'

'How should I know? Whatever people who work for insurance companies do, I suppose. He's part of the management team, I imagine. He hasn't been in this part of the world long. Before he came down here he lived in London.'

'Convenient. And let me guess, he's now in rented accommodation.'

'Until he can buy a place of his own, yes.'

'Which, to be honest, Jo, I think it's unlikely he'll ever do. He won't be here long enough.'

I was getting very wound up, to put it mildly.

'Anna,' I said, banging down the kettle. 'If you've got something to say, come out and say it. Just don't keep hinting that Tom is some kind of fraud.'

'All right.' She met my eyes directly. 'Tom *is* a fraud, as far as you are concerned.'

My stomach contracted. 'He doesn't work for an insurance company. Is that what you're saying?'

'He does work for an insurance company,' Anna said. 'But not as a manager. Not even as a pen-pusher. Tom – who used to be a policeman, by the way – is one of the itinerant squad. His job could take him anywhere. At the moment, it happens to be Bristol.' She paused, her face crumpled a little, as if she was on the verge of tears. Not for herself. For me. 'Tom is an insurance investigator,' she said. 'He looks into cases where it appears his company have been taken to the cleaners by people making fraudulent claims. He's here because he's investigating the payment they made on Michael's death. They suspect he isn't dead at all. Now – are you going to pour yourself a stiff whisky, Jo? Or am I?'

Shock ran through me in ice-cold waves. No – ice-hot. My legs seemed to have turned to jelly. My heart to have stopped beating.

Oh, no – not Tom. Please God, not Tom.

Anna was thrusting a tumbler into my hand – she'd located the whisky, poured me one and added a splash of water, and I hadn't even noticed. I held it between my hands, incapable of so much as raising it to my lips.

'I can't believe it,' I said. 'I don't understand.'

But I did. That was the whole trouble. I understood only too well. Little things he'd said came to me, fitting together. Tom had been using me. Cultivating me. Worming his way into my life to try and find evidence that his employers had been defrauded into paying out on Michael's life when Michael was not dead at all.

'I am so sorry, Jo,' Anna said. And I could see that she was. She looked dreadfully upset, fluttering round me, the picture of contrition. 'I'd have given anything to spare you this. But I had to tell you. I couldn't let you go on thinking . . .'

172

Thinking that I had found someone who cared for me. Someone who was concerned about me. Loved me.

'Oh, have a drink for goodness sake,' Anna urged me. I raised the glass to my lips obediently. My hand was shaking so badly it clattered against my teeth.

'You need to sit down.' Anna steered me towards a chair and sat down beside me, taking my hand and squeezing it. 'You've had a terrible shock, Jo. But I had to tell you. You can see that, can't you?'

'How do you know?' I asked. 'How did you find this out?'

But I knew that too, even before she explained. Another flash of clarity in the distorting fog of shock and disbelief.

'Dave found out,' Anna said. 'He was asking questions before he had his accident. As you know, Dave lost his memory when he was knocked off his motorbike. But now it's all come back. You remember I told you he kept asking about you? I was teasing you that you and he were having a fling? Well, he was getting snatches of what he'd found out. First all he knew was that he was worried about you for some reason. Then . . . well, he remembered. He wanted to tell you himself what he'd found out, but he's not up to it, Jo. And in any case, it wouldn't have been right for you to find out something like that in a hospital ward. You needed to be in your own home, with a friend here to look after you.'

'So what exactly did Dave find out?' My voice was curiously flat, emotionless, matter-of-fact. 'Do I have any more nasty surprises to come? Like I buried someone else thinking it was Michael?'

'Oh, Jo!' Anna looked shocked. 'How can you say such a thing?'

Five minutes ago I'd have wondered that myself. Now, suddenly, it was as if scales had been stripped from my eyes. The certain knowledge that I had been a gullible fool where Tom was concerned had shattered my belief in my own judgement. Time after time I'd come across evidence that pointed to Michael not being dead at all and I'd been unable to bring myself to believe it. Now, suddenly, I knew I could no longer ignore it.

'Clearly the insurance company have some reason for

thinking he's not dead,' I said. 'They paid up at the time without question. Something has made them suspicious. And why would the police have all this information? I presume it was through police sources that Dave pursued his enquiries?'

'Well, yes . . . yes it was, of course. But I'm sure they're mistaken . . .' Anna was becoming more distressed than ever. 'I'm sure Michael would never have done something like that. Or been involved in the things they say he was . . .' Her voice tailed away miserably.

'I was sure of that, too,' I said in the same hard voice. 'I was sure of my husband and I was sure of Tom. It seems I was wrong on both counts. It doesn't say much for my judgement, does it?' I swivelled and met her eyes, forcing her to look at me. 'So what exactly are they saying? Though I've got a pretty good idea.'

Anna looked startled. 'You knew?'

'No, of course I didn't.' I twisted the whisky glass between my hands, which were still shaking. 'I've been doing some investigating of my own. I didn't tell you about it because you've had enough on your plate. But I've found out that Michael and Adam are directors of a company called Best Sun. A timeshare operation of some kind, based in Tenerife. I assume that's what Dave found out, too. That they had some kind of scam going with local villain Kenny White.'

Anna's eyes flicked away from mine again. 'Amongst other things . . .'

I braced myself. 'What other things?'

'Oh, Jo . . .' Anna shook her head. 'I don't know that I should be telling you this at all. The Fraud Squad is involved. Dave could get into terrible hot water over this. Until their investigations are complete, it's all very hush-hush . . .'

'Anna, this is my husband we're talking about.'

'I know, but . . . Look, Dave didn't tell me all the details. He might not even know them himself. It's not his department, after all. He probably had to pull strings to find out as much as he did. All I know is that there's more to it than just the timeshare business. And that things have come to light that made the insurance company suspicious. There must be some collaboration between them and the police,

174

maybe because as I mentioned before, Tom used to be in the job himself. I really don't know. But there is this suggestion that they paid out when . . .'

'When Michael wasn't dead at all.' I could hardly believe the matter-of-fact way I was talking about this. Whether it was the effect of the whisky or whether it was that I had begun to accept that I, too, had been the victim of a terrible and heartless scam, I don't know. But right now it was as if I'd detached myself emotionally from this part of it at least. The real kick in the stomach was that Tom had deceived me too. That nothing that had happened between us was real at all. That all the time he'd just been stringing me along. When he'd asked me out. When he'd shown concern for me. When he'd made love to me . . . Physical pain, sharp as a knife thrust, twisted in my stomach and a dull ache bled from it, suffusing every part of me.

'Jo – they're wrong about Michael,' Anna said. 'They must be! I don't know where they got the idea that he'd done . . . this awful thing. Whether it started with the police investigation and they alerted the insurance company, or whether it was the other way around. But just because Michael is still listed as a director of this timeshare company doesn't mean he's still alive.'

'I tried to tell myself that too.' I pressed my fingers against my temples and massaged them up into my hairline. 'I persuaded myself that Adam just hadn't bothered to update the website or had some reason for wanting to leave Michael's name on it. Then I got a phone call from some man in Yorkshire – or Lancashire – one or the other. He said he'd found Michael's passport in Spain. Who but Michael would have been using his passport? Who but Michael himself would have had it? I've looked amongst his things – it's definitely not there. And it always was. Now you say that there's other evidence that's alerted the insurance company and the Fraud Squad. You don't have to be a genius to work out what that might be, do you?'

Anna looked bewildered, shrugging helplessly.

'Well, he must have a source of income, mustn't he? Bank accounts somewhere. Presumably he's still drawing an income from this timeshare company.'

175

Anna shook her head. 'I don't believe it, Jo. For a start, if he did fake his own death, he'd be cleverer than to leave a trail like that. He'd have sorted himself out a new identity, not swanned around the world under his old one . . .'

'Perhaps there was some reason he couldn't. Or he didn't think it was necessary,' I interrupted.

'And Adam would have to be in on it too,' Anna went on. 'Besides, if it wasn't Michael in the car the night of the accident, who was it? You're not suggesting, surely, that Michael and Adam bumped someone off just so that they'd have a body? Put Michael's ring on his finger and watch on his wrist and set fire to the car so he'd be unidentifiable? No one would take a risk like that – certainly not Michael and Adam.'

'There was someone else with them that night,' I said. 'Kenny White. He's known to be dangerous and ruthless. Dave told me that himself. It's also suspected that he's got a policeman or two in his pocket. Which would smooth his path when it came to pulling off a stunt like that. And he was definitely involved in the attempt to abduct Molly.' I was chewing my lip now, trying to make all the incidents fit together. Think the unthinkable. 'If Michael didn't die that night, if he wanted to disappear for some reason, if he is actually still alive, still involved with Kenny White, then perhaps . . . perhaps he was behind it. He wants Molly with him, and it was a stunt to get her.'

'Oh, Jo . . .' Anna covered her mouth with her hand for a moment, breathing hard again. 'But what about Adam? Why has he disappeared?'

'I don't know, but I'm beginning to think the worst. All this while I've been assuming that it was Adam who drew Michael into all this. Now I'm wondering if it was the other way round. Perhaps Adam knew too much – or found out too much – and became a danger to them. Or maybe he just got a conscience. It could have been a tip-off from him that sparked the investigation.'

'Or he got wind of it and decided to make himself scarce.'

'I think something has happened to him,' I said. 'From what I can make out the sort of people involved in something like this wouldn't think twice about disposing of anyone who might queer their pitch. Apparently the timeshare business is noted for it. Gang wars between rival outfits, people who step out of line or even sleep with someone else's wife . . . they don't care who gets hurt as long as their empires are safe. It's like the old days of the Krays in the East End.'

'Jo, you can't seriously be suggesting that *Michael* . . .?'

I let my breath out on a shaky, bitter laugh.

'If I knew the man who was my husband – Molly's father – so little that he could actually put us through such a terrible trauma by faking his own death, then I didn't know him at all. Anything is possible. And you can't ignore the fact that something terrible has happened to everyone who starts poking into the facts . . . begins to get close to the truth.' I buried my head in my hands. 'I know, I know . . . I can't believe I'm saying this either, but I can't get away from it any longer, Anna. I can't go on kidding myself.'

Anna put her arm round me. For a few minutes I slumped like a sack of potatoes while despair bubbled up inside me like a witch's brew in a cauldron. I still found it almost beyond belief that Michael could be behind all the terrible things that had happened. My Michael? All my senses cried out that it just wasn't possible. And yet, now, I'd allowed myself to be taken in yet again. By Tom. What kind of fool was I?

But however I continued to rant against it, the events that had so traumatized me were indisputable. And the conclusions were beginning to be inescapable, though I still hoped desperately that I was wrong. But until the truth finally emerged, I wouldn't know for sure. Wouldn't be able to move on.

Move on to what? a treacherous small voice inside me asked. I'd thought I'd been lucky enough to find someone to move on with. That I had something to look forward to when this whole nightmare was over. Now I knew differently. But still I had to know the truth about Michael. For my own sanity. I raised my head, looking at Anna.

'Did Dave say how far on the police were with their investigations? If they're anywhere near a conclusion?'

'He didn't say. Just that it was a really complicated enquiry and it was ongoing. But these things are bound to take time, Jo. They won't want to go off half-cocked.'

Determination surged, giving me a sense of purpose, making me feel better, momentarily at least.

'In that case, I'm going to go on seeing what I can unearth myself. The more leads I can provide them with, the sooner it will be over. One way or another.'

Anna looked very worried. 'But these people are dangerous, Jo. You said so yourself. I don't want anything happening to you. And you've got Molly to think about too.'

'Michael would never harm her,' I said with absolute certainty.

'No, but it sounds as if this Kenny White is a nasty piece of work. And there may be loose cannons in the organization.'

She was right, of course. Though I had no proof whatsoever that something dreadful had happened to Adam, there was no disputing that Alison was dead – and I was more certain than ever that she had not taken her own life. And someone had died in Michael's blazing car, and I was beginning to think that was no accident either. I couldn't take chances with Molly's safety. But neither could I sit back and do nothing.

'Anna.' I met her gaze directly. 'Would you have Molly for a few days? I know it's a lot of ask, but she's no trouble really. I need to know she's safe – and I need to be a free agent myself, too. I think I might go to Tenerife . . .'

'Jo!' Anna looked more worried than ever. 'If these people are capable of such terrible things here, in England, what will they be like on their home turf?'

'England is Kenny White's home turf,' I pointed out. 'It's Michael who is in Tenerife – if he's still alive. That's what I have to find out. And,' I added with more bravado than I felt, 'I don't think he'd harm me either. Will you have Molly, Anna? She can miss a couple of days of school this week and then it's half term. Please!'

Anna exhaled her breath over her top lip. 'When do you want me to have her?'

'Tomorrow? I could bring her over to you. To be honest, the sooner she's out of this house the happier I'll be. I think somebody was in here whilst we were away at the weekend.'

'What!' Anna exclaimed, shocked, and I realized it was the one thing I'd failed to fill her in on.

'I can't be sure, but when we got home the front door was unlocked. I must have left it open. And I'm sure somebody had been in, wandering about. There was dried mud on the carpet in Molly's bedroom.'

'You left the door open?' Anna was frankly incredulous.

'I must have done. All I know is that it was unlocked when we got back.'

Anna sat forward, looking at me intently. 'But you thought you'd locked it?'

'Well, of course I did! I wouldn't have been likely to go off and leave an open house for burglars if I'd known, would I?'

'Perhaps you did lock it,' Anna said. 'Perhaps someone opened it with a key and left in a hurry. Perhaps *they* were the ones who left it unlocked.'

A shiver ran over my skin.

'Michael would have a key,' Anna said. 'Wouldn't he?'

'Well, of course he *had* a key . . . but just now, Anna, you were arguing that Michael would never . . .'

'I can change my mind.' Anna's lips were pursed. 'No one else would have a key, would they?'

'No . . .' I broke off.

Tom had a key. I'd given it to him to let himself back in on Friday night and I hadn't asked for its return. He'd had no opportunity to break in over the weekend – he'd been in Devon with me – and no opportunity either to give it to someone else. But he'd been gone rather a long time when he went home to collect his things. Long enough to get a copy made and hand it to a colleague who could come in and have a look around for whatever evidence it was insurance investigators looked for whilst Tom kept me safely out of the way. Could he have got it copied on a Friday evening? I didn't know. I didn't even know for sure that anyone had been in, or whether I'd left the door open by mistake myself. My gut instinct was that they had, but it could be that I was now so paranoid I'd reached the point of seeing spectres where none existed. I could no longer trust Tom. I could no longer trust Michael. I wasn't even sure I could trust myself.

Either Michael had been in the house, or one of Tom's

colleagues had, or no one had. I knew nothing for certain any more. The one thing I did know was that I could not take any chances with Molly's safety.

'Would you take her home with you now?' I asked.

'*Now?* But she's fast asleep, isn't she?'

'It'll be an adventure for her.'

'What will you tell her?'

'I don't know,' I said. 'I'll think of something.'

When Anna had left with a sleepy Molly bundled into her dressing gown, Manuel cuddled close in her arms, and her Minnie Mouse suitcase, packed with a few changes of clothes and her toiletries, in the boot of the car, I stood for a moment in the doorway, fretting and bereft, but also relieved. Molly would be safe with Anna. No one had seen her leave; no one would think to look for her there. And I was free to do whatever I had to do to find out what the hell was going on.

I'd go to Tenerife. To whatever office Best Sun was using there. It was risky, but I thought I could get away with it. None of the employees would know me and if I posed as a tourist looking to buy a timeshare I could ask questions without arousing suspicion. The only person who could blow my cover was Michael himself. And if I ran into him I'd have the answer to one of my most pressing questions.

Would he be there, sitting in some inner sanctum? Might he see me through a one-way window and me not see him? The very thought that he might be there, very much alive and living the good life on an income conned out of gullible tourists made me feel sick. I'd never thought I could wish my husband dead, but I wished it now whole-heartedly. Losing him had been indescribably dreadful. I'd thought I'd never get over it. But at least I had memories, of love and tenderness and happy times shared, of a life we'd built together. But if he had done this terrible thing I would have nothing.

I prayed a silent prayer that when I asked about the directors, mentioned Michael's name, I'd be told that he was dead. That his name was still on the website by default. That he'd never been actively involved . . .

A sudden thought occurred to me. It was several days now since I had told Tom what I'd found about Best Sun. If he'd reported back to his company they could well have sent someone to Tenerife to do exactly what I planned to do now. It could already be all over. Perhaps that was what was keeping Tom busy tonight – filling reports to finalize his investigation. Perhaps that was the reason he hadn't needed to see me. He'd found the answers he wanted. He didn't need me any more.

The pain jolted my heart again. Strange that it was Tom's betrayal that was hurting me the most. Perhaps because I'd come to accept the loss of Michael over the last two years. My life with him was my past. Tom, I had thought, was my future. Now I knew different. He had simply been using me to try and find proof that the claim on Michael's life had been fraudulent. Ruthless had been the word used to describe Kenny White by a number of people. It could apply equally well to Tom. How could he have done it? How could I not have known? I'd been right, that first evening when we met, in thinking he was tailing me. It had been him who was watching the house and who had followed me, panicking me into running on to the verge and getting a puncture. He'd seen his opportunity then, and presented himself as my knight on a white charger. He had gained my trust and insinuated himself into my life.

That much I could almost understand. At that point he'd been doing a job. What I couldn't understand was how he could have taken the pretence to such lengths. He must have realized I knew nothing. That I was totally spooked by everything that was happening. But still he'd gone on with the charade, pretending concern for me in the hope that I'd provide him with the key. And perhaps I had.

Suddenly I was angry. Outraged and furious. How dare he? How *dare* he? And how much more did he know that I didn't? What had he kept from me with his silken words? Did he know for sure even as he was making love to me that my husband was still alive? As he charmed Molly? As he let me fall in love with him?

I grabbed the phone, my hands shaking with rage, and dialled the number of his mobile. Even as I did so I was thinking – why didn't it ring bells with me that he gave me no land line number? That he had given me no address? How could I have become so involved when I knew so little about him? His friends? His family? His past?

Only now, when it was too late, could I see just how gullible I'd been. Vulnerable. An easy touch. I'd made it so damned easy for him and I was furious with myself too for being such a fool.

'Hello.' The sound of his voice, which had been capable of arousing such desire in me all by itself, now ratcheted up my anger another notch.

'I hope you're pleased with yourself,' I said fiercely.

'Jo?' He sounded startled. 'Is that you? Are you all right?'

'No, I am not all right!' The fury trembled in my voice. 'How could you, Tom? How could you do it to me?'

'Jo – hang on a minute . . .'

'You have been deceiving me, Tom. All along. Leading me on because you think I'm living the good life on a pay-out stolen from your damned company. Haven't you? Haven't you?'

A small pause. Then: 'How do you know?'

So he wasn't even going to bother to deny it.

'How could you *do* it? You are utterly despicable!'

'Jo – wait. It's not like that . . .'

'Oh, really? Well, let me tell you it's how it looks from where I'm standing. Have you got what you wanted? Have you found Michael in Tenerife? Or did he get wind that you were on his trail and disappear again? I certainly hope so. I hope if he *is* alive you never find him. Not because I want your damned money – your thirty pieces of silver. I just don't want to see you profit from such filthy tactics. To pretend you were interested in me is bad enough, but to worm your way in with Molly too – a little girl who had already lost her father . . .' Words failed me.

'You've got it all wrong, Jo.' He cut into the hiatus in my tirade. 'Let me come over . . . talk to you . . .'

'Oh, so you *haven't* got what you want?' I flashed. 'Well, dear me, what a shame!'

'Jo – please, give me the chance to explain . . .'

'I don't want to hear your explanations. And I don't want

182

to speak to you or see you ever again.' I slammed the phone down.

And then I burst into tears.

Fifteen

Keep busy. That was the best thing to do. I went online and shopped around for a flight to Tenerife. I couldn't get one out of Bristol until Thursday and I didn't want to wait that long. Now that I'd decided on a course of action, I was impatient. This whole thing had been hanging over me for far too long already. In reality, it was only a few weeks. It felt like a lifetime. And besides . . .

I was aching for Molly already, to feel her firm little arms wound around my neck and smell the clean soapy scent of her hair and skin fresh from a bath. My daughter was the only thing in the world that mattered now. I wanted her back with me, under our own roof, living a normal, busy, everyday life. If we still had a roof over our heads by the time this was over! If Michael had defrauded the insurance company and they demanded all the money I'd been awarded be paid back, I didn't know how the hell I would manage. But I wasn't going to worry about that now.

I found a flight out of Heathrow leaving the next day and booked it. Then I went upstairs to pack. The small case was still in a corner of my bedroom – I hadn't put it back in the loft since returning from Devon. Remembering the weekend I'd just spent with Tom brought all my wretchedness flooding back. And the anger. I wouldn't think about that either. Just take one step at a time, I told myself.

I threw a couple of T-shirts and a flippy skirt into the suitcase, added a halter-necked sun top and a pair of shorts. If I was going to pose as a holidaymaker, I needed to look the part. It wouldn't hurt to have a bit of a tan either. I thought I had the remains of a tube of self-tanning cream left from last year, and located it in the bathroom. If I used it I'd have to wait a couple of hours before going to bed or I'd get it all over the sheets, but I couldn't imagine I'd sleep much anyway.

I undressed and got into the shower, standing for long minutes with my head tipped back so that the water cascaded over the full length of me, as hot as I could bear it. I felt the need of it, as if cleansing my body could also cleanse the inner me, wash away some of the pain, the soiled feeling of having been used. After I'd shampooed my hair and soaped myself from head to toe I turned the shower to cold, gasping as the icy needles pricked my hot skin. But the shock treatment seemed to be working. I felt invigorated, refreshed, and full of determination. I'd been a victim long enough. Time to take control of my life. Whatever I might have to face, I'd do it. Anything had to be better than the quicksands I'd been sinking into these past weeks, helpless as my world collapsed around me.

I turned off the shower, stepped out, dripping, on to the bath mat. And heard something I shouldn't have heard.

For a moment it didn't register as anything in particular, just a dull thud from somewhere in the house. I froze, adrenalin pumping. Then it came again, and I recognized it. A door slamming against the frame as if a sudden draught had caught it. A draught? The doors were locked and the back door was bolted too – I'd made sure of that. The downstairs windows were all closed – the only one open was here in the bathroom, letting out the steam from the shower. There shouldn't be enough draught to cause an inside door to bang. But if someone had opened the front door . . .

I thought of what Anna had said about someone letting themselves in with a key while we were away in Devon. Had they? And had they now let themselves in again? Was there someone in the house?

I froze, every nerve alert, listening. Nothing. I grabbed my towelling robe from the hook on the airing cupboard door, pulled it on. And heard another sound. The creak of a stair. There was one that always creaked.

Pure ice-cold terror flooded through me. I cursed myself for not having brought the phone or my mobile with me. I looked around wildly for something with which to defend myself. In a bathroom? Fat chance! The only thing to hand

185

was a long handled back brush. I grabbed it, pathetic as a weapon, but the feel of the wood in my hand lent me courage.

I could have shot the bolt of the door, I suppose, locked myself in until the intruder had gone – until morning if necessary. But I didn't. If someone was in my house I was going to confront them. It could only be Tom – though I didn't think he'd had time to drive the fifteen miles out of Bristol since I'd spoken to him – or a colleague of Tom's. Or Michael. They were the only people with keys.

The blood pounded in my veins. Clutching the back brush like a baton I pulled the door wide open. Went out on to the landing.

Nothing. In the low level lighting cast by the energy saving bulb, the landing was just as it should be. Deserted. I looked to left and to right, at the bedroom doors, all ajar. Crept to my room first, snapped on the light. Empty. Across the landing to Molly's room, switched on the light there. Same result. I repeated the exercise with the other bedrooms. The first floor of the house now blazed with light. But it revealed nothing. No intruder. Nothing untoward at all. But I had to be sure.

I inched down the stairs one step at a time, my fingers still tightly curled around the handle of the back brush. Empty hall. Empty living room. Empty kitchen. Tension began to seep out of me, replaced by reaction. My bated breath came out on a sob.

You're imagining things. What you heard was nothing more than the house settling. Or air in the pipes.

I put down the back brush feeling a little foolish and poured myself a whisky. I'd have to stop turning to the bottle when this was over. But just now I badly needed the comfort it brought. Taking my drink with me I headed back upstairs. I was still on edge, my nerves taut as bowstrings, and when the telephone in the hall rang just as I was passing it – a loud, old fashioned beep rather than the softer tone of the one in the kitchen – it made me jump out of my skin. I set my glass down on the hall table and lifted the receiver, half expecting it to be Anna, reporting on Molly. Or maybe even Tom, trying to weasel his way round me. It was neither.

I recognized the voice at the other end instantly – I'd heard

186

it enough times. But I could scarcely believe the evidence of my own ears.

'Jo?' he said. 'It's me.'

My own voice came out on a sharp breath, sounding as incredulous as I felt.

'Adam?'

'Jo,' he said again. 'You are there, then.'

'Yes, of course I am.' I didn't say that tomorrow I wouldn't be, that I'd been going to go to Tenerife looking for him and Michael and answers. 'Adam, where have you been? We've all been so worried about you. And the most awful things have happened.'

'Jo – I have to see you.' He cut across my garbled response. 'It's very important.'

'Where are you?'

'I'm just around the corner. I was on my way to you, but I thought I'd ring first, given that it's so late. I thought you might have been in bed.'

'No – I'm not in bed. But I was in the shower. Adam, what is going on?'

'I can't go into it on the phone. I'll explain when we're face to face.'

And you have a hell of a lot of explaining to do! I thought.

'Give me five minutes to get dressed.'

'Will do. I'll see you shortly.'

I dashed upstairs, throwing on the clothes I'd taken off a while earlier, fingers fumbling with buttons and zips in my haste.

Adam, at least, was alive. In spite of everything, it was the most enormous relief. There had been too many sudden and violent deaths. And perhaps at last I was going to get some answers as to what was going on. Without going to Tenerife. Here, in my own home.

The head lights of a car arced across my bedroom window. I pulled on a sweater and ran down to open the door.

'Jo.' He attempted to embrace me, the usual brief platonic hug and the obligatory air kiss. I drew back. I might be relieved to know that he hadn't suffered some grisly end at the hands of the White gang or Tenerife timeshare barons, but I didn't feel like going through the motions of pretended affection for a man who had been part of the enormous deceit that had been practised on me.

'Come in Adam,' I said tautly. I stood aside for him to do just that and locked the door behind him.

I'd shut up the living room for the night but the lights were still on in the kitchen. He headed for it with all the familiarity of a man who'd been here many times before.

He was looking, I thought, very fit, very brown. He was always tanned from the time he spent in the sun but now the tan appeared deeper than when I'd last seen him and in the bright artificial light thrown by the spotlights in the kitchen the hairs on his muscular arms, bleached blond, gleamed like threads of gold.

'I just don't believe this, Adam,' I said. 'I thought something terrible had happened to you. Alison thought so too . . . have you heard about Alison? She's dead.'

'Yes.' Adam rubbed the back of his hand across his mouth. 'Yes, I know. It's terrible.'

'She was so worried about you,' I said. 'She was pulling out all the stops to try and find you. Where the hell have you been, Adam? Why didn't you get in touch?'

'I couldn't,' he said shortly.

'Why not?'

'Jo,' he said. 'You don't want to know. I mean it. For your own safety. The less involved you are in this mess the better. If Alison had left well alone, she might still be alive.'

A chill whispered over my skin. 'I knew it.' I said it more to myself than to Adam. But he heard me and his eyes narrowed, questioning me. 'I know she didn't kill herself,' I said. 'That's what they're saying – that it was suicide. But I've never believed that. I've always thought Alison was murdered because of something she found out. It's all to do with the timeshare business, isn't it? And the White gang.'

I saw Adam tense. The muscles in his arms corded suddenly and there was a watchfulness, not just in his eyes, but every fibre of his body. 'She told you.'

'No,' I said. 'She didn't tell me anything. She said she needed to be sure of her facts first. But since she died I've been doing some investigating of my own.'

'Shit, Jo . . .'

'Yes. Shit.' I was in no mood to pussyfoot around any more. 'I expect you can guess what one of the things I found out was.'

He gave a slight shake of his head. Liar! I thought.

I looked him straight in the eye. 'Is Michael with you in Tenerife?'

I was expecting to see a look of guilt. What I saw was shock and incredulity.

'*Michael?*' It was there in his voice too. Undeniable. Certainly not feigned, unless Adam was Sir John Gielgud reincarnated. 'What are you talking about? Michael is dead, Jo.'

The first wash of relief had made me go weak inside, but I couldn't let it go so easily. 'Then why is he still listed as a director of Best Sun? Which, incidentally, I knew nothing whatever about until very recently.'

'Oh God.' Adam ran a hand through his hair. 'Oh, Jo – I'm sorry. That's down to me. I never removed his name. For business reasons. It's too complicated to explain . . .'

The corners of my mouth tightened as Adam took a further dive in my estimation and I snorted softly. Some legal wangle, I supposed. Tax evasion maybe. How dare he? How dare he keep Michael 'alive' for his own dubious ends and put me through hell?

But there were other questions still unanswered – and plenty of them.

'What about his passport?'

'His passport?' Adam echoed.

'Yes – his passport. Someone phoned and told me they'd found it in Spain. They thought he'd be worried about it. Can you imagine what I thought when I took the phone call? Have you been using that too? Did you need it to keep up this fiction that Michael was still alive?'

I was fuming, all the uncertainty that had been tormenting me boiling up inside me and escaping in steaming rage.

'I don't know anything about that.'

I wasn't at all sure I believed him. There was a shifti- ness about him suddenly that reminded me of a little boy caught with his hand in the biscuit tin. The passport had been useful to him, I supposed. A back-up for the deception

189

he was perpetrating in the pursuit of making money from this timeshare company. He just didn't want to admit it to me.

I locked my eyes with his again. 'Then how can you be certain it's not Michael who has been using it?'

'Because Michael is dead, Jo.' I was still staring him out; he shrugged suddenly, the guilt he must have been feeling exploding into bluster. 'All right – I did have his passport. I found it in his office desk when I was clearing out. I thought it might come in useful.'

In his office desk. What the hell had it been doing there? Had Michael intended to make a trip to Spain or Tenerife without telling me? Would he have made some excuse to me about having to go away on business for a day or two if the accident hadn't happened first? Would he have told me eventually? Or was he too ashamed at what he'd got himself mixed up in to be able to bring himself to admit it to me? I was still angry – angry with Adam and with Michael too. But the most important thing – the only thing that really mattered, little as I liked the rest of it – was that it hadn't been Michael using his passport. I had not spent the last two years of my life mourning a man who had simply abandoned me and his daughter.

'I don't have it any more,' Adam was saying. 'My briefcase was stolen. The passport – and a lot of other stuff – went with it. That's the reason I'm here actually . . .'

'You mean you want something else of Michael's so you can continue this pretence that he's still alive?' I said angrily. 'You must be joking! You'll have to go to your friend Kenny White and ask him to help you out. I'm sure he knows people who can provide you with forged documents.'

Adam's eyes narrowed. 'Kenny? What do you know about Kenny?'

'I know you're in cahoots with him and his brother Barrymore. I've seen the Best Sun website, remember? And I know he was at the golf club with you and Michael the night of Michael's accident. What happened that night, Adam? Something did, I'm sure of it. Michael was a careful driver. He wasn't reckless, he wasn't a young lad showing off to his pals. Yet that night . . . I've never understood how he came to have such a terrible accident. But I think now that you know. And I think I have a right to know too, don't you?'

'Don't go there, Jo, please,' Adam said. 'I feel bad enough as it is. I should never have let him get into the car, the state he was in. I should have stopped him.'

'And why was he in such a "state" as you put it? Let me guess. He wanted out of your grubby scheme and you wouldn't have it? I knew something was worrying him those last weeks – and now I know what it was. Did it all come to a head that night? That's what happened, isn't it? Michael finally baulked and told you he'd had enough. But you wouldn't cut him free. You couldn't have him rocking the boat.'

I could see it all in my mind's eye now. Michael saying he wanted nothing more to do with Best Sun. Adam – to whom he was somehow so important that he had 'kept him alive' for 'business reasons' even after he had been killed – threatening him with the loss of his job if he pulled the plug. I saw Michael, worried and furious, slamming out of the meeting, driving like hell to get it out of his system. Not concentrating on the road. His mind on Adam and Kenny White and the mess he had got himself into . . .

'No wonder you took it upon yourself to keep an eye on Molly and me,' I fumed. 'Because you had Michael's death on your conscience. You knew you were responsible.'

'Jo . . .' A muscle worked in Adam's cheek, his hands clenched. 'I am so, so sorry.'

'And so you damned well should be!' I retorted furiously. 'My husband is dead because of you and your greed. As for this pretence for the sake of the company that Michael is still alive – you realize you've put me through hell? I've even been targeted by insurance investigators . . .'

'What?' Adam started.

'Oh, yes.' I wasn't going to elaborate, tell him what a fool I'd made of myself. 'And I've been targeted by the Whites too, though I've no idea why.'

Adam had changed colour. Not even the deep tan could conceal the fact that the blood had drained from his face. He was definitely nervous of the Whites – and who wouldn't be? Another piece of the jigsaw slipped into place as I remembered the e-mails I'd found on his computer – Kenny White demanding to know where he was. And later banging angrily on the door of the office. A man with a mission.

'You've fallen out with them, haven't you?' I said. 'That's why you went missing – to keep out of their way. And they thought I might know where you were. But you have no idea of the lengths they were prepared to go to. They even tried to abduct Molly.'

'What?'

'A woman tried to get her to go with her in her car with some cock and bull story about me being taken ill. And I know she is connected to Kenny White – I've seen him in the car Molly described. Can you believe it? That they would try to snatch an innocent seven-year-old child? Because of you, Adam. It all comes back to you and this scam you're embroiled in.'

'Where is Molly now?' Adam asked.

'It's a little late in the day to start showing concern, isn't it?' I flared. 'She's out of harm's way, hopefully. I'd booked myself on a flight to Tenerife to try and find out what the hell is going on, and she's staying with Anna.'

'With Manuel to comfort her?' He half-smiled. Trying to worm his way back into favour, I supposed. Reminding me of the efforts he'd made to ease his conscience, like buying presents for Molly. As if a damned stupid teddy bear could make up for the loss of her father. Or for involving us in the fallout from his dodgy business enterprise in partnership with ruthless and dangerous criminals.

'Don't try to get around me, Adam. I am so angry I could kill you. Oh . . .' I pressed my hands one each side of my head, pushing my hair back behind my ears with a furious gesture. 'God, I need a drink.'

'I must say I could do with one too,' Adam said ruefully.

'Quite honestly, Adam, I couldn't care less what you want.'

'Jo, I am truly sorry about all this.' He was still trying to placate me. 'I had no idea you and Molly were going to be dragged into it.'

'Well, we have been.'

'I know, and I'm worried for you. The Whites are dangerous people if you get on the wrong side of them, or they think

192

their empire is being threatened. You've seen what happened to Alison. She found out too much and started interfering and she paid the price.'

I felt chilled. It was no more than I'd suspected, but to hear Adam confirm it was not suicide terrified me. 'You do think they murdered her then?'

'Not a doubt in my mind. Look – I know you're furious with me, Jo, and I can't say I blame you. This whole thing is my fault for being greedy and getting mixed up with the wrong people. But please . . . try to put that to one side for the moment. I want to look after you now, make sure things don't go from bad to worse. Michael is dead and Alison is dead and no amount of remorse on my part will bring them back. But I sure as hell want to make sure the same thing doesn't happen to you and Molly. So get us both a drink and let's see if we can work something out. Or do you want me to get them for you?'

'No, thank you. I can do it.' I was still too angry with Adam to want him treating my home as if it was his too, but it was clearly going to be a long night. This was far from over yet. I still didn't know why Adam had come here . . . unless it was to warn me. But warn me of what? I still didn't understand what it was that Alison had discovered that had made her such a danger to the Whites that they had disposed of her, and by the same token, what it was that put me in the frame for similar treatment? There was more to it. There had to be.

'I think the best thing is to call the police,' I said, plonking the whisky bottle and a couple of glasses on the table.

Adam shook his head. 'The police can't help you, Jo.'

'You don't want them involved because you don't want to go to jail,' I said shortly, unstoppering the whisky bottle and pouring two generous measures.

'True enough, I don't. But it's you I'm thinking of. The police can't give you protection 24/7 for the rest of your life. And in any case, Kenny has friends . . .' Adam took a long pull of his whisky. 'Besides, you have Molly to think of, remember.'

As if I could forget . . . I took a gulp of my drink myself. Goodness knows, I needed it!

193

'I have a suggestion to make,' Adam said. 'The only way to guarantee your safety – and hers – is for you to come back to Spain with me. I've got a plane chartered on standby at a private airfield not far from here. Let's go and collect Molly and get the hell out of here.'

I stared at him in disbelief. 'Tonight? You must be joking!'

'I was never more serious in my life, Jo.'

'Take Molly to Spain? Away from her home, her school, her friends? And anyway, what would be the point? The Whites are in Tenerife too. It would be out of the frying pan into the fire.'

'I said Spain, not Tenerife. I have a nice little bolt-hole there, that none of the Whites know about. Not my villa – a place in the mountains. Where do you think I've been these past weeks?'

I took another healthy drink. 'A place in the mountains,' I echoed stupidly.

'Yes. I bought it derelict – did it up. Even had a swimming pool installed. You'd be comfortable there, Jo. And safe.'

I shook my head in disbelief. 'Adam, this is totally ridiculous. I haven't the slightest intention of going on the run to Spain. Why should I? I've done nothing wrong. This is England, for God's sake. I'll go to the police first thing in the morning. If I need protection, they'll give it to me, I'm sure. But I honestly can't see why I should even be in need of it. Why the little I know makes me a danger to anyone. All I found out is already in the public domain. On the Internet. It makes no sense at all . . .'

'Jo – you have to take my word for it. Because of Michael, you are involved, whether you like it or not. And the Whites are dangerous people to cross. For Molly's sake, if not for your own . . .'

I tossed back my whisky, poured another. It was giving me confidence.

'Adam, I am going nowhere unless I know the reason why. I want answers. How did all this come about, for a start?'

'Best Sun, you mean?'

'If you like. You'd better start filling me in, Adam.'

He sipped his drink. 'OK. Well, you're already aware of

the set-up. Timeshare sales. Kenny put up the money to get it started and his brother is the front man. I was invited to become a director. I've done business with Kenny for years.' I raised a questioning eyebrow; he ignored it, refusing to elaborate. 'It was a golden opportunity, far too good to pass up. Timeshares, the way we handle it, are a real money spinner. All our operatives are paid commission only, so no sale – no income. You'd be surprised how that concentrates the mind. They are really very good at what they do, and it's surprisingly easy to hook punters. You collar a couple. Give them both a scratch card. The first one is a loser. "Oh, sorry. Not lucky this time." But the second one, taken from the bottom of the pile is a different story. The operator rubs the card and gets very excited. Not only has it won "the star prize", but he gets a good bonus into the bargain. All the couple have to do is go with him to the office and they'll crack a bottle of champagne and hand over the prize. It's a con trick, of course, to get the punters in for a presentation, but you'd be surprised how common sense deserts normally level-headed folk when they're in the sun and feeling good. Before the champagne bottle is empty they've either bought into Best Sun, or turned over their existing timeshares – for a nice little administration fee, of course. I tell you, there are fortunes to be made in this game.'

'It's utterly despicable,' I said.

'You're entitled to your opinion. Mine is that if these people are stupid enough to part with their hard-earned cash so easily, they're fair game. Not my problem. And I like the life they help me to live. I like the sun. I like the golf. You may not approve of the way I make the money to live that sort of life, but . . .' Adam shrugged carelessly.

'I certainly don't approve,' I said. 'And I find it hard to believe Michael did either. How did you drag him into this in the first place, Adam? Did you threaten him with the loss of his job if he didn't play ball?' Adam was silent, and I knew I'd hit the nail on the head. 'What I don't understand though is why his involvement should be a threat to us now.'

'You know too much. Just as Alison did.'

'No, Adam, it doesn't hold water.' I was beginning to feel a little woozy, but not so woozy that I couldn't see the flaws

I'd already pointed out. 'The Best Sun website is there for anybody to see. This sort of scam, as far as I can make out, is perfectly legal in Tenerife, if not in England. If there's any sort of trouble, all you have to do is hop on a plane – and the same goes for Kenny White. With the money to be made over there, I'm only surprised he isn't already living there in a secure villa with a private golf course.'

'He has plenty of business interests here that have nothing whatever to do with timeshares,' Adam said. 'He runs with the big boys. You hear of a big robbery in the area, a security heist or something of the kind, chances are Kenny has an interest in it. Anyway, the sun doesn't suit him. Believe it or not, he actually likes England. And he's prepared to go to any lengths to make sure his freedom to go on living here and making his money the way he always has aren't threatened.'

'How can you continue to do business with someone like that, Adam?' I asked incredulously. 'If you really think Kenny White had her killed, how can you do it? Alison worked for you. She idolized you. To be honest, I can't see her being the slightest threat to Kenny White, whatever she'd found out. She'd know that you were involved with him, and were likely to be implicated. She'd never do anything to cause trouble for you.'

'Perhaps she got greedy.' There was something about the way he said it, coldly, speculatively, that made my skin crawl.

'There's still something you're not telling me, Adam.'

He moved impatiently, draining his glass and getting up. 'We don't have time for all this, Jo. Come on, let's go and get Molly and be on our way. My plane won't wait for ever.'

'I already made myself clear. I am going nowhere with you, Adam, unless you come up with a very good reason why I should. Michael has been dead for two years – I still don't understand why I should suddenly be in danger because he was drawn into this sordid business.'

Adam looked at me speculatively for a moment, then poured himself another whisky and sat down again. 'OK, Jo – have it your way. You want to know – I'll tell you. But you're not going to like what you hear.'

'I know that!' I snapped. 'I don't like any of it.'

'Just shut up and listen. Like I said, I don't have much time.' Adam had never used a tone like that to me before. He was metamorphosing before my eyes from a charming, good natured friend into someone I did not know at all. Someone who was beginning to frighten me. 'I told you, I've done business with Kenny for years. Helped him out with disposing of the proceeds of his criminal activities by passing money through the books of the estate agency and the insurance part of the business.'

'Money laundering.' I said it softly, almost to myself, astonished at the murky waters Adam had swum in.

'If you want to call it that,' Adam said casually. 'The trouble is, Kenny isn't the most generous of men. He wasn't rewarding me anywhere near adequately for the risks I was taking for him. So I decided to cream some off. Open a few offshore accounts of my own that he knew nothing about. Some of them are in Michael's name.'

'In Michael's name?' I was outraged. 'That's the reason I've been targeted by the Whites, is it? And the reason why you decided you needed to keep Michael alive?'

'Got it in one. Anyway, things were going fine until a few months ago when Kenny rumbled that I'd relieved him of a small fortune. I think I have Barrymore to thank for that. Barrymore shares his brother's trait for being mean – he was withholding the lion's share of the profits from Best Sun – and I decided to set up a rival company of my own. Barrymore was suspicious of where my capital was coming from – they put their heads together and realized it was Kenny's money. Hence the falling out.'

'And the reason he was so anxious to talk to you.' I thought of the e-mails, the angry way he had tried to barge into Adam's office.

Adam pulled a rueful face. 'You don't fall foul of the Whites if you can help it. I decided to make myself scarce until I'd managed to get my new company going and sorted out secur-ity arrangements for my own safety. Then disaster struck. I told you my briefcase was stolen – well, there was something in it – along with Michael's passport – which was very important to me. A computer memory stick with all the information I needed to access the offshore accounts – IDs, passwords, the lot. At first I thought it was one of the Whites who had taken it – that I'd lost my nest-egg – but it soon became clear it wasn't. It was just unfortunate – a sneak thief, who presumably chucked the passport away in disgust, and never realized the significance of that little memory stick. A fortune in his hands, and he never knew it . . .' He smirked.

'Anyway,' he went on, 'fortunately for me, I'd made a copy of that memory stick, just as insurance. When I realized Kenny wasn't in possession of the original I knew that my investments were safe. I just couldn't get at the money without the details on the memory stick. I was in Spain – and the copy was in England.'

'And that's why you're back.'

'Absolutely. I'm not leaving without it, Jo.'

I frowned. I was feeling muzzy again. Too much to drink on an empty stomach. Information overload. And still so many questions.

'Where is it? What's it got to do with me?'

Adam smiled, but it was a parody of the friendly smile I knew so well.

'Haven't you guessed, Jo? It's hidden in Manuel. The bear I gave to Molly.'

Sixteen

Manuel. The bear who went everywhere with Molly. The key to a fortune was hidden inside Manuel. Unbelievable as it seemed, yet it explained so much and I knew Adam was speaking the truth.

'So that's the reason we've been targeted,' I said tautly. 'It wasn't because of Michael at all. You used Molly because you thought you'd be able to access the key to your fraudulent account any time you needed to, but your partners in crime would never think of looking for it in a bear owned by a little girl. That is the most despicable thing of all, Adam. How could you place her in such danger? And how did the Whites come to know where it was, anyway?'

Adam smiled smugly. 'They don't know.'

I frowned, the muzziness threatening again. 'What are you talking about? Of course they know! The woman who tried to abduct Molly is one of them. I know. I've seen Kenny White in her car.'

'Yes, possibly you have. Sonia is Barrymore's wife. But she wasn't trying to get the bear for him or Kenny. She was trying to get it for me.' Adam poured more whisky into both our glasses. It occurred to me that he was trying to get me drunk and, though I could have used another sip or two, I ignored it stonily.

'For you. Barrymore White's wife was trying to get the memory stick for *you*. Why would she do that?'

That smile again. How could I ever have been taken in by it? 'Sonia and I . . . well, how shall I put it? She's an attractive woman. I'm a red-blooded man. We've been enjoying one another's company for some time now. Unbeknown to Barrymore, of course. But we had plans for her to leave Barrymore for me when I cut loose with my own company.

And I can't do that until I can access my capital.'

'Kenny's capital.'

He ignored that. 'I was reluctant to blow my cover and come back to England. I was trying to keep out of Kenny's way and if he found out I was here he'd have my balls on his barbecue. So Sonia came over, supposedly for a little holiday, staying with her brother-in-law, to try and get it for me. Unfortunately she's a bit of an airhead. One bungled attempt was all she could come up with.' He shook his head regretfully. 'Not very clever. Alerting you, alerting Alison, and nothing to show for it. I don't know what the hell she thought she was playing at. So in the end there was nothing for it but for me to take a chance and come over myself.'

'But . . .' I was really struggling with this now. 'If the Whites don't know about the bear, why are Molly and I in any danger from them, Adam? Why have you been trying to talk me into going back to Spain with you so as to be safe from them? All you had to do was take Manual and you'd have had what you wanted.'

'I couldn't get it though, could I?' Adam said, patiently almost, as if I was a stupid child. 'It's never where I expect it to be. It wasn't here last weekend, when the house was empty. And it's not here tonight.'

A firecracker exploded in my brain. There *had* been someone in the house while we were away in Devon. And again tonight, when I was in the shower. Adam. Presumably along with Michael's passport, he'd helped himself to Michael's spare key. And used it to get in and look for the damned bear.

'You broke into my house!' I was furious. 'How dare you, Adam?'

'It would have been best all round if I could have just taken Manuel,' Adam said, regretfully almost. 'As it is, I'm afraid you now know a great deal too much. Just as Alison did. I thought I could trust her to help me. I thought she was besotted enough with me to do as I asked without asking too many questions. Silly girl. She got very upset when I explained what I wanted and I couldn't have that. I don't like it when people who know too much get upset. You can never be sure what they'll do or say.'

200

Another firecracker. And with it a wash of utter disbe-lieving horror, turning my blood to ice. Alison had been happy, excited, on the day of her death. Claire had thought she had a date. Now I knew the reason for her elation, and who her date had been with. Adam. The man she'd thought the world of and been so worried about. And in the last resort . . .

'It was you, wasn't it?' I said. My lips felt stiff and numb. 'You killed Alison, didn't you?'

He shrugged carelessly, this man who had been my husband's friend and partner and who I now realized I'd never known at all. 'We do what we have to do. Now, I really think we've wasted enough time, Jo.' He got up, moved around the table towards the counter where the phone stood. 'Ring Anna now – tell her to have Molly and Manuel ready, and we'll go and pick them up.'

'You are joking!' I don't know if it was the whisky giving me courage, or the adrenalin that came from realizing I was alone with a man who had killed at least once, but for some reason I was beyond being afraid. 'You really think I'd go along with this, knowing what I know now?'

'Your choice, Jo. I hoped we could do this the easy way. But if you insist on being stubborn . . .'

Out of the corner of my eye I saw something gleam reflected light where it shouldn't have been. Jerked my head towards it. And at the same moment felt cold steel against the base of my throat. A knife. One of my own kitchen knives. And Adam was holding it against my throat.

My stomach contracted, turned to liquid as the fear belat-edly kicked in. I shrank away. But Adam's solid frame was behind me, his arm hooked around my neck.

'The phone, Jo.' With his free hand he reached for the handset, held it for a moment just out of my reach. 'Tell Anna we're coming for Molly, for her own safety. To have her ready for us with her things. *All* her things. Don't say anything else. Don't try to warn her, or you know what will happen. You won't be around to tell anybody about the bear, or anything else. And I shall get what I want one way or another. I don't want Molly to get hurt, but if that's what it takes . . .'

201

The threat was clear enough. Adam had killed before; he'd kill again – anyone who stood in his way. I didn't care about myself if it would keep Molly safe but it wouldn't. He'd get to her and I wouldn't be there to protect her. I'd be dead, like Alison and all I now knew about Adam and how dangerous he was would be dead with me. Somehow I had to play along with him, play for time, think of a way out of this. I was stone cold sober now, but it wasn't helping me.

Adam depressed the button for a line. 'Is Anna's number programmed in?'

I nodded wordlessly; the blade pricked my throat. He was scrolling down with one hand; I wondered if I could knock the knife aside, knew that even if I could I had nowhere to go. He held the phone up to my face. It was ringing. Ringing endlessly. Perhaps Anna was in bed – she often went early. I could imagine her coming to, wondering what the hell was going on. Or would she sleep through it? What would Adam do if she didn't answer?

'Hello?' Anna answered, her voice sounding thick and anxious.

The knife pricked my throat. 'Anna . . . it's me – Jo.' Trying to work out a way to alert her without Adam knowing. Thick head. Slow brain. 'I'm coming for Molly . . .'

'*Now?* Jo, she's fast asleep . . .'

'I know. But it's important, Anna. We have to go away – tonight . . .'

I know what I'll do. I'll go to the door and I'll snatch Manuel away from Molly and I'll push her back into the house. Adam can have the damned bear. He can do what he likes to me. Just as long as Molly is safe. How dare he threaten Molly? How dare he?

The knife pricked my throat again. Adam was getting impatient, jumpy.

'I'm taking her to Spain with me. Just have her ready. And her things. Especially her teddy bear.' The words came out in a jumble.

'Jo – are you all right?'

The knife dug deeper. 'I'll see you soon,' I managed.

Adam snatched the phone away, disconnected the line and tossed it on to the counter. 'Come on. Let's go.'

He urged me towards the door with the knife still at my throat. With that part of my brain that was functioning in overdrive I realized why he was in a hurry now. He was afraid Anna's suspicions might be aroused – that she might call the police, even. He would be banking on the fact that it would take some time for a patrol car to get from wherever it might be to way out into the country. That we could beat them to it. If Anna *did* call them. He was taking one hell of a chance.

Could I delay him somehow? He'd have to take the knife from my throat to drive. But even if I was stone cold sober I'd be no match for Adam, and I wasn't stone cold sober. I'd had an awful lot to drink. Terror might be clearing my head, but I wasn't sure how dextrous I would be when push came to shove. I only hoped I would be able to wrench the teddy bear from Molly and push her back inside the house, yelling at Anna to raise the alarm. As a plan it wasn't much. But it was the best I could do.

Adam's car was parked on my drive; he bundled me towards it. And to my utter amazement, I saw by the light of the streetlamps that there was someone in the passenger seat. It looked like a woman.

Adam opened the door and the interior light allowed me to see her properly. Blonde hair, elegantly coiffed. Pretty face – too much make-up. Lashings of gold jewellery.

The woman who had tried to snatch Molly.

'What the hell is going on? What's she doing here?' The woman's voice was brittle; it jarred with her immaculate appearance.

'Snags. Change of plan.' Adam bundled me into the back seat, held me, half lying across the seat, gesticulating to the woman with the knife. 'Get in the back with Jo. If she tries anything, use this.'

'Oh, no bloody way! What d'you think I am? This is going way too far . . .'

'Come on, Sonia – just do it. If Jo behaves herself no one will get hurt. Move, you silly bitch! Let's get the hell out of here.'

The woman swore again, moved reluctantly, took the knife from Adam and slid into the seat beside me, still arguing.

I felt the first glimmer of hope; with a woman I stood a chance.

'Where are we going anyway?' she demanded shrilly. 'What's happening?'

Adam was in the driving seat, gunning the engine. 'Where d'you think we're going? To get the memory stick, of course. The kid's staying with friends, and she's got the bear.'

The car lurched right on the road throwing the woman against me. Her perfume was overpowering, turning my already queasy stomach.

'Adam! Slow down for Chrissakes!' It came out between gritted teeth. I held on to that nugget of hope. Sonia wasn't happy, that much was clear. I wondered if she knew about Alison.

'Oh, shut up, Sonia,' Adam snarled. 'If you'd got the bear from the kid none of this would be necessary. You're about as much use as a chocolate fireguard.'

'Don't talk to me like that!' Sonia snapped. I held off from mentioning Alison; it seemed Adam was doing quite a good job of alienating her all by himself. 'I won't be talked to like that.'

'Go back to your husband, then. Go back to Barrymore. Though I don't know what sort of a reception you'll get. He won't take kindly to knowing you and I were at it under his nose. Or that you thought I was the better bet for making the fortune you want to keep you in Botox and champagne.'

'You bastard!'

'A murderer too,' I said. 'Did you know that? Did you know he . . . ?'

'And you can shut up, Jo, too.' Adam turned to look at me, the car swerved violently. 'Just shut up, or I swear I'll . . .'

Headlights appeared suddenly, cutting a swathe through the rear window of the car, so bright they dazzled me when I glanced at them over my shoulder. They were lighting up the offside of the road so that the hedges were illuminated in a brilliant shimmering green, iridescent and ghostly. The offside. As if the car was trying to overtake us . . .

Adam swore. 'What the hell?' He moved towards the middle of the road, a quick, jerky manoeuvre, and there was a sharp jolt and an ugly crunch of metal on metal as the following car collided with the rear offside of his car immediately behind me.

'It's Kenny!' Sonia's voice was high pitched, almost hysterical. She was looking out of the rear window, her face a mask of terror.

'You stupid bitch – what did you say to him?' A sudden surge of power like g-force hit me in the stomach as Adam's foot went down hard on the accelerator and the car shot forward.

'Nothing! I didn't say anything! Christ, Adam . . .'

The headlights behind were keeping pace, still swerving towards the centre of the road, looking for a chance to overtake again. Adam's car skidded around a bend in the lane, the hedge, thick and dark against the night sky leaped out at us.

Déjà vu. Headlights. Speeding cars. Tom following me. Someone following Michael. Two cars – it looked like they were racing – or road rage. Someone chasing Michael. *Adam* chasing Michael . . . The sure knowledge exploded in my fuzzy brain like a Catherine wheel on Guy Fawkes Night. Adam hadn't just let Michael go that night. He'd followed him. Ruthless Adam. Crazy Adam, maddened by greed . . .

No time to think. The car slewed round another bend, tyres screaming on tarmac, throwing me deep into the corner of my seat. Sonia, screaming at Adam, fell across me. A whitehot pain shot from my right knee to my calf.

For a moment I didn't realize what it was, but when I touched my leg my fingers came away warm and wet. I looked down. I couldn't see the gash that I would later discover was about four inches long, but something glinted briefly in the well of the car, illuminated like day by the following headlights. Sonia was hanging on to the headrest of Adam's seat, pulling herself upright, still yelling at him. She no longer had the knife in her hand.

I didn't stop to think. I reached down instinctively, wriggling my hand between my injured leg and the door of the car, feeling for the knife I could not now see though I knew it was there, trying to anchor my feet to prevent the swaying of the car from throwing it out of my reach. I scrabbled wildly and my fingers encountered steel. I grasped it, slid along to reach the handle, somehow wriggled my arm free again and inched it up into my lap. My heart was pounding; I could scarcely breathe. But I had the knife. I didn't stop to wonder if I would use it. I knew I would. On Adam. On Sonia. On anyone who threatened my daughter.

Another bend. We seemed to be losing the following car; the lights had dropped back a little. I braced myself against the wild swaying, gripping the knife so hard the wooden handle bit into my palm. Waiting, waiting for the right moment. *Get this right. You have only one chance . . . Threaten Sonia, he'll take no notice. Use it on Adam, he'll crash the car. You have to wait . . .*

Adam swore again, suddenly and loudly, and simultaneously stamped on the brake. The car slewed and jolted so violently that I crashed against the back of his seat, jarring my shoulder, and Sonia catapulted forward into the gap between the front seats. There was something blocking the road ahead of us; in the light of the headlamps I could see what looked like a Range Rover straddling the lane. And the following car was right behind us again, so close now that its blazing lights turned night into day. Sonia was trying to free herself from between the seats; Adam's airbag had inflated – he was trapped behind it. And I still had the knife.

This was it. This was my chance. I pulled myself upright, oblivious to the pain in my shoulder and my slashed leg, poised for a moment gathering my strength and resolve. And then, before I could do a single thing, all hell broke loose. Dark forms rushed the car from both in front and behind. Adam's driver's door was wrenched open and someone was dragging Adam from the car. A big man, bull-necked, close cropped head.

'Kenny – for God's sake . . .' Adam's protest was cut short as a huge fist caught him square in the mouth. He went down, out of my line of vision, was dragged to his feet, knocked down again. There were at least three men surrounding him, giving him one hell of a beating from what I could hear of it.

Adam had driven straight into a trap. Afterwards, when I had time to think about it, I supposed that Kenny, in the following car, had called on reinforcements by mobile phone and they had blocked the road. But at the time I could think of nothing but that the memory stick with the information that would give access to a small fortune was in Molly's teddy bear. The Whites would want it every bit as much as Adam – and they were just as dangerous. If they knew where it was. And it was always possible Sonia had put them up to this. When they'd finished dealing with Adam they might well make for Anna's – and there were three of them. I had to take the chance to get away; try to get to Anna's before they did.

I couldn't get out of my own door – the fracas was taking place on my side of the car. Somehow I scrambled over Sonia's legs – she moaned, protested, shifted. I ignored her pleas for help. She'd tried to abduct Molly, damn her. Let her stew! My only concern was getting away, getting to my daughter. I wrenched open the car door, half-fell out on to the road. Sonia was pulling herself up now, groggy, but scrabbling for my arm and screaming for Kenny. I wrenched myself free. My legs buckled and I went down on to my knees. But I still had the knife. And I'd use it. Dammit, I'd still use it if I had to . . .

Suddenly the night sky strobed blue. I jerked up, looking around. Behind us. It was coming from behind us, the flashing light illuminating the hedges. Coming closer. I staggered along the length of the car that had chased us, began to run along the lane. A police car rounded the bend – the most welcome sight I'd ever seen in my life. I stood in the middle of the road, arms outstretched and waving. It screamed to a halt. The passenger door opened, a uniformed figure jumped out and ran towards me, followed almost at once by the driver.

'Don't let them go!' I was sobbing now. 'Don't let them get to Anna's!'

Then my legs had given way beneath me and I crumpled down on to the tarmac. No fear, strangely, that these policemen might be on Kenny White's payroll. All my old faith in the law intact. They looked to me as solid and dependable as Dave. The cavalry had arrived. And I was truly grateful.

207

Seventeen

It might have been any Sunday morning. Me in the kitchen, doing necessary chores, Molly in the living room redressing her Barbie doll in between watching a DVD. Except that it was a new Barbie outfit and a new DVD – I'd felt like treating her because I was so grateful she was here with me, safe and sound, and I was putting a joint of beef in the oven for the same reason. Except that Gwenda Stone had been here for the last hour, taking yet another statement from me and filling me in as far as she was able on developments regarding Adam and the Whites.

I'd made one statement on the actual night, in the oasis of harsh electric light that was an interview room at the police station, before a police car brought me home, but I'd heard nothing since then and I'd been chewing my nails wondering what was going on and whether my tormentors were safely in custody.

'I'm sure they are,' Anna had comforted me when I'd collected Molly the next day. 'Judging by what they said when they came here last night and took away that damned bear, I should think it will be some time before any of them are walking the streets again. Especially Adam. That bastard, Jo! Thank goodness I twigged something was wrong and dialled 999.'

'Thank goodness you did or I might be the one behind bars – for stabbing somebody. I would have done it, you know.'

'The bastard!' Anna had said again, vehemently. 'It would have been no more than he deserved. But – oh, my God, Jo – it doesn't bear thinking about. He murdered Alison in cold blood just because she got in his way and he would have done the same to you. People he knew – people who trusted him. It's beyond belief.'

'He's sick,' I had said. 'He must be.'

'Corrupted by greed. But he was so good at hiding it – you'd never have guessed for a moment that he . . . Do you think he murdered Michael too? Put something in his drink to make him drive recklessly that night?'

'I don't know. It's all too much like a gangster film.'

'He must have put something in Alison's drink – drugged her, then—' She broke off, pressing her hand over her mouth. 'If he has access to that sort of substance, then he could easily have slipped something into Michael's drink too. And then . . .'

'I don't suppose we'll ever know for sure. But I am certain it was his car that was chasing Michael that night. I think Michael had threatened to expose the whole scam – not just the timeshare, but this other business too – the money laundering. I think Michael only found about it a few weeks earlier – that was the reason he was so worried. If only he'd said something to me! But he didn't. He had a showdown with Adam and Kenny White, and they couldn't risk him blowing the whole thing wide open.'

Anna had been silent for a moment, shaking her head as if it was still all too much to take in. Then she'd added: 'And what about that terrible woman? The one who tried to abduct Molly? She's Kenny White's sister-in-law, you say?'

'Barrymore's wife, yes. She and Adam were having an affair – planned to set up home together, by the sound of it, when he'd got his new empire going. She came over from Tenerife to try and get the memory stick for him. She was staying with Kenny and the car she was driving was most likely hired – that's why no one recognized it. But she's not a very good criminal – thank goodness. Adam called her an airhead. He got desperate enough to risk coming into the country himself. I think it's possible he might have approached Alison, hoping she'd help him to get the bear from Molly. But Alison wasn't the push-over he'd thought she'd be. When she realized just what sort of a man he was she refused to do as he asked and he realized she could expose him – both to Kenny White and to the police. I don't know which he was more worried about.'

'Well, it's over now, Jo,' Anna had said.

'Yes.' But I'd known it wasn't, not quite. I'd known the chances were I'd have to relive it all a few times yet – that there would be more police interviews and that I'd probably have to stand up in court and give evidence. And this morning I'd been proved right when I'd looked out of the window and seen Gwenda Stone, as solid and motherly as ever, coming up my path.

'How are you doing?' she had greeted me.

'I'm fine.' It wasn't quite true. In my fragile state it had been tempting to give in to Anna's suggestion – no, forceful insistence – that I should stay with her for a day or two. But I'd wanted to overcome the cold shiver of fear that ran through me every time I thought of being alone in the house with Molly and start getting things back to normal, for Molly's sake if nothing else. I had to face up to it sometime; it might as well be sooner as later.

I'd taken Gwenda into the kitchen and made a cup of tea.

'So – what's happened?' I had asked when we were sitting down at the table.

To my surprise, Gwenda was a little cagey.

'What I can tell you, Mrs Lansdale, is that Adam Garratt is facing charges in relation to abducting you at knife point,' she said. 'And he's been charged with Alison's murder.'

'He's in custody?' I wanted to hear it from the horse's mouth.

'He won't be going anywhere soon, don't worry. Not that he'd be in a fit state to go far, even if he was free. He spent the night and half of Friday in hospital, and he's still looking pretty sorry for himself, I can tell you. He took quite a beating.'

'And the Whites?'

'Common assault. Grievous bodily harm.'

'They'll walk then.' I felt myself tense, though I didn't think the Whites would be any further danger to me or Molly.

Gwenda's mouth had twisted up in a tight smile. 'I wouldn't bank on it. I have a feeling birds are going to be singing once the lawyers start pointing out that police co-operation can result in lighter sentences. A falling out between thieves usually ends in tears. And thanks to the evidence in our hands since we recovered the teddy bear I think the whole lot of them will be going down for a very long time.'

'The off-shore bank accounts, you mean,' I said.

She shot me a look, then tightened up like a clam. 'I'm sorry, but I can't discuss that with you, Mrs Lansdale. It's more than my job's worth.'

'Why are you here then?' I asked.

'To go over your account of what happened. Fraud Squad will want to interview you regarding the other matters.'

Fraud Squad. I felt sick. Accounts in Michael's name. No wonder they wanted to interview me. I just hoped I could convince them he had played no part in this business. That the evidence they turned up would prove it.

When I'd made another statement and signed it, there was one more question I wanted to ask Gwenda Stone, though I wasn't sure how to phrase it, or how it would be received.

'Look – this is really awkward but . . . more than one person mentioned to me that there might be policemen in Kenny White's pocket. There's no possibility, is there, that Dave's accident might not have been an accident at all . . . that he was asking too many questions, just like poor Alison, and someone dealt with him? That couldn't have been Adam. I don't think he was back in the country by then. But I can't help wondering if someone deliberately knocked him off his motorbike. As a patrolling officer he would be quite a distinctive target.'

Again I saw her face shut, the professional mask sliding back into place over her normal open, friendly expression.

'It's possible someone has been working undercover with White. Again, it's not my department, so I wouldn't know. Fraud Squad can be pretty secretive. But I think you can rest assured Dave's accident was just that. A stolen car has turned up, burned out, in a quarry, and we think it's the one that was involved in the hit and run. Just a joy rider, Mrs Lansdale. Some stupid boy who stole a car, drove it recklessly, and then panicked when he realized he'd hit a policeman.'

'Well, that's a relief . . .' I still wasn't totally convinced. It seemed too much of a coincidence to me. But I guessed it was just one more thing I'd never know for sure.

Then Gwenda had left, and I'd cleared away the tea cups,

continuing with my chores, glad, for once, of ordinary, mundane routine.

'Mummy! Mummy!' Molly came running into the kitchen at that moment, interrupting my thoughts, her voice piping over the whir of the blender as I mixed batter for the Yorkshire pudding. 'Tom's here!'

'What?' I switched off the blender abruptly.

'Tom . . . !' And she was off again, dashing to the front door to greet him.

'He's got a nerve!' I said aloud. But my heart was beating too fast and there was a tremor in my stomach.

I followed Molly along the hall. She already had the door open and was on the drive, hopping up and down with excitement as she waited for Tom to get out of the car. I hadn't enlightened her as to the fact that he'd been deceiving us. The occasion hadn't arisen, and in any case I hadn't known how. Bad enough I'd had to explain that she wouldn't be seeing Adam any more, that he was a bad man. I'd shrunk from destroying her faith in human nature by telling her that Tom, too, had only been using us. She was seven years old, for goodness sake. Plenty of time yet for her to learn the hard way that people are not always what they seem.

'Molly,' I said severely, 'go into the house.'

'But Mummy . . . Tom . . .'

'Just do as I say.'

'Mummy . . .'

'Go!'

Puzzled, pulling a face at me that involved curling her lip and giving me a hard stare, she went. She's learned that when I use a certain tone of voice she'd better obey me – or else. But I knew that I was going to have to answer the questions I didn't want to when I'd seen Tom off.

He came around the front of the car, holding his hands up in a gesture of truce and looking chastened. 'Don't shoot, Jo.'

'What the hell are you doing here?' I challenged him. 'I thought I made it clear. I don't want to see you – ever again.'

'Oh, you made it pretty clear.' His tone was rueful. 'I don't give up so easily though.'

'Well, you're batting for a lost cause,' I said, vehement,

bitter. 'There's no way your insurance company is going to get back the pay-out they made on Michael's life. I didn't defraud them. Michael didn't defraud them. My husband is dead. So you can get back in your car and drive right out of my life.'

'Sorry. No can do.'

'Why the hell not? You've got your result – even if it isn't the one you hoped for. Case closed. You're through here. You've got what you want.'

'The result *was* the one I hoped for,' Tom said. 'From the minute I saw you too frightened to death to back your car off that bank, I hoped I was barking up a gum tree. But I haven't got what I want.'

'What do you want then?' I demanded, exasperated.

He dropped his hands to his sides; his eyes met mine directly.

'What the hell do you think I want? You.'

The wind went out of my sails. My heartbeat had quickened again; somewhere inside I was melting. A flicker of foolish hope. My senses remembering the way it had been between us. And my head telling me not to be a fool again.

'You expect me to believe that?'

'Not really. But I hope you will.' He caught me by the arms, forcing me to look at him. 'Do you really think I'd have taken you and Molly for a weekend away – gone to bed with you – all for the lousy pittance they call a salary – if I hadn't wanted to?'

'It was a pretty big pay-out.'

'Not that big. I investigate fraud, Jo. I'm not some kind of gigolo.'

'You tricked me,' I said. 'You followed me that first night when I set out to go to Anna's. You'd been watching the house before that, just waiting for your opportunity. And when you got it – boy, did you take it.'

'I have to hold my hands up to that,' he agreed. 'Up till then, it was just another job. I was following you to see if there was any chance you were in contact with Michael. I admit it.'

'And you stopped to help me and asked me out so that you'd be in a good position to find out as much as you could.'

Tom whistled through his teeth. 'You really don't have much of an opinion of me, do you? Ulterior motive or no ulterior motive, I could hardly just drive off and leave you to it when I'd caused you to have an accident, could I? Well, it's not something I would do, anyway. Asking you out? I was telling myself at the time that it was purely for professional reasons, but even then I knew damned well it wasn't. I wanted to see you again. Simple as that.'

'You deceived me.'

'Not about the way I felt. But professionally I was in a very sticky situation. Falling for a woman whose husband I was supposed to be investigating. I couldn't tell you. Couldn't blow my cover. Though I did come close when we were in Devon.'

A picture flashed before my eyes. The two of us sitting on the swing seat. Tom saying we had to talk; that I knew nothing about him. Me replying I knew all I needed to know. Not wanting to spoil the special moments we were sharing. Kissing him. Maybe he had been going to tell me then . . .

'I didn't want to upset you unnecessarily either,' Tom went on. 'I knew by then you honestly believed your husband was dead and you'd be devastated if he wasn't. And I didn't want some other investigator coming in with both feet. I decided to stick with it, hoping I could find proof that Michael really did die in the accident. Get the insurance company off your back once and for all and—'

'And for your own reasons.'

'I must admit I was hoping for selfish reasons that would be how it would turn out, yes.'

'But you had no scruples about romancing a woman who might not be free.'

'If your husband could do something like that to you, he didn't deserve you,' Tom said bluntly. 'Besides all that, I knew that the Fraud Squad were carrying out their own investigation. I thought, foolishly and egotistically, perhaps, that if things turned ugly you could use a friend.'

I stared at him narrowly. 'How did you know that? About the Fraud Squad, I mean?'

He shrugged. 'I used to be a copper until an accident on duty rendered me unfit for active service. I took a bullet in

214

a drugs raid that went wrong. I didn't fancy being relegated to a desk job for the next twenty years, so I handed in my warrant card and made a career change. But I still have friends in the job. And through them I knew that Michael was under investigation. There was a bit of a trade-off in information. That there were off-shore accounts in Michael's name, for instance, that were still active.'

'He wasn't part of that.' I was defensive suddenly on Michael's behalf. 'Adam will have blackmailed him into it – if he knew about it at all. I shall tell them that when they interview me. And they'd better believe it.'

'Better not mention to them that I mentioned it to you,' Tom said. 'Anyway, that's not the reason I'm here.'

'Why are you here?' I don't know why I had to ask. I already knew the answer.

Tom's hands slid down my arms till they were holding mine.

'Will you forgive me, Jo? Can we start again?'

'Oh, Tom!' His hands felt good on mine, the contrite expression on those very rugged features was turning my spine to liquid. I remembered how good we'd been together, how he'd reawakened emotions I'd never thought I'd experience again. They'd been real, never mind there had been things Tom had kept from me. And quite suddenly I knew without doubt they'd been real for him too. He'd been facing his own dilemma, his own demons, but he hadn't been using me. I wanted to believe that. I would believe it. We can never know everything about the people we love. We can only trust. And I trusted Tom.

A small sound from behind me attracted my attention. I swung round and caught a glimpse of sunshine on a fair head before it ducked out of sight.

'Molly!' I said sharply. She emerged, a little sheepish. 'How long have you been there?' I demanded.

'Not very long . . .' Her face was solemn; her eyes darted to Tom. 'Isn't Tom coming in? Why are you still out here?'

'We had things to talk about.' I glanced at Tom, raised an eyebrow. 'And I think Tom might be coming in now. As long as you promise not to plague the life out of him.'

The smell of roasting beef met us in the hall.

'Are you hungry?' I asked.

'What do you think?' He hesitated. 'I do have a bottle of wine in the car. I bought it just in case I got lucky . . .'

'Oh, you!' But I was laughing. Tom had that effect on me. 'Well, at least now I know what it is you want me for.'

Molly was dancing ahead, Tom was behind me. I felt his lips touch my ear.

'Don't you believe it,' he said, too soft for her to hear.

He went back outside to collect his wine and I called to Molly. 'Can you set an extra place?'

'For Tom? Is he staying then?'

'Yes.'

I hoped he would be staying for a very long time.

Postscript

He stayed. In fact, we've been together ever since. Call me an optimist, but I can't see us splitting up now. If we could get through all that, we can get through anything.

Molly adores him and he adores her. He bought her another bear to replace Manuel – but thank goodness it does not wear sunglasses or a sun hat. She calls him Loopy and she loves him every bit as much as she loved Manuel, perhaps more, because he came from her hero – Tom.

The cases against Adam and the Whites haven't come to court yet, but Adam was remanded in custody, and I know now there's no danger to us from the Whites. Gangsters they might be, but they weren't the ones who murdered indiscriminately, maddened by greed. In their own way, I think they have certain standards of behaviour.

And just as a matter of interest, a certain Superintendent Bunter Williams took early retirement a few weeks later. Full pension, according to Dave. Not a whisper of impropriety. Just a sudden decision that it was time for the pipe, slippers and golf clubs. Funny that . . . Oh, well, like some other things, I suppose we shall never know the full truth. We can only have our suspicions . . .

And our hopes for the future and our dreams. I know now that even when things seem darkest, there is always light at the end of the tunnel. I know that though we may not know all the secrets of those closest to us, we must trust them, and trust too our own intuition, our own hearts. And if we are sometimes mistaken – well, that is part of living. The important thing is not to lose faith.

I almost lost my faith in Michael, yet a small unshakeable part of me refused to accept the evidence that was mounting against him. I trusted Adam, and it nearly cost me everything. Two sides of a coin.

As for Tom . . . I'm going to trust him. With my life, and with Molly's. I know he will never let me down.